# THE GIANT-SLAYER

## ALSO BY IAIN LAWRENCE

*The Séance*
*Gemini Summer*
*B for Buster*
*The Lightkeeper's Daughter*
*Lord of the Nutcracker Men*
*Ghost Boy*

### The Curse of the Jolly Stone Trilogy
*The Convicts*
*The Cannibals*
*The Castaways*

### The High Seas Trilogy
*The Wreckers*
*The Smugglers*
*The Buccaneers*

# THE
# GIANT-SLAYER

## Iain Lawrence

DELACORTE PRESS

All rights reserved. Published in the United States by Delacorte Press, an imprint of Random House Children's Books, a division of Random House, Inc., New York.

Delacorte Press is a registered trademark and the colophon is a trademark of Random House, Inc.

Visit us on the Web! www.randomhouse.com/kids

Educators and librarians, for a variety of teaching tools, visit us at www.randomhouse.com/teachers

Library of Congress Cataloging-in-Publication Data
Lawrence, Iain.
The giant-slayer / Iain Lawrence. — 1st ed.
p. cm.
Summary: When her eight-year-old neighbor is stricken with polio in 1955, eleven-year-old Laurie discovers that there is power in her imagination as she weaves a story during her visits with him and other patients confined to iron lung machines.
ISBN 978-0-385-73376-2 (hardcover)—ISBN 978-0-385-90393-6 (lib. bdg.)
—ISBN 978-0-375-89374-2 (e-book)
[1. Poliomyelitis—Fiction. 2. Storytelling—Fiction. 3. Imagination—Fiction. 4. People with disabilities—Fiction. 5. Medical care—Fiction. 6. Fathers and daughters—Fiction.] I. Title.
PZ7.L43545Gid 2009
[Fic]—dc22
2008035409

The text of this book is set in 11-point Century.

Book design by Marci Senders

Printed in the United States of America

10 9 8 7 6 5 4 3 2 1

First Edition

For Mom—
I miss you.

# CONTENTS

# CHAPTER ONE

## THE GIRL WHO SAW THE FUTURE

When Laurie Valentine was six years old she got out her crayons and drew the future.

She started with an island in the shape of a potato, and in the middle she put a range of mountains in a zigzag line. She drew a crooked river crawling down toward the coast, green forests and a scarlet lake, a smear of yellow for a meadow. Here she put a white cross, there a lion with wings on its back.

It was a Thursday morning in 1950. Laurie was kneeling on a kitchen chair, her elbows on the table, while her nanna—Mrs. Strawberry—did the dusting in the living room. The house smelled of furniture polish.

"I need that table now," said Mrs. Strawberry. She came into the kitchen with her rags and feather duster, and stopped behind the girl. "My, what a pretty picture."

"It's not a picture, Nanna," said Laurie, looking up. "It's a map of my life. It shows all the things I'm going to find when I go exploring."

"So what's the squiggle?" asked Mrs. Strawberry. "That red thing by the castle?"

"I don't know," said Laurie. "But I think I'll have to fight it when I get there."

Mrs. Strawberry laughed. "What an imagination you've got." She rubbed Laurie's hair and turned away. "Now clear the table, honey. It's nearly time for lunch."

Laurie picked crumbs of blue crayon from the river. "Do you want to know anything else about my map?" she asked.

"It's probably best if you put it away," said Mrs. Strawberry. "After all, we should keep it safe for your father. He'll certainly want to see *that* when he comes home."

"Can I put it in the atlas?" said Laurie. "It's a map, and—"

"Yes, that's a good idea."

"Because it should be with all the other maps."

"Yes, I understand," said Mrs. Strawberry. "I know what an atlas is for."

Laurie had been smiling. But without another word she returned her crayons to the box, standing them as neatly as pickets in a fence. She climbed down from her chair, carried her map in both hands to the living room, and stuck it among the pages of the big blue atlas, between Antarctica and the index.

◆ ◆ ◆

"You've never seen a child so lonely," said Mrs. Strawberry that night. She was sitting with her husband on the front porch of their small white house. He was on the glider, she on the wooden chair with her knitting on her lap.

"It's tragic, don't you think," she said, "for a girl to grow up without a mother?"

"I suppose it is," he said with a sigh. They had had the same conversation many times before.

"So tragic, the mother dying in childbirth," added Mrs. Strawberry.

Her husband nodded. "Yes, indeed."

"I don't know why he never remarried. I feel sorry for the both of them." Mrs. Strawberry took up her needles and tugged on the wool. "That poor Mr. Valentine, he's so darned busy. It's good work, of course; why, it's the work of saints he does, raising all that money for polio. But I wish he had more time for Laurie." She began to work the needles, and they ticked as steadily as a clock. "It's like he's trying to save every child in the country, and forgetting his own."

"That *does* sound sad," said Mr. Strawberry, as though following a script.

"She's so much like him. Smart as a whip," said Mrs. Strawberry. "Shy and quiet too. You should see how she plays. She takes every book from the shelf and stacks them into walls, talking away to herself a mile a minute. She always arranges the books in the same way—in a square—

but one day it's a castle, and the next a sailing ship, or a fort or a covered wagon. It's all imaginary, you see."

"Yes," said Mr. Strawberry.

As always, Mrs. Strawberry finished with a clack of her knitting needles and some final words. "That child lives in a land of make-believe."

◆ ◆ ◆

There were pictures everywhere of Mrs. Valentine—black-framed photos that stood like little cardboard tents on the mantelpiece and radio, on the sideboard in the hall, on every windowsill and table. But to Laurie these were images of strangers, of twenty different women all fading into brown and yellow.

Sometimes, in the night, she could hear her father talking to the pictures.

He was her hero: the second smartest man in the world. Only Santa Claus knew more than Laurie's father. He raised money for the March of Dimes, but she thought of him as some sort of soldier. He was always talking about fighting.

"We're waging a war against polio," he would say. Or, "We've won the battle, but the fight goes on."

His uniform was a brown suit, his helmet a gray fedora. Every morning, as soon as Mrs. Strawberry arrived, he put on that hat, gave Laurie a kiss, and hurried away to catch the bus. And Mrs. Strawberry, still holding her handbag, still wearing her gloves, would make sure that the knot on his tie was perfectly straight, that he hadn't forgotten his briefcase.

"People think your father's scatterbrained," she told Laurie. "But he's so busy with big ideas that he doesn't have time to think of little things."

Laurie thought of herself as one of those "little things." Mr. Valentine never had time to play with her. He spent his evenings in the armchair, smoking his pipe, reading the papers he brought home from work. He didn't like noise, and he didn't like music, so the house was very quiet, the only sounds the rustle of his paper.

But for a few minutes before her bedtime, Laurie was allowed to sit on his lap, and the smoke from his pipe coiled round the two of them like a gray rope. She liked to fiddle with his tie clasp, watching reflections twist on the gold.

On the day she drew the map, Laurie brought the atlas to his chair. She put it on his knees and climbed up beside him. It was such a big book that it hit his pipe when she opened it. Then she nestled against him and started telling him all the things about the map of her life.

"Isn't that wonderful?" he said. But he wasn't really listening.

◆ ◆ ◆

Laurie grew up to be quiet and shy.

She grew up wearing glasses as big as windows. They kept sliding down her nose, and she spent all day poking them into place with her middle finger.

She grew up afraid of daffodils.

To her, the yellow flowers were the beginning of summer, the start of polio season.

Because her father worked for the Foundation, he knew all about polio. But because he didn't have time for little things like Laurie, it was Mrs. Strawberry who made the rules: "Don't share food with others. For heaven's sake stay away from the drinking fountain. And never, ever use a public toilet." From spring until autumn, Laurie's world shrank to the size of an atom. She was banned from the movies and the bowling alley, from the swimming pool and the playground. Anywhere that children gathered, Laurie Valentine was not allowed.

"I know you think I'm a horrible old woman," said Mrs. Strawberry every year. "But it's for your own good because you can't take chances with polio. I've probably told you a hundred times, it was polio that took my little sister."

Laurie had heard the same story every year, nearly word for word.

"One day she used the public toilet, and that was it. The next week, she was gone. Infantile paralysis. It was a dreadful, awful way for her to die, and I'm not going to let it happen to you."

Laurie sometimes argued, but she always obeyed her nanna. She stayed away from the pool and the playground and everywhere else, and her summers were sad and lonely. But so were the winters, the springs, and the autumns. Laurie Valentine didn't have a friend in the world until 1955.

◆ ◆ ◆

His name was Dickie Espinosa. On the first day of March he moved into the house at the end of the block, the smallest in the neighborhood.

He appeared on the street that day with a buffalo gun, a coonskin cap, and a buckskin jacket with fringes down the sleeves. He looked just like every other boy in the city in that spring of 1955; the only unusual thing about Dickie Espinosa was that he didn't go to school with the other Davy Crocketts. A tutor called at his home four days a week, a woman as skinny as a stick.

Dickie Espinosa was eight years old, three years younger than Laurie. She met him on a Saturday, in the little Rotary park on the corner. A creek came tumbling out of a culvert there, dashed across the park, and slipped into another culvert, as though afraid of open spaces. Laurie was launching twigs two at a time into the stream, pretending they were rowing boats racing. She looked up and saw him in his Davy Crockett clothes, skulking along the creek. He had a wooden tomahawk stuck in his belt and the big popgun in his hands. He said, "Howdy, stranger."

From that moment, it seemed, they were friends. If Laurie wasn't in school or asleep, she was playing with Dickie Espinosa. He spent time at her house, but she spent more at his. Down in his basement, Dickie had a little world of his own, four feet wide and eight feet long.

The tracks of toy trains ran through towns and fields, into tunnels through the mountains, over spindly bridges across deep canyons. Tiny people seemed frozen at everyday tasks: a boy fishing at a pond, a woman hanging laundry on a line. There were cars on the roads, cows in the fields. There were ducks on the painted glass of the pond, and even decoy ducks among them, and a hunter—nearly invisible—lying with a gun in the grass nearby.

"Keen!" said Laurie the first time she saw it.

That day, Dickie scurried in between the sawhorses that held up the little world. He plugged electrical cords into sockets, scurried out again, and started flicking switches.

Lights came on in the buildings. A windmill's vanes went slowly round, and a watermill began to turn on a spillway at the pond. There was a hum that grew louder, and Laurie had a funny feeling that the people would suddenly start to move, to go about their business in the town. But of course they didn't. Dickie worked the controls, and the trains went whirring through the mountains, through the forests, through the fields. Crossing gates flashed as they opened and closed in a ringing of bells.

Dickie dashed back and forth, adjusting things. Then he waved Laurie over to stand beside him, and he gave her the controls of one of the trains. He showed her how to slow it down and speed it up, how to set the switches that would steer it where she wanted.

It was a passenger train that he'd given her, and Laurie guided it from station to station. At first she didn't stop anywhere near the platforms, and she and Dickie laughed at the idea of all the passengers getting angry. They acted out the people shouting at the train, shaking their fists at the stupid engineer. But soon she got the hang of it, and as her train went round and round she made up stories about the plastic people who never really moved to get on and off. She said one was a farmer on his way to town for the very first time in his life. And she followed him along, past simple things that were—to him—as strange as rocket ships and time machines.

Laurie led Dickie all over the neighborhood, through every park and vacant lot. He called it "scouting," and he did it in his coonskin cap and the jacket with the fringes. He said the hollow that the creek ran through—from culvert to culvert—was "like the valley of the Shenandoah." When the weather was cold or rainy, they stayed inside, inventing long stories about the train-set people.

"Why don't you go to school?" she asked him once. "How come you got a tutor?"

"My mom was worried," he said, " 'cause I missed so many days at my old school."

"From getting sick?"

Dickie shook his head. "From getting beat up."

In March, just after St. Patrick's Day, they played at the Shenandoah until it was nearly dark. Laurie saw the first daffodils showing yellow on the banks of the creek and stomped up and down the slope, trying to stamp them out. She squashed them into the ground.

When she got home, Mrs. Strawberry's white gloves were arranged on the sideboard as always, ready—like a fireman's boots—to be slipped on in a jiffy. Nanna's voice called out from the kitchen, "Is that you, Mr. Valentine?"

"It's me!" shouted Laurie. She kicked off her muddy shoes. But her socks made damp splotches up the hall and into the kitchen.

"Where have you been?" asked Mrs. Strawberry. She was bending over the table, setting out the silverware. When she looked up, her mouth gaped open. "Why, look at you! You're soaking wet," she said.

Laurie saw that the ends of her sleeves were dark with water. Her knees were wet as well. "We were playing in the creek," she said.

"You were *what*?" Mrs. Strawberry pointed through the doorway. "Go wash your hands."

"I just washed them in the creek," said Laurie.

"That's not a creek; it's a sewer. Now go," said Mrs. Strawberry.

Laurie didn't move. She was older now, not so easily scared by a nanny. As though Mrs. Strawberry suddenly saw the change herself, she grew quiet and serious. "Look," she said, "it's nice you've got a friend; I'm pleased for you. But summer's coming on, and you know what that means. I've probably told you this a hundred times, but—"

"Oh, brother." With a big sigh, Laurie looked up at the ceiling.

"Don't roll your eyes at me, young lady," said Mrs. Strawberry.

"I know all about your sister and her stupid toilet seat," said Laurie. "I know all about polio too, 'cause we studied it in school. And guess what? You can't get it from a toilet seat."

"What's the matter with you, Laurie?" Mrs. Strawberry looked horribly sad, as though she'd been slapped in the face and was trying not to cry. "It's *my* sister we're talking about. I think I know better."

The front door opened, and into the house came Mr. Valentine. Laurie looked tauntingly at Mrs. Strawberry. "Ask Dad."

"No," said Mrs. Strawberry. "Don't bother your poor father the moment he comes through the door. Let him get settled at least."

But Laurie was already out of the room, marching down the hall. She reached her father as he was sliding his hat onto the shelf in the closet. She poked her glasses. "Dad, can you get polio from a toilet seat?"

He looked puzzled, frowning at Laurie's wet clothes. Then he glanced up as Mrs. Strawberry came into the hall, and he suddenly understood. He'd heard the story himself nearly as many times as Laurie. "That's a good question," he said. "I don't think anybody knows exactly how polio is passed, but—"

"Dad, you know it's impossible."

Of course he knew, but he didn't want to say so with Mrs. Strawberry standing there. "The important thing," he said, "is not how you get polio. It's how you *don't* get it."

"Well, you don't get it in March," she said. "Tell her, Dad. You can't get polio playing in the creek in the last half of March."

"Now, you must know better than that." Mr. Valentine sat down in the chair to take off his shoes. "It's unlikely, but not impossible. It's never too early for polio."

"Oh, Dad!"

Mr. Valentine seemed old and small as he looked up from the chair. "Do you realize how well the war is going? How close we are to victory?" he asked. "There's no doubt the vaccine will work. Nearly two million Polio Pioneers are proving that, and the results of the trials are better than expected. I know it's hard sometimes to stay away from pools and creeks and things. But if you just hold out for a few more months we'll have unconditional surrender."

Laurie suddenly saw her father as a little man trying to sound like General Patton. She felt embarrassed for him, even sad. But she laughed in a cruel way.

Mr. Valentine turned red in the face. "The rules are for your own sake," he said flatly. "You're still a child, though you may not think so. As long as you live in this house, you'll live by the rules."

Laurie glared back at him. "So you're both against me now? You're ganging up to wreck my life."

Mr. Valentine sighed. "Honey, nobody's against you. And nobody's ganging up."

But that was how she felt. So she turned and bolted from the room. She ran up the stairs, slammed her door as loudly as she could, and threw herself facedown on the bed.

It was half an hour before Mr. Valentine went up and knocked on the door. He sat at the edge of the bed, as stiff and straight as a toy man.

"We've been fighting polio for a hundred years," he said. "In another month we'll have the silver bullet. You'll get a vaccination and never have to worry about polio again. And that will happen before summer." He ran his fingers down his tie, smoothing it out. "You've waited so long already, can't you hold on for a few more weeks?"

"I don't know," she said.

"Well, you can. And you will." He'd never been so firm as he was just then. There were even hard lines on his face, wrinkles on his forehead. "Polio scares me to death, Laurie. I see all the children with braces and crutches. *You* see them too: the ones who'll never run again, the ones who'll never walk, the children in wheelchairs. Well, *I* see the ones in rocking beds, on treatment boards, in iron lungs. So many of them, and another thirty thousand every year. Can you imagine how it haunts them that they got polio just because they went to a *swimming pool*, or something as frivolous as that?"

"I dunno." Laurie had seen plenty of children on crutches, but of course she had never talked to them.

"Well, I'm sure it does. How could an hour of play be worth years in braces or a lifetime in an iron lung?" He shook his head in bewilderment. "I can't tie a string to you, Laurie, and keep you in sight. All I can do is ask that you follow the rules."

She shrugged and mumbled. She wanted to remind him, purely for spite, that he was only a fund-raiser, an organizer, that just because he worked for the Foundation didn't mean he was an expert on polio. Laurie didn't think her father really knew what he was talking about at all.

But he did.

It was never too early for polio.

# CHAPTER TWO

## THE GIRL IN THE IRON LUNG

Laurie believed that she could feel the virus moving through her body. She could see it, in her mind, crawling like a little worm along the tunnels of her nerves.

Sometimes she could tell *exactly* where it was, when her skin began to prick and tingle, and in this way she traced its path through her body. She thought it was making for her brain, and every night she went to sleep praying that she would be able to stand up in the morning, that she wouldn't be spending the *next* night in an iron lung.

Just as her father had said, she began to wish with all her heart that she hadn't gone to the creek that day, and then that she had never met Dickie Espinosa. A picture of him kept popping up in her mind at the strangest times: Dickie in his silly coonskin cap, Dickie with that stupid buffalo gun.

She didn't dare tell her father—or even Mrs. Strawberry—what was happening. But both of them saw that something was wrong. Yet it was many days before Mr. Valentine knocked again on Laurie's bedroom door and crept mouse-like to her bed.

She was sitting cross-legged on the covers, doing her homework. "The Ballad of Davy Crockett" was playing—again—on her radio. She was sick of that song, she had heard it so often.

Mr. Valentine turned off the radio. "Honey, what's the matter?" he said. "Are you mad at me?"

She shook her head.

"Are you lonely? I know that boy hasn't been around recently, and—"

"That's not it." Laurie stared at her schoolbooks. Her tears made them look wet and blurry. Suddenly, it was all too much. She looked up and blurted out, "I think I've got polio."

She thought he was fainting, or having a heart attack. His face turned perfectly white, and his breath made a horrible gurgling gasp. His hands shook as he reached out to the wall to steady himself. He closed his eyes and just stood for a moment like that, trembling very slightly. Then at last he asked, "Where does it hurt?"

"It doesn't hurt," she said. "Not really. But I can feel it inside me, Dad." She touched her throat, at the base of her neck. "I think it's right about here."

"Your arms? Your legs? Do they hurt? Do you have a fever? A headache?"

{15}

"No, Dad," she said. "Nothing like that."

He looked bewildered. "What makes you think it's polio?"

She told him straight out, then called him by a name she hadn't used since she was tiny. "Because Dickie's got it, Daddy."

Mr. Valentine sat down on the bed. He listened as Laurie told him all about the day at the creek and how she'd found out about Dickie. "I didn't see him for a couple of days," she said. "So I went to his house. And Mrs. Espinosa wouldn't even open the door at first. She shouted at me to go away. I thought she was ashamed, that Dickie had done something awful. I asked where he was, and she said, 'He's at Bishop's, in an iron lung.'"

"Dear God," said Mr. Valentine.

"I was supposed to tell you, Dad, but I was scared," she said.

"How long ago was this?" asked Mr. Valentine.

Laurie couldn't remember exactly.

"It must be more than a week," he said. "Is it more than two?"

"Nearly three," she said.

He smiled just the tiniest smile. "Then I think you're all right."

"How do you know?" asked Laurie.

"That's the way polio works," said Mr. Valentine. "It can't stay hidden. The symptoms have to show up very quickly."

Laurie wiped her nose with the back of her hand. "What will happen to Dickie?" she asked.

"You would need a Gypsy with a crystal ball to tell you that," said Mr. Valentine. "Even his doctors won't be certain. He could be back on his feet any day, or in hospital the rest of his life. It's unpredictable."

"Can I visit him, Dad?"

Mr. Valentine turned away, closing his eyes. "Oh, honey, I don't know."

It was safe enough, and he knew it. There was no reason why she *shouldn't* go and visit, but he didn't want to say so. In his head he understood that polio wasn't contagious for long, that she couldn't possibly catch the disease from Dickie. But in his heart he didn't want her to go, for all of a sudden he was full of doubts. What if it wasn't exactly true that polio couldn't be spread that way? What if something went wrong? Even he never touched the children in the polio wards, though he wasn't proud of it. Secretly, he didn't even like to stand too close to them. He had seen too many doctors keeping their distance, too many nurses hiding behind masks and gloves. For the first time he wondered: did the scientists know more than he'd been told? He was a mere fund-raiser, a tiny cog in the giant March of Dimes.

"Can I, Dad?" asked Laurie.

He swallowed hard, his Adam's apple bulging. He felt that it would betray all that he knew to say no, but he wasn't brave enough to say yes. He had lost a wife; he couldn't stand to lose a daughter too.

"I want to see him, Dad," said Laurie.

"I'll tell you what," said Mr. Valentine. "If Mrs. Strawberry says yes, it's fine with me."

He was pretty sure what the nanny would say, and he

wasn't disappointed. Mrs. Strawberry put her hands on her round hips and shook her head at Laurie.

"A polio ward? Are you out of your mind?" she said. "If it's up to me, a polio ward is the last place on earth you'll visit, young lady."

◆ ◆ ◆

The hospital was only a few blocks from Laurie's house. Going the long way home from school took her through the grounds, along paths where mothers pushed their baby carriages, past a pond where people sat on benches to feed the ducks and squirrels.

She had often gone to Bishop's Memorial, sometimes with Mrs. Strawberry. There was a bench at the pond that had been their favorite when Laurie was a little child.

From there, between the weeping willows, she could see the windows of the fourth floor, where the polios lived, and she had often sat staring at them, trying to imagine what was inside: a room full of iron lungs; another stuffed with braces and crutches; all the polios staggering and lurching down the halls. Only once had anyone ever looked back at her—a boy with blond and curly hair, a boy so pale and thin that he'd looked like a prisoner. She had thought of him ever since as the prince in the tower, and the image of him gazing down from the window was as sharp in her mind as a photograph. Though she had looked up many times, hoping to see him, he had never been there again.

On the day in April when she walked through the north gate, Laurie had the grounds to herself. It was a drizzly afternoon, with puddles on the pathways. No mothers pushed their carriages; no one fed the ducks.

Laurie passed through a tunnel of willow branches, looked up at the fourth-floor windows, and kept on walking.

The building was enormous. It looked more like a fort than a hospital, more like a castle stripped of turrets and banners. At the top of a ladder, a gray-haired gardener was battling the ivy, as he did on many days. Leaves and stems rained down on the lawn and the path.

There were birds in the trees, traffic on the street. The tires of cars and trucks made a sizzling sound on the wet road. A sleek red car, a Starlight, came up the curving entryway and slipped behind the building, heading for the parking lot where the doctors had their spaces.

Laurie passed under the covered entrance and up to the row of doors.

As soon as she stepped inside, everything seemed familiar. The hospital smell, the odd hushing of every sound, reminded her of the time she'd had her tonsils out. She remembered struggling against doctors who had rushed her away on a gurney, holding her down as the bed rolled along. She could remember with perfect clarity the hum of the wheels, the hurried slap of the doctors' shoes, the way the lights had flashed past on the ceiling. One of the doctors had pressed a mask on her face and told her, "Count backward from ten." She had held her breath, afraid he was trying to kill her. But at last she'd had to breathe, and the next thing she knew, she was coming awake in the night with a sore throat.

She'd found herself in a strange bed in a strange place, feeling frightened and alone. She had started crying in the night, and kept on crying until a nurse finally came by and told her sharply, in a voice like a witch's, "Keep it up, honey, and you'll tear out your stitches."

◆ ◆ ◆

In the lobby was an information desk, where a lady sat at a switchboard. She had silver hair, a red sweater, and lipstick so bright that it made her mouth look like an axe wound.

Laurie told her, "I came to see Dickie Espinosa."

The lady looked down at a big binder. She turned the pages. "Do you know what room he's in?"

"No." Laurie poked her glasses. "I think it's the one with the iron lungs."

"Oh, dear." The lady looked sad. "Are your parents with you?"

"No. My nanna's at home; my dad's at work," said Laurie.

"You came on your own to visit your friend?"

Laurie nodded, sending her glasses sliding down again.

"Hold on a minute." The lady called for a nurse, and the one who arrived a few minutes later was twice as pretty and half as old as Mrs. Strawberry. She had super-curly hair as black as coal, with a white cap pinned high on top, but tipped back like a sailor's. A heart-shaped watch was hanging upside down on her breast.

She said her name was Miss Freeman. "I'm from Polio," she said, as though the disease were a country. "So you're friends with Dickie? You must be Laurie Valentine."

"Yes," said Laurie.

"I feel like I know you already, he's said so much about you. How you played in the creek and called it the Shenandoah. How you played with the train people. He's been hoping you'd come and see him."

"I was kind of scared," said Laurie.

"Well, sure you were. Who wouldn't be scared?" Miss Freeman was as cheery as a songbird. "We had a boy whose parents *never* came to visit, not once in four years, because they were too afraid of taking polio home to his sister. They couldn't understand that it's only contagious for the first few days."

"My nanna's like that," said Laurie.

"She doesn't know you're here?"

"No way. She'd go ape."

Miss Freeman grimaced. "You know, I really shouldn't let you up there without your parents saying it's okay," she said. "But if Dickie knew you came and I didn't take you up, it would bust his little heart. So I'll do it this once. All right?"

"Thank you," said Laurie.

They took the elevator, standing side by side to watch the lighted numbers change above the door. As the 2 went out and the 3 came on, Laurie asked, "What's it like in Polio?" And Miss Freeman said, "Whatever you're thinking, it's different."

The elevator shimmied as it crossed the third floor. Laurie could only imagine the polio ward in black and white, as she'd seen at the movies, in the March of Dimes. She imagined long rows of iron lungs, a dozen nurses moving about in silence, somebody pitching up and down on a rocking bed, kids in braces learning to walk all over again.

A chime sounded as the elevator stopped. The doors slid open, and Laurie looked out at a green wall, at a poster with a picture of a little boy striding away from his cage of a bed, cured of his polio. He was marching like a soldier, below a huge slogan that said, "Your dimes did this for me!"

"Come on," said Miss Freeman. She stepped out of the elevator, into the hall, with Laurie behind her.

They had gone only a few steps when Laurie heard the scream of a child. It came from somewhere around the next corner, and was followed by another scream, from a different child, and the rumble of wheels turning fast. Miss Freeman moved closer to the wall but didn't slow down. Behind her back, she motioned to Laurie with her fingers. "It might be best if you got out of the way," she said.

Laurie pressed against the wall. She thought a gurney was coming, pushed by running doctors. But round the corner came a wheelchair, moving so fast that it careened on two wheels. In the seat was a girl with long hair, her arms driving the wheels so fast that the spokes looked like solid silver. The chair swerved, then straightened, and the girl looked back and screamed again—a sound of happy fright.

Behind her came a boy. But not in a chair. He was lying on a platform with four little wheels, like something a mechanic would use to roll himself under a car. He was paddling with his feet as he pushed with his hands, and he rolled round the corner like a pinball.

The girl hurtled past. She raised a hand for a moment, high above her head. "Hi ho!" she shouted as she barreled past.

The boy followed behind her, laughing all the time. His platform spun sideways, and he paddled and kicked like a frantic swimmer caught in a current. He hit the wall and bounced away. "Hi, Miss Freeman!" he cried.

Miss Freeman waved as he passed. "See what I mean?" she asked Laurie. "There's usually a wheelchair race or something going on. Last week I saw eight kids in one chair, all piled up like a pyramid."

"Really?" asked Laurie.

"Sure. Sometimes it gets kind of crazy."

◆ ◆ ◆

Laurie followed Miss Freeman around the turn in the corridor, past a large room where many people—mostly children—were busy with different things. A girl with braces on her legs was pushing a doll in a stroller. A boy was using Lincoln Logs to build a sprawling cabin. Others were watching television, staring at a tiny screen in an enormous wooden cabinet.

The corridor turned again. Laurie looked through half-open doors at identical wards, at tall hospital beds with wheels on the legs and railings on the sides. She passed room after room, turned again, and went on to the end of the corridor. The last door was propped open. Miss Freeman stopped just before it.

"This is the respirator room," she said. "It's not so much fun in here."

Her expression had changed; she wasn't smiling anymore. Laurie could see only a corner of the room through the doorway. She heard a hum and whir of machines, a steady whoosh of air.

"Now listen," said Miss Freeman. "When you see Dickie it's going to be a bit of a shock. You'll feel pretty bad for him, but don't let him see it. Okay? If you think you're going to cry, just go look out the window. It won't do him any good to think people are sorry for him." The nurse looked at Laurie. "Can you do that?"

"Okay," said Laurie.

"There are two others in here as well," said the nurse. "They've been here quite a while, and there's one I think might never come out. But don't feel sorry for *them* either, because they're not as alone as you'll think. They get visits from actors sometimes, from magicians and clowns."

Miss Freeman took a step toward the room, then paused again. "These are the bravest kids you'll ever find anywhere," she said. "You know the story of David and Goliath? Well, these kids, they're all Davids to me; that's how I think of them. They got knocked down something awful, but every day they get back up—even if it's only on the inside—and keep throwing their little stones."

Miss Freeman rubbed her nose with the back of her hand. She sniffed and said, "I'm sorry. I get mushy about it." Then she went breezing in the open door, her voice happy and excited. "Hey, Dickie! Guess who's here."

◆ ◆ ◆

Laurie had never seen an iron lung, except in the films for the March of Dimes. Now four of them were right in front

{24}

of her, and she could hardly believe how big they were, how high they stood on their framework of metal legs. They reminded her of the Martians' spaceships from *The War of the Worlds*, the big cylinders that had smashed into Earth with tiny creatures inside them. There was a blond-haired girl in the first one, a boy in the second, little Dickie in the third. But only their heads stuck out from the ends of the metal tubes, resting on pillowed shelves. It looked as though their bodies had been swallowed by the cylinders, because the metal things seemed so much alive. The huff and puff she'd heard was the breathing of the machines. Their rubber lungs worked below their bellies, and she watched them stretch and shrink, fill and empty.

The fourth machine was vacant. Still and quiet, its lungs frozen, it seemed to be dead. Or waiting.

Laurie saw this all in a moment, in the time it took the children to turn their faces toward her. Dickie grinned. "Oh, boy," he said. "It's Laurie."

The others just stared: the boy in the middle with a curious look, the girl with no expression at all. Their skin was pale, their faces gaunt. Dickie said, "Laurie's my best friend." And the girl said, "Whoop-de-doo."

Laurie hurried past her, and past the boy, to stand beside Dickie. Just as the nurse had warned, it was a shock to see him lying on his back, trapped in the iron lung. Around his neck, sealing the opening, was a rubber collar that pulsed with the breathing of the machine—in and out, like the throat of a frog. He was so small that he moved a little distance with every mechanical breath—drawn in, pushed out—as though the machine were a short, fat snake that was forever trying to eat him. But he seemed as happy as ever, a big grin on his face.

"Boy, it's neat you came," he said.

They looked at each other as the respirator hummed and puffed. Dickie had his coonskin cap and his wooden tomahawk hanging on the front of his iron lung. Struts and brackets held a mirror above his head, tilted so that he could look back at the big window in the wall. Along the brackets were cream-colored envelopes stuffed with checklists and medical charts. Between them someone had put up a little picture of Fess Parker, cut from *TV Guide*.

It made Laurie sad to see the cap and the tomahawk, and to think that Dickie couldn't even reach up and touch them, with his arms sealed inside the respirator. It seemed mean to Laurie to dangle those things in front of him—but always out of reach—like a carrot in front of a mule.

His grin, she saw, was fading away. He looked worried now as he stared at her. She forced herself to smile again, but it was too late. Dickie turned his head aside.

Already, Laurie wished that she hadn't come to Bishop's. She didn't know what to say, and neither did he. They just looked at each other, and then at everything else *except* each other.

"Wow. Some friend," said the girl in the iron lung.

Miss Freeman came up beside Laurie. "Dickie's not planning to stay around very long," she said, smiling down at him. "He wants to be at Disneyland on opening day, and you know, I think he's going to make it. When the first steamboat heads off to Frontierland, Dickie's going to be right at the front. Aren't you, Dickie?"

"You bet!" His grin was back already. "I can move my fingers, Laurie. Want to see me move my fingers?"

"Of course she does," said Miss Freeman. She guided Laurie to the side of the iron lung, where narrow windows were spaced along the metal. Inside, Dickie was covered by a white sheet. His naked feet and ankles poked out at the bottom, his bare shoulders at the top. His right hand rested at his side.

"You watching?" he asked.

Muscles strained in his neck. His face flushed red with the effort he was making. But his hand lay perfectly still.

His mouth stretched into a grimace. His eyes closed; a straining sort of grunt came from his throat. Then the tips of his fingers twitched.

They rose a quarter of an inch from the mattress. They straightened just a tiny bit. Then they fell back into place, and Dickie seemed exhausted. He was immensely proud, but utterly worn out.

To Laurie, it was the most pathetic little effort she had ever seen. Just weeks before, Dickie had been running down the Shenandoah, bounding from bank to bank with the fringes leaping on his jacket, the raccoon tail flapping from his cap. And now all he could do was twitch the tips of his fingers? She couldn't understand why it made him so proud.

But Miss Freeman squealed with delight. "Oh, Dickie!" she said with a clap of her hands. "That's wonderful. You're on your way to Disneyland for sure."

Dickie looked at Laurie with such a grin that he might have just hit a home run in a stadium full of fans. "Did you see it?" he said.

"Yes," said Laurie. "That was great." She paused a moment. "But, you know, I think—"

She was going to say *I think I should leave now*, but again Miss Freeman stepped in. "*I* think you should meet the others." And she started with the girl.

◆ ◆ ◆

Her name was Carolyn Jewels.

She was maybe fourteen, and though her face was very thin and very pale, she looked as pretty as a movie star. Her hair was like Rapunzel's, a golden braid that tumbled from the pillow nearly to the floor. She looked not at Laurie but up at her tilted mirror.

"Carolyn's been with us for almost eight years," said Miss Freeman. "We're going to have a heck of a party next month, aren't we, Carolyn? A real blowout."

"Sure." The girl could talk only when the iron lung was breathing out, when the bellows were shrinking below her. "We'll all do the cha-cha."

"Oh, Carolyn!" Miss Freeman rolled her eyes. She let out a little sigh, but never stopped smiling. "You don't want Laurie to think you're a sourpuss, do you?"

The bellows filled, then began to shrink again. "I couldn't care less," said Carolyn.

◆ ◆ ◆

The boy in the middle was older than Dickie but younger than Carolyn. His skin had shrunk around his bones, and

{28}

his scalp showed white as snow through the short hairs of his flattop haircut. It was obvious that he had a huge crush on Miss Freeman. He gazed at her with the dumb look of a sheep.

"Hi, Miss Freeman," he said.

"Hello, Chip." The nurse took a handkerchief from her sleeve and dabbed the boy's chin. There was a line of spittle there, dried and crusty. "Chip came in last summer. He's learning to breathe on his own. And his legs are fine; no trouble there. So it shouldn't be long till he's walking out."

The front of his iron lung was covered with so many pictures that they overlapped like crazy shingles. Most were postcards from different places, and magazine pictures of automobiles, mostly woodies and pickups and slim little sports cars. But set among them were family photographs—some in color, some in black-and-white—of people doing simple, everyday things. Right in the middle of the bunch, a man and a boy stood in front of an open garage, with a strange sort of car in the shadows behind them. The man was wearing a T-shirt with a pack of cigarettes rolled up in the sleeve. He was resting a hand on the boy's shoulder and he had his head back, laughing. The boy was about eight years old, strong and tanned. But his face was so smeared with black grease that he looked like a war-painted Indian.

"Chip gets heaps of mail," said Miss Freeman. "His dad's always sending him a picture or a postcard or something."

Laurie was fascinated by the photograph. It was hard for her to see how that greasy kid had grown up to be the thin rake of a boy in front of her. The kid looked so healthy, so strong, that he might have been a different person altogether.

"Chip's a mechanic," said Miss Freeman.

Again, Carolyn interrupted. "Not a real one."

"Well, real enough for me," said Miss Freeman. "Chip and his dad are building a car together. Can you imagine that, Laurie? Actually building a *car*?" She made it sound like the eighth wonder of the world. "It's a hot rod, isn't it, Chip?"

"Stripped-out Model B," he said. "Flathead Ford."

"Wow," said Miss Freeman.

"Ten-inch cam."

"My goodness!" She put her hands on her cheeks. "One day you'll take me for a ride, now, won't you?"

"Sure."

"I know—you can take me to Disneyland." She smiled, and that made him blush. "We can all go. You and me and Dickie . . ."

"Oh, boy!" cried Dickie. "Can Laurie come?"

"I'm sure there's room for everyone. What about you, Carolyn? You want to go to Disneyland?"

The girl could talk only in short sentences, in bursts of words with the bellows wheezing between them. "You'll need long . . . extension cords."

"Yes," said Miss Freeman. The happy conversation had fizzled, like a fire doused with water. The bright little sparks in Dickie's eyes were gone. "Thank you, Carolyn."

◆ ◆ ◆

Miss Freeman lifted the watch from the front of her blouse. "My, look at the time," she said. "I'm supposed to be downstairs."

{30}

Laurie turned to go with her, afraid of being abandoned in the room of iron lungs.

"Oh, Laurie, there's no need for you to leave just yet," said Miss Freeman. "You can stay and visit with Dickie if you want. I'll check in every once in a while and make sure no one gangs up on you."

Well, she couldn't say no. But she took the nurse's advice and went quickly to the window. She looked down at the pond and the grass, at the distant gate in the wall. A black Cadillac with stubby fins was just pulling out onto the street, and she wished she were in it.

"What do you see?" asked Carolyn Jewels, behind her.

"Nothing," said Laurie.

"Clean your glasses, four-eyes."

There was a laugh from Chip. Laurie blushed. "Well, it's kind of raining," she said. "There's a car going out—"

"What kind of car?" asked Chip.

"A Cadillac. A Park Avenue, I think."

"That's boss!" he said. "They're keen."

"The gardener's picking up all his bits of ivy; he doesn't look very happy. There's a brown duck in the pond, but no one's sitting—"

"What pond?" asked Chip.

"The one right there." Laurie pointed. "With the benches around it."

"He can't see it, you stupe," said Carolyn.

Laurie turned toward the respirators. She could see three faces hovering in the slanted mirrors, reflected from the pillows. They seemed to float there, just above the round machines, like the disembodied head of the Wizard of Oz.

"I came in the dark," said Chip. "In an ambulance."

"Well, it's not much of a pond," said Laurie. "It's got willow trees around it, and benches for people." She looked again through the window, trying to see what Dickie and the others would see in their mirrors: the sky and the clouds; maybe the very tops of the highest buildings, the peaks of the hills in the distance. They could never look down at the grass, never watch the squirrels or the ducks or the mothers with their babies. The shadows slid across the grass unseen by them, shrinking in the mornings, growing in the afternoons. The sun was always hidden.

"My nanna used to take me to the pond in a stroller," said Laurie. "That's my first memory: throwing bread for the ducks when I couldn't even throw as far as the water. I remember how they waddled out, like they were angry. We called it Piper's Pond."

"Why?"

"I don't know." She had never thought about the name. "Maybe there was a man who played the bagpipes there. Way before the war."

"What did he look like?" asked Dickie.

"No one ever saw his face."

This was how she and Dickie had told their stories of the train people: one asking questions, the other inventing answers. It made Laurie feel more comfortable to be doing it again, and now she put her forehead on the glass, her palms on the windowsill. In her mind she could see the piper down below her, with long tassels streaming from the horns of his bagpipes. It wasn't daylight anymore. She was looking out at a chewed-away moon that turned the water to silver, the piper to a dark silhouette. "He wore a white mask that made him look like a ghost," she said. "It covered his eyes and his cheeks, just a white mask with one black teardrop painted on the cheek. And he played the same song all the time. He played 'Danny Boy,' slowly, under the weeping willows."

"Why?" asked Dickie.

"He was mourning," she said. "For a girl that he loved, who drowned in the pond."

"That's bull," said Carolyn.

"Oh, it's just a story!" Laurie heard the angry snap in her voice, and regretted it right away. She could hear the machines wheezing behind her, and imagined herself in Carolyn's place, lying for eight years on her back, seeing the world upside down in a mirror. Wouldn't she too find it hard to be nice to people?

"I'm sorry," said Laurie.

Carolyn didn't answer. The motors whirred on the iron lungs, the bellows groaned and filled.

When it seemed that no one might ever speak again, it was Dickie who started talking.

"Laurie makes up stories all the time," he said. "She used to tell about the train people. About Davy Crockett. Boy, she told good stories."

His voice was high and happy. He beamed at Laurie in his mirror. "Could you tell us one now?"

# CHAPTER THREE

## A GIANT-SLAYER IS BORN

More than anything Laurie wanted to please Dickie. But when he asked her to tell a story, she didn't think that she could do it.

"Please?" he said. "Tell about a dragon. And a guy like Davy Crockett."

Laurie Valentine had made up stories all her life. She *lived* in stories that she narrated constantly in her head. But it was completely different to tell a story to people she didn't know. "How would it start?" she asked, with an odd-sounding laugh.

"Once upon a time," said Dickie. "Like that." He breathed with the machine. "Once upon a time. There was a man named Fingal."

"Why Fingal?" asked Laurie.

"I dunno." Dickie grinned wider than ever. "I like that name."

"Well, you're right. There *was* a man named Fingal," she said. "He kept an inn called the Dragon's Tooth, at the foot of the Great North Road."

◆ ◆ ◆

The inn was made of black timber and white plaster. It was two stories high, and the chimney at the top had a slab of stone set into it, as a resting place for any passing witch.

There was a parlor with a big fireplace, seven rooms upstairs, and a stable around the back. Just to the south, the Great North Road split off from the High Road. It headed past the Dragon's Tooth and into the wilderness, into a forest as thick as the hair on a dog's back, as black as night even at noon. When the Great North Road curved to the right and went into that forest, it didn't come out again for a hundred miles. Many of the people who went along it *never* came out again. So every traveler—no matter where he was heading—stopped at Fingal's inn. He found others there, sitting in front of the fire, and the ones going north asked the ones going south for news about thieves and trolls. On their way in, and on their way out, the travelers touched the dragon's tooth.

◆ ◆ ◆

"Why?" asked Dickie.

"For luck," said Laurie.

"What did it look like?"

"It was five feet long," she said. "A bit bigger than me. It was like a thick saber, hung sideways from chains above the door, just inside the parlor. Where it curved down in the middle, it was worn to a shine by the fingers of the travelers."

"Like who?" asked Chip.

"Oh, the woodsmen," said Laurie. "And the wandering knights, and the ones who went searching for gold. And the unicorn hunters, and the minstrels, and the dragon slayers. The only ones who never stopped at the inn were the Gypsies and the gnome runners. *They* passed right by, up the Great North Road."

"Where did it go to?" asked Chip.

"No one really knew," she said. "It was a mystery."

"How come?"

"Because no one ever returned from the end of it."

"That's so dumb!" Carolyn Jewels was glaring at Laurie in her mirror. Her beautiful face seemed hard as marble. "If no one got to the end," she asked, "how did anyone build it?"

Laurie liked little puzzles like that. She smiled as an answer came right away. "That was a mystery too," she said. "The road was so old that no one remembered who made it, or when. The people believed that it went up into the land of the giants, but nobody knew for sure."

"Who were the giants?" asked Dickie.

"Well, one of them was called Collosso, and he was the worst of all. He was the tallest, and the meanest, and the cruelest. He ate babies for breakfast, tossing them into his mouth like peanuts."

"I like that." Dickie grinned ghoulishly in the mirror. "Start over with the giant. Okay?"

"Start over?" asked Laurie.

"Yes, please. With Collosso."

◆ ◆ ◆

Once upon a time, there was a giant named Collosso. He lived at the edge of the earth, in a castle made of white stone. He kept a thousand slaves to do his work, and a thousand more for dreadful entertainments.

On most mornings Collosso went out of his castle with a basket on his arm. He strode across the land at a hundred feet for every step, filling his basket with food. He plucked sheep from the fields, and cows from the pastures; he took the farmers too, scooping them up as they ran for their lives. He chased them hunched over, his arms reaching out, like a monstrous boy hunting beetles. He uprooted whole trees of apples and figs and pears, shaking them into his basket. Along the way he snacked on dogs and cats, on chickens and gryphons and gnomes.

Every person and every animal lived in fear of Collosso. Even the birds kept glancing around, watching the far horizon, for at any moment the giant might appear. He could stride across a hill, or come sweeping through a forest like a farmer through a field of wheat, crushing the trees to make a path. The people set out offerings of fruit and bread and butchered sheep, hoping to keep Collosso away from their homes and farms. But it never worked. So every three or four years, someone would stand up in a village square and announce that he was setting out to kill the giant. He would hold a pitchfork in the air and ask, "Who will come along?" But always he would end up going alone, never to return.

Collosso laughed at those men who came to kill him. He never squashed the giant-slayers, but took them alive and kept them in his toy box, to amuse himself with at night. He was so big and powerful that nothing could scare him. Thirty years he lived without a twinge of fright, without a single thought of danger.

Then, one night in midsummer, a black storm rose in the mountains.

It began at midnight, with a rumble of thunder no louder than the purring of a cat. But an hour later it was shaking people from their beds with a terrible din and a roar of wind.

From end to end, the sky flashed silver. Bolts of lightning cracked the clouds apart, shot toward the ground, and set the forests aflame. Sparks flew half a mile high, and the colors of the fire shone in the clouds, until it looked as though the air was burning. Animals ran in shrieking herds, deer and wolves together, rabbits and foxes side by side.

Through it all, Collosso slept. The flashes of lightning lit his enormous face, making black shadows round his eyes and mouth. Thunder boomed through his castle, and smoke flowed in through every window, and down in their cages the slaves were screaming. The toys were screaming too. But Collosso didn't stir, though it seemed the end of the world had arrived. He snored softly in his bed as the storm passed over.

It was the final roll of thunder that woke the giant. The

storm had swept a hundred leagues to the south, and the sound was so faint that a pine cone falling in the forest could have drowned it out. But with that tiny noise, Collosso sprang up in his bed. Six tons he weighed, yet in a flash he was upright. His heart, the size of a mule, kicked wildly in his chest. For the first time in his life, Collosso was terrified.

Far below his castle, the forests crackled as they burned. Trees exploded with puffs of yellow flame, and a blizzard of sparks whirled through the sky. Collosso stood at his window, pale as death in the shifting colors of the flames.

Somewhere in the land, beyond the mountains and the forest, beneath that final thunderbolt, a boy was breathing his first breaths. Collosso knew it as surely as he knew anything. A giant-slayer, that night, was born.

◆ ◆ ◆

"Gee, who was it?" asked Dickie. His iron lung wheezed and hummed. "What was his name? The giant-slayer?"

"Don't be a stupe," said Carolyn. "It was Fingal."

Laurie looked at the girl through the mirror. She didn't mind if Carolyn listened to the story. She didn't even mind that the girl tried to seem bored and pained, as though she wasn't really listening at all. But it bothered her very much that Carolyn had guessed so easily that Fingal was the giant-slayer. So Laurie changed her story.

"Well, it wasn't Fingal," she said, as though the thought were crazy. "It was the *son* of Fingal."

"Gosh!" said Dickie. "What was his name?"

"Jimmy."

Carolyn put on a petulant, doubting look. "Jimmy the giant-slayer?"

"Yes, that's right," said Laurie.

◆ ◆ ◆

Jimmy was born in the thunderstorm. The same clap of thunder that had woken Collosso was the first sound that the baby heard. For him it was monstrously loud, an ear-splitting crash right over his head. Down in the parlor, Fingal watched in fear as the rafters shook and a snowfall of plaster fell upon him. But Jimmy didn't cry. He didn't wail or shriek; he just lay in his mother's arms, pink and wrinkled, like a wise old man.

At the moment of his birth, the wolves began calling from the forest. They sang and they howled, more wolves than ever had sung at once. Jimmy's mother, hearing them, pulled the blankets over herself and the baby. She lay shaking in the bed while Jimmy laughed and kicked against her.

Although she must have had a name, no one could remember ever hearing it. She was Fingal's wife—the Woman—no more than that. Thin as a whip, with hard lines in her face, she had a nose like the blade of an axe. She was always telling her husband what to do, and when to do it, and when to do it again if he hadn't done it right.

Jimmy wasn't the firstborn child. He was neither the second nor the third, but he would never meet the others. A sister had drowned, and another had been squashed by the giant, while his only brother—Tom—had simply disappeared.

Fingal's wife told anyone who asked that Tom had struck out on his own, up the Great North Road to seek his fortune in the mountains, but as he was only six years old at the time, that seemed unlikely. Fingal believed the gryphons had got him. "There's nothing that gryphons like better than boys," he said.

"Well, gryphons won't get this boy," said Fingal's wife. "My little Jimmy won't be eaten, and he won't be squashed. He's my little treasure."

*Treasure?* thought Fingal. He muttered under his breath, careful not to be heard. "*Woman, you're mad if you're thinking that babby's a treasure.*"

Fingal was a mean-hearted man, and to him the child was a cost, an item he recorded on the debit side of his ledger. On the day that his son was born he drew a narrow column that he headed "Jimmy," and there he recorded in minuscule writing—because even ink cost money—every expense, from diapers to mashed peas. He had started columns for his other children, and began this one in the same way—with a huge sigh, as though he believed it was bound to be a wasted effort. As he wrote he kept moaning, "All debits, no credits. What's the use of a babby?"

◆ ◆ ◆

"What about the giant?" asked Dickie, in his iron lung. The bellows worked below him. "Did Collosso go looking for Jimmy?"

"No, he didn't," said Laurie.

"Was he scared?" asked Chip.

Dickie's head nodded slightly on the pillow. "I think so."

"Well, you're right; he was," said Laurie. She shifted her feet, leaning back against the windowsill. "Collosso was scared to death of the giant-slayer."

♦ ♦ ♦

For days, the giant fretted in his castle. He stood at the ramparts, staring across the mountains, over the valleys, toward fields and forests. From sunrise to darkness he stood and stared, leaning his elbows on the great stone blocks.

It was all he could think about, that a giant-slayer was out there. The idea worried away at him, as though an animal gnawed at his innards. At night he dreamed about the giant-slayer, then woke in the morning more frightened than he'd been the day before. On a Sunday afternoon, as he had on many Sundays, he took out his entertainments. He lifted the lid and saw the people cowering inside. Some held on to each other, some raised their hands toward him for mercy, and many sat hunched and quivering in the corners. Just weeks before, the sight would have made him laugh uproariously. But now he only slammed the lid in place again and pushed the box away.

"Curse him. Curse him," said Collosso. "I cannot bear this any longer."

Right then, the giant got up from his chair. He put on his jaunty red hat and went out from the castle. He strode to the south, over the pass and down a valley, then west across the foothills. People scurried away, hiding in ditches, diving into cellars. Collosso didn't stop to crush them. His arms swinging, his great thighs shaking, he marched along with his enormous boots smashing all in his path. Flights of white swans rose from fields and copses, and he swatted at them as though at mosquitoes.

He went straight to the marshes, to the home of the Swamp Witch. He believed that she had lived a hundred years in the mud, and knew everything there was to know. He had gone to see her twice before, the first time to ask how long he would live. She had taken a frog and pulled off its legs, then stirred the pieces in the mud, reading the patterns they made. Then she had looked up and told him mysteriously, "You shall live to the end of your days." Three years later he had gone again, to see if she could turn his hair from curly to straight, because he believed that giants looked best with straight hair. Again she had killed a frog and cast its pieces. "Wear a red hat," she'd told him.

The journey would have taken any man a year, but Collosso was there in hours. He stomped down the long slopes of barley and corn, through a forest of pines, to the edge of a swamp that seemed to stretch on forever.

It was believed that the marshes were bottomless. It was said that an ancient city—with streets of gold—lay drowned in the swamp. A famous legend told of 'the lost army' that had marched out to find the city, only to vanish in the mud. Its leagues of men, its hundreds of horses, its wagons and chariots had disappeared in a moment, along with seven siege towers nearly as tall as Collosso. Some said that the witch had eaten every man and horse.

Well, the stories weren't utter nonsense. Collosso strode out into the mud and sank to his ankles. Then he sank to his knees. Then he sank to his waist. As thick as tar, the mud sucked and oozed around his feet, and the black water swirled in torrents behind him.

When the water was up to his armpits and getting deeper with every step, Collosso found the Swamp Witch. She had a little round house, like a beaver lodge, of sticks and mud, with a smoke hole at the top, and a little round door in the front. Collosso tapped on the top of the house, and the ducks and the alligators slipped away among the reeds.

The witch came oozing from the mud behind her house. She was clotted with filth. Her hair was long, her face all wrinkles. She had the eyes of a lizard and the hands of a frog—each finger webbed at the base, tipped at the end by a fleshy knob. Her throat bulged as she breathed, and her voice was a croak.

"I knew you were coming," she said. Her neck filled like a red balloon.

"You sensed it?" asked Collosso.

"I *heard* it." She was looking up at the face of the giant, into the caverns of his nostrils. "You wake the dead with your splashing."

Her voice drifted off across the marshes, through the bulrushes and the grasses. The birds were silent, the frogs as well, and the water beetles stood as still as possible on their trembly legs.

"I had a dream," said Collosso. "A horrible dream."

"Of what?"

"A giant-slayer."

The witch pulled herself from the mud and sat in a chair

of woven reeds. She felt nearly sorry for the giant because he looked so scared and worried. He didn't seem to notice that he was sinking into the swamp, a little deeper every minute. The water now was nearly at his shoulders.

"I had a dream. Or a vision," said Collosso. "I saw the giant-slayer born of thunder. Oh, witch, is it true?"

"It is true," said the witch.

"How do you know this?"

"Because you dreamed it."

"Oh, curse my powers!" The giant looked up at the sky. His great fists came out of the water and he held them high above his head, as though trying to shake the clouds. "Curse me!" he roared again.

Alligators swung their tails and backed away, their round eyes blinking. Snakes slithered off through the grass, and the crayfish scuttled deeper in the mud.

"Help me, witch!" said Collosso. He settled more deeply in the mud. The black water closed over his shoulders, and his huge head seemed to float there in its red hat. "Please," he said. "What do I do?"

"Go home to your castle," she told him in her croaky voice. "Wait for the slayer to come."

"Will he kill me?" asked the giant.

"He will try," said the witch. "But remember this: as long as you are living, you cannot be killed."

This gave the giant a strange comfort. For the first time in a fortnight, a smile came to his face. The deep lines of worry smoothed away from his eyes, and he muttered to himself: "As long as I am living, I cannot be killed."

"Now go," said the Swamp Witch. "Hurry home to your castle."

She was sliding feet first from her chair, vanishing into the swamp. But Collosso cried out, "Wait! There's more. That wasn't the end of my dream."

"What else did you see?" she asked.

"He came to find you. I saw him with you in the swamp, and in my dream he spoke to you." Collosso tried to shift his feet. The water crept higher up his neck. "He bade you to point the way to my castle. He said, 'I mean to kill Collosso. I will do him in a flash.' Oh, witch, what does it mean?"

"Many things," she said. "But this above all: you must protect me, for your dream must be fulfilled. The giant-slayer must come to see me."

"What will you tell him?" asked Collosso.

"Whatever you like."

The giant sighed a mighty sigh. His breath flattened a field of rushes, scattering ducks and blackbirds. "Send him to my castle. Tell him I am waiting," he said. "And tell him this: before that day is done I will crush him in my fingers like a nit." Again his hand came out of the water. He pressed his fingers together, as though already crushing. Then he turned around and waded home, with the water churning into monstrous waves until he reached the solid ground. He went full of joy, so happy that he actually skipped across the foothills, over the black ground of burned forests. He sang to himself as he crashed through the dead trees. "As long as I live, I cannot be killed."

Straightaway, Collosso put his slaves to work. "Build me a lookout tower half a mile high," he commanded. "Dig me a moat half a mile deep. Fill it with pitch and tar, and build me a drawbridge to cross it."

Collosso collected more slaves, and more after that. He put them all to the task of strengthening his castle. "Hurry," he told them. "The giant-slayer is coming."

◆ ◆ ◆

In her iron lung across the room, Carolyn sighed as loudly as she could. "That's so dumb," she said. "It would take years to finish."

"He knew that," said Laurie. "Collosso figured he had twelve years before the giant-slayer would be old enough to come after him. In all that time, he never rested for an hour."

◆ ◆ ◆

On Jimmy's first birthday, Fingal lit a candle and went down to the basement of the Dragon's Tooth. He pulled the bung from a half-emptied cask of brandy and ladled water through the hole. It was a job that he'd done every morning for seventeen years, and it always made him happy. He liked the smell and the gurgling sound, the flash of his candlelight on the pouring water.

He worked in shadows, for the basement was a gloomy place, the home of rats and spiders. Every now and then he paused to sample the thinning brandy, then smacked his lips and started again. He cackled as he worked, overcome by the thought that he was turning water into gold.

The cask was nearly full when Fingal heard the Woman

shout. *"Fingal!"* The sound, though faint, took him by surprise.

"Oh, mercy, what now?" he said to himself. "I'll never have a moment's peace with a babby in the house."

She shouted again. *"Fingal!"*

"All right, all right, I'm coming," said Fingal.

He slammed the bung in its hole and rolled the keg aside. Then, with a sigh, he made his way up the back stairs and through the parlor.

There were only three travelers that day at the inn. They sat in a row, close to the tiny fire: a minstrel, a shepherd, and a dealer in the fine carpets that were woven by trolls. The shepherd was poking with his crook at a pile of embers no bigger than an anthill, while the minstrel shivered beside him. Outside, the day was warm and sunny; it was fear that chilled the travelers, for all three were about to set off up the Great North Road.

"Is there trouble, innkeep?" asked the shepherd as Fingal passed behind them.

"There's always trouble," said Fingal. "That's what comes with a babby."

At the top of the inn, the Woman's room was in darkness. The shutters were drawn and latched, and the Woman lay in her bed with the sheets pulled up to her chin.

"What's the matter, Woman?" asked Fingal.

She didn't say a word, but only shifted her eyes toward the window. Jimmy's crib—standing there—was empty.

"The babby?" said Fingal hopefully. "Has it wandered off?"

"No, you fool." The Woman shifted the blankets so that

Fingal could see Jimmy sleeping beneath them. "There's someone outside."

"Who is it?" asked Fingal.

"How should I know?" She shook her head, as though he was stupid. "Why don't you look and see?"

Fingal's ears turned a bright red. But he tried to keep his temper. "I was in the basement, Woman," he said slowly. "Did you have to bring me all the way up here so that I could look out your window?"

"Well, how else could you look out of it?" she asked with a cluck of her tongue.

Fingal fumed. Sixteen years he'd been married. He'd done the Woman's bidding night and day. But, suddenly, he'd had enough.

"Woman, you're a layabout," he told her.

Her mouth fell open. She stared at him, aghast. Flat on her back, covered from chin to toes, she lay there and looked at him. The only sound in the room was her breathing, hard and steady.

"All day you lie there," said Fingal. "Well, if you want to know who's outside, get up and look. Shift yourself, Woman. I'm sick of the sight of you."

◆ ◆ ◆

"Hardy har har. That's so funny I forgot to laugh," said Carolyn.

She lay like Fingal's wife, staring up from a hard bed as rubber bellows whooshed and wheezed. "You think I'm lazy? 'Cause I asked you what was outside?"

{49}

Laurie felt rotten. She'd forgotten that that was how everything had started, with Carolyn asking what she could see from the window. All she had wanted to do was make Dickie forget where he was for an hour or two, to free him from his iron lung. Instead, she had sealed them all more tightly.

In the tilted mirrors she could see the three faces. Dickie had his eyes closed, but his skin was pulled into wrinkles by the things he was thinking. Chip had turned his head to the left, and only Carolyn was staring right back. "He's polio, isn't he?" said the girl in the iron lung. "Your dumb giant."

Dickie's eyes opened now. Chip rolled his head to look at Caroline.

"Well, guess what?" said Carolyn. "He can't be killed. You can never beat polio."

"I didn't mean that," said Laurie.

"Just get out of here." Carolyn looked away from the mirror. Her long braid swished like the tail of an angry cat.

Laurie imagined how frustrating it would be if you couldn't wave your arms when you were angry, if you couldn't run away from anything. Without another word, she left the room. Though Dickie called out to stop her, she didn't look back. She ran for the elevator.

She heard the chime as she rounded the last bend in the hall. She saw the doors open and Miss Freeman come out.

"Laurie," said the nurse, surprised. But with one look, she somehow understood. "Did Carolyn tell you to leave?"

Laurie nodded.

"That happens a lot. It's not your fault."

The elevator doors were wide open. Laurie wanted to push her way past the nurse.

"Carolyn likes people to think that she's strong and brave," said Miss Freeman. "But inside, she's a frightened girl. Just a sad and lonely girl with not very much to look forward to."

"You said she's getting better," said Laurie.

"Oh, there's lots of ways she can make improvements." The doors closed and the elevator hummed as it started down. "If wishing was medicine, Carolyn would have been home a long, long time ago. What she needs right now is a little understanding. She craves that, though she'd never admit it. Not many people come to visit Carolyn."

"No wonder," said Laurie.

Miss Freeman smiled. "If you showed some interest, it might surprise you what could happen."

"I think I should go home now," said Laurie.

"Of course," said Miss Freeman. "But if you want to come back and see Dickie again, I think I could allow it."

"I'd like to," said Laurie. "Sometime."

"Saturday would be terrific."

◆ ◆ ◆

For the rest of the week, Laurie kept thinking about the polio ward and the iron lungs. She kept seeing the faces floating in the mirrors: Dickie Espinosa smiling as though he had no worries at all, Carolyn Jewels turning angrily aside. The first image made her happy, the other made her miserable. She wanted to talk to someone about it but didn't dare say a word to her father.

At the Valentine house, it was a week like any other. Mrs.

{51}

Strawberry came and went, never particularly happy nor particularly sad. Mr. Valentine commented on stories in the newspaper, about Eisenhower and the atom bomb. On Saturday morning he settled at the dining table with his tax forms and a shoebox full of receipts. He grumbled about the tax man. "I slave away while he gets richer."

Laurie went out right after breakfast. She said she would be at the library, but of course she went back to the hospital.

Miss Freeman came down to the lobby, and all the way up on the elevator she fussed with her hair and her little white cap. She pulled out all her bobby pins and held them in her lips as she put everything back in order. "I don't know how you plan to spend the day," she said, mumbling past the pins. "But don't think you have to be everybody's entertainment. You don't need to do a song and dance." She looked at her reflection on the elevator's shiny wall. "Chip likes to read his car magazines, so maybe you can turn the pages for him if it isn't much trouble. Carolyn would drop dead if she knew I told you this, but she likes to hear about the movie stars. If you could mention something about Marilyn Monroe or Rudy Vallee or—"

"I don't know anything about them," said Laurie.

"Well, it doesn't matter."

The number 4 lit up. Laurie felt the elevator slowing. "Last time," she said, "I started telling them a story."

"Well, I guess you could always do that," said Miss Freeman. "I would think they get their fill of stories from books and things, but I suppose you never know."

There was no one racing wheelchairs that morning. In the

big room at the bend of the hall, everyone was crowded in front of the television, cheering as a tiny Roy Rogers galloped across the screen on Trigger, his palomino. On the little round screen, his white hat was the size of a pencil eraser.

In the respirator room, Carolyn and Chip and Dickie lay in their row, in the steady pulse of their machines. The mirrors above them had been turned around, and on their backs were metal clips and straps. Carolyn had two books fastened to her mirror, held side by side in the fastenings. Chip had a car magazine, Dickie a comic book. All three twisted their necks to look toward the doorway.

It was clearly Miss Freeman's first visit to the room that day. She went in all happy and chirpy, talking about the weather, about things she'd seen on the way to work. All the time, she kept moving between the iron lungs, looking into each of them through the windows in their sides. She unfastened the clips on the mirrors and turned over pages.

"Who's this?" she asked Dickie as she put his comic back in place. "This man with the black hat?"

"Gee, that's Clay Harder," said Dickie.

"Is he a bad guy?"

Dickie laughed. "Boy, I don't think so! He's the Two-Gun Kid."

It was a surprise for Laurie to see what Carolyn was reading. On the left side of the mirror was *Silas Marner,* and on the right was *The Catcher in the Rye.* Both were too difficult for Laurie, and she thought they made her story of a giant-slayer seem silly and childish. It seemed no wonder that Carolyn wasn't interested.

Miss Freeman brought a wooden chair for Laurie to stand

on, to turn the pages. "I'll be back in an hour or two," she said, and left the room.

Laurie sat with Dickie, reading the comic aloud. But every few minutes Chip or Carolyn asked for pages to be turned, and she had to drag her chair along the iron lungs.

She was clumsy with the clips. *Silas Marner* tumbled from the mirror, hitting Carolyn square in the forehead. When the same thing happened with *The Catcher in the Rye,* Carolyn lost her patience. "Just leave me alone!" she snapped. "Get away from me."

"I'm sorry," said Laurie. She felt as awkward as a hippopotamus.

As though to comfort her, Chip said, "Come look at this hemi."

Laurie stood at his side. There were four pictures on the pages of his magazine, and she had no idea where the hemi was, or even *what* a hemi was. So she looked instead at the wonderful clutter of photographs as he rambled on about valve stems and piston rings—a few words at a time. She looked at the boy and the man, at the boy in a soapbox racer, at the boy flying a kite, at the boy playing football. She tried to arrange them chronologically in her mind, hoping to track the life of a child who would one day end up in an iron lung. But the pictures wouldn't fit in any order, because the boy kept changing.

She became so lost in the pictures that she forgot about Dickie and the Two-Gun Kid. She forgot about *everything,* until Carolyn spoke up beside her: "So . . . who was outside?"

Laurie didn't understand.

"You stupe," said Carolyn. "The inn. The *Woman*. She said there was someone outside."

Laurie wasn't sure why Carolyn brought up the story. She wondered if the girl was jealous of Chip, or just bored half to death by *Silas Marner*. But whatever the reason, Carolyn saved the story.

And by doing that, she changed the lives of all of them.

# CHAPTER FOUR

## THE STORY OF CAROLYN JEWELS

F ingal was standing very close to the window. When the Woman told him to look out, all he had to do was straighten his arm and open the shutters. But he didn't move.

"You want to know who's there, get up and look," he said.

The Woman grew furious. She shouted at him to open the window. She commanded him to do it. But he stood there like a stone man, until she finally got up and barreled past him, leaving Jimmy on the bed. She wrenched the latch and flung the shutters wide.

Up through the window came the jingling sound of a harness, the stomp and snort of horses. The Woman leaned out, looking nearly straight down at the roadway. The back of her nightdress lifted from the floor, showing stockings that had been darned so many times that they were nearly all patches.

The sight of the Woman's legs made Fingal want to take hold of her ankles and tip her through the window. He could see himself doing it—so clearly that he imagined the rough feel of her stockings, the great weight as he levered her over the sill. Then she snapped at him—"Come and look!"—and the picture dissolved. He squeezed in beside her at the open window.

Down below him was a fancy carriage, trimmed with gold. Its four black horses wore helmets of silver, and the harnesses glistened with jewels. Fingal had never seen a finer carriage in all his life. He thought the King himself must have come to visit, so he carefully spat on his fingers and smoothed his hair into place.

The driver was wearing a uniform of scarlet, black, and yellow. He had a pair of round goggles that he whipped off and placed on the seat. They left white circles round his eyes, for his face was caked with gray dust. Then he climbed from his seat and opened the carriage door.

Fingal peered down. He saw a long, black boot of shiny leather. On the toe was a cap of silver, and at the other end of the boot was a thin and wretched man with a small hat and voluminous cloak. His neck seemed as narrow as a pipe stem, while his nose was enormous, every bit as red as the driver's bright tunic. He paused on the step and blew into a white handkerchief.

"Who's the fancy Nancy, then?" asked the Woman.

"It's the tax man," said Fingal, annoyed. He had combed his hair for nothing. "I'd better go and meet him."

He hurried down the stairs, arriving in the parlor just as the travelers were leaving by the back door. The tax man looked over Fingal's books, then helped himself from the cash box. He demanded that the Woman come downstairs, and when he saw little Jimmy in her arms, he whipped out a folding ruler and measured the length of the giant-slayer. Then he blew his nose a second time, levied a tax on the child, and dipped again into the cash box. In a big black book he recorded the population of the Dragon's Tooth Inn:

One Fingal
One Woman
One baby, twenty-two inches

◆ ◆ ◆

Fingal had many faults. He was mean and stingy, and he didn't bathe very often. He was sly as a fox, as homely as a hound. He was boastful and full of himself. He was rather stupid, if the truth be told. But one thing he wasn't was lazy. Each day Fingal rose with the sun and worked until dark, when he paused just long enough to eat his supper. Then he labored on by candlelight, counting and sorting his coins.

He had little time for Jimmy. Tending the baby was the Woman's job. But there came a day when the Woman had to go to the market along the high road, and she left little Jimmy with Fingal.

There were two travelers in the parlor, one a gryphon hunter heading south, the other a woodsman going north. The hunter was filling the woodsman's head with stories of the dark forest and of the mountains at the edge of the world. The woodsman, all a-tremble, was drinking glass after glass, so Fingal spent half his time pumping the beer engine and the other half trotting back and forth to the table.

"Fingal, you'll have to mind wee Jimmy," said the Woman. She put the baby carefully into his arms. "Now hold him tight."

"Oh, don't worry. No babby was ever held tighter," said Fingal. But as soon as the Woman was gone, he put the baby on the floor.

Jimmy was a crawler. His little arms and legs pumped madly as he dashed toward the door, racing to catch his mother.

Fingal snatched him up and brought him back. But the baby only crawled away again and sat screaming at the door. So Fingal chopped a hole in the side of an empty brandy keg to make a cradle for his son. He stuffed the boy inside and set it on the polished top of the bar, where the drafts of wind from door and chimney kept it rocking merrily.

At noon the door flew open. The cradle rocked, and into the parlor came an old man with a stooped back, using a walking stick to balance himself. He heaved the door shut and stood squinting into the gloomy parlor. He had a white moustache that fluttered as he breathed.

Fingal called out from the bar, "Are you going north or south, sir?"

"North," said the old man.

"Mind you touch the tooth, then. For luck," said Fingal. "Put a coin in the offering box, and you'll be safe as houses."

The man had to use his walking stick to touch the tooth. He fumbled with his coins. But he bought his luck and got himself seated.

Fingal went to serve him. "What takes you north?" he asked.

"Trolls," said the old man.

Fingal had no idea what business a man could have with trolls, but he certainly didn't care enough to ask. He brought the man an ale, then perched himself on the stool behind the bar.

To him, travelers were like snakes. If you tossed snakes in a pit, they couldn't stop themselves from tangling together, and travelers were the same. They shouted back and forth, then leaned toward each other, and finally the old man got up to join the others.

He took the long route past the bar, where he stopped to fill his glass. He slammed it down and swabbed his arm across his moustache. At his elbow the cradle rocked, with little Jimmy gurgling inside.

The old man smiled. "There's a baby in there," he said, as though Fingal might not have noticed. He made silly goo-gly faces into the brandy keg as Fingal filled the glass. He puffed air against his big moustache, making it ripple like a snowy caterpillar. When he got his change—a six-sided Rhodes—he slipped it into the cradle, down at Jimmy's feet. "For luck," he said with a wink. "Tip a baby, and fortune follows."

*Stupid old fool,* thought Fingal. *You could have bought him for that. And the cradle as well.* But he only smiled and nodded. Then he poked the cradle with his fingertip, to make it rock in a tempting fashion.

The woodsman was next to put a coin in the cradle. He hoped to travel along with the old man, and so was quick to please him. And the gryphon hunter, not to be left out, tossed another Rhodes into the keg.

Fingal's eyes were gleaming then, bright with the shine of gold. When the Woman came home from the market and ran to collect little Jimmy, Fingal steered her away. "Here, leave the babby with me," he said. "He's a wee pleasure to have about, that babby. I'd miss him like the devil."

The Woman was delighted. She went up to her bed and had the first good sleep that she'd had in a year. From her room upstairs she could hear the cradle rocking and the baby laughing inside it.

Fingal made up a sign that night: *Tip a babby; fortune follows.* In the morning he salted the crib with a few copper Constantines, to add a musical jingle to the pitching of the cradle. By evening, Jimmy was sloshing about on a bed of coins.

Salting the cradle became a daily ritual, a chore as happy as the watering of the ale or the draining of used glasses back into bottles. From then on, no traveler passed through the inn without slipping a coin into the keg. Shepherds and hunters, nobles and thieves, they all touched the tooth and tipped the baby. For the first time, the "Jimmy" column in Fingal's ledger began to show a profit.

Fingal was finally a happy man. But of course it didn't last. There came a day when Jimmy didn't fit in the cradle. For a week or more, Fingal had been jamming him into it, like a cork into a bottle. But now, no matter how he squeezed and pushed, it was no use. His little boy—sadly—was longer than the keg.

Fingal replaced the keg with a small barrel. But even as he did it, he knew it was at best a temporary solution. The barrel was only two inches longer, and Jimmy was steadily growing.

◆ ◆ ◆

"Don't let him splint his legs," said Chip.

"What do you mean?" asked Laurie.

Chip was wincing. He had listened to the story quite happily up to now, just lying with his eyes closed, his mouth in a peaceful smile. Now he tried to turn his head far enough to look at Laurie. He said, "I don't want Fingal to splint the baby's legs."

"Why would he?" asked Laurie.

"That's what they did. To polios."

"They did it to me," said Carolyn.

Above the girl's head, *The Catcher in the Rye* was sagging from its clips. Laurie took it down and put it away. She turned the mirror in its frame so that Carolyn could see the sky and trees outside the window. "What's it like?" she asked. "Splinting."

"It's like a torture," said Carolyn. "Remember the old iron maiden? It's just like that." Splinting, she said, was something that Cotton Mather would have done to a witch in Salem if he'd been cruel enough to think of it.

Her iron lung breathed in and out, and she talked in the whoosh of air. "First," she said, "there's nothing more painful than polio. It eats away at your nerves. Then the muscles start to wither. They shrink and tighten. Your legs and arms go crooked; they twist like corkscrews. Your knees bend backward. Your arms look like gnarly little sticks.

"The doctors say, 'We'll help you.' First thing they do, they stick a tube in your spine. They suck out some of the fluid. That's the only way to make sure you've got polio. But they don't tell you if you've got it or not; they don't tell you anything, 'cause you're just a kid. They go away, and you don't know when they're coming back. You think maybe they'll never come back, but they do."

Carolyn wetted her lips with her tongue, then went on as before, talking in snatches between the breaths of her respirator.

"They put wooden splints around your legs. Or they put on plaster casts, or metal things that look like armor from a knight. They pin you down like a butterfly to make sure your bones won't bend. But it happens anyway, and then they start to operate.

"They put you to sleep and smash your legs. They break your bones, then straighten them out and stick them together with pins. They put on the splints and casts again. They bind your legs so tightly that the bones can't grow. And maybe they leave out a bit so you won't have one leg that's longer than the other, 'cause they sure don't want you to look weird.

"They tell you, 'There! Now you'll be better.' It hurts so much that you wish they'd take away the splints and casts

{63}

and leave you alone. But you trust the doctors; you think you must be getting better. Then they come back and tell you, 'Well, we have to operate again,' and it all starts over.

"By then you hate the doctors. You think there's nothing in the world more scary than a doctor."

At the window, Laurie nodded. "Yeah, I know!" she said loudly. "When I was five I had my tonsils out and—"

"Big deal. Big hairy deal," said Carolyn. "It's not like tonsils."

"That's not what I meant," said Laurie.

"How can you say that? How can you be so stupid?" Carolyn glared at Laurie. "I hated my doctors. I wished they would die. They stole me, you know. That's what they did. They took me away from my mom and my dad, and they locked me up in hospital."

It came into Laurie's mind to say, *They were just trying to help you.* But, still stung by Carolyn's reaction to her tonsil story, she was careful not to say anything wrong. "How did it start?" she asked.

The machine pulled air through Carolyn's mouth. The rubber collar that sealed her neck vibrated very slightly. Talking slowly, keeping time with the iron lung, she sounded like a poet with a breathy chorus in the background.

"When I was a kid Daddy called me 'kitten.'

"Wherever we went, he leaned sideways. Bending down to hold my hand.

"We went to the store and the zoo. To the park and the pool.

"We were always alone. Just me and my dad. That's the way I wanted it."

Her eyes were red and wet. She rolled her head against the pillow, trying to blot her own tears.

"I was six years old. Dad took us to a cabin on a lake. There were cottages all around. Everybody swimming all the time.

"There must have been a thousand people," she said. "Maybe more. But no one else got polio. I was the only one."

In that way, in little sentences or phrases, Carolyn told her story. It was the first time that she had done it, from beginning to end.

"One morning," she said, "I felt sick. Hot and creepy. My mother said it was too much sun. She made me stay in bed.

"The sheets hurt me. Just the weight of the sheets. When I cried, Mom said, 'Don't make a fuss. You're barely even sunburned.' She waited three days to call a doctor."

Carolyn described the doctor as a smelly old man with white hair in his ears. "He had lollipops in his shirt pocket," she said. "I could see the little sticks poking up. He pulled out a purple one and held it toward me, and he was disappointed when I didn't want to eat it. 'Well, I'll leave it on the table here,' he said.

"Then he opened his black bag. He took my temperature and tapped my chest. He looked in my ears with a flashlight on a stick. He told my mom, "It's a summer cold. Nothing to worry about.' He said, 'Let her rest a few more days. She'll be as fit as a fiddle.'"

That afternoon, said Carolyn, her arms stopped working. When the sun went down she was having trouble breathing. Her father flew into a rage, ranting about the doctor. "He seemed twenty feet tall," she said, looking up at the mirror above the iron lung. "His voice shook the room. I thought my bed was whirling round and round."

She didn't remember clearly what happened after that. "I was in an ambulance. We were rushing along gravel roads, shuddering over potholes. There was a little bump when we came onto pavement."

Soon, said Carolyn, the darkness of the country gave way to city lights. She remembered the coolness of the air as the ambulance doors were opened, and looking up to see people looming all around her, frightening figures in gowns and gloves, with masks on their faces. "All I could see were their eyes."

Beside her now, Chip was silent. No one made a sound as Carolyn talked.

"The next thing I knew, I was sealed in an iron lung," she said. "There was a hole in my throat, and a tube stuck inside it. Air was going in and out with horrible whistles and gasps."

The next days seemed hazy to her now, she said. She had slept and woken, and slept again. And then a priest was standing at her side, clothed as black as a crow. He was holding something above the iron lung, moving his hand in the sign of a cross.

"It was the last rites," she said. "I was dying."

She described how he muttered the strange Latin words, how his hand moved up and down, back and forth. "I thought when he finished I would die," she said. "I wanted to signal to him that I was still alive. But I couldn't call out. I couldn't move a hand to warn him. I could feel my fingers, my toes, my arms and legs, but couldn't make them work."

Every muscle in her body was burning hot, she said. But her skin was all prickles and ice.

"Then it was morning. There was sunlight in the room, and a bird was singing somewhere," said Carolyn. "A nurse in white was moving round the iron lung. Her shoes were squeaking.

"When she saw me, she smiled. It was the most beautiful smile."

Now Carolyn too smiled up at her mirror. She told how the nurse ran to the hall, shouting, "She's awake! She's awake!" and then ran back again to hold the girl's face in her hands, to stroke the blond hair that was then nearly as short as a boy's.

"Her hands were warm," said Carolyn. "She kept saying, 'I knew you'd pull through. I just had a feeling you would.' I tried to talk, but no sound came out. Then the nurse put her finger on the end of the plastic tube, and suddenly there was air passing through it, into my mouth, over my lips and gums and teeth." Sucked with lovely coolness down her throat, it filled her lungs, and as the bellows pumped below her machine, Carolyn spoke for the first time in ten days.

"I asked, 'Where's my daddy?' That's all I cared about. He was out in the hall. He had been there every night," she said. "When he came in, he looked as old and worried as Rip Van Winkle. All he did was cry. He just stood beside me, crying."

Laurie asked, "Was your mother there?"

"No, but she came right away," said Carolyn. "She was in a hotel down the street."

Laurie looked at Carolyn with a new understanding. Chip

had turned his head away, and little Dickie was staring up toward his comic of the Two-Gun Kid but not reading the words or seeing the pictures.

"That was more than seven years ago," said Carolyn. "They moved to a new city. They moved again. Dad bought a company, and that took them even farther away.

"I have a sister now. She's three years old. I only saw her once.

"They went to Niagara Falls. To the Grand Canyon. To California.

"And I haven't left this room. Not once in all that time."

Dickie tipped his head toward her. "They couldn't take you," he said.

"Think I don't know that?" asked Carolyn. "Think I couldn't figure it out?"

"I mean, you shouldn't be mad. Boy, it's not their fault."

"Oh, shut up," said Carolyn.

Laurie stepped away. "Do they still come to visit?" she asked.

"Oh, they did at first." Carolyn talked about it as Laurie moved along the row of iron lungs, to Chip's and then to Dickie's, taking down the magazine and comic book, flipping mirrors over.

For a week, said Carolyn, her father and mother had come every day to the hospital. Each time they brought a tiny bunch of flowers, or candy that she couldn't eat. They always asked how she was doing, as though they couldn't see that she was just the same. Then they had to go home; Mr. Jewels had to go back to work.

"Dad started coming by himself. All that summer, he

came every weekend," said Carolyn. "In the fall it was every *second* week. By the end of winter it was once a month.

"And now . . ." She sobbed and sniffed. "It's maybe once a year. He came last month, and stayed for less than an hour."

"Were you mean to him?" asked Dickie, piping up above the huff of the respirators. "Did you get sore at him?"

"Mind your beeswax," said Carolyn.

But Dickie kept on, with the serious expression that made him look so much older. "Did you shout at him? Then not even talk at all? Boy, I bet he looked so sad."

"Well, good for him!" she snapped. "Why shouldn't he be sad?"

"'Cause he came to see you," said Dickie.

"You stupe. He didn't *want* to come. He *had* to," said Carolyn. "He hates coming here."

She looked mean now, not pretty at all. Her face had set into hard lines, her forehead into rows of wrinkles.

"You should be nicer to people," said Dickie. "Then they'd be nicer to you."

"You should shut up," said Carolyn.

She and Dickie might have argued all day if not for the boy between them. Chip lay for a while with his eyes closed, his teeth gritted, as though he hoped to block out the sound. Then he tossed his head back and forth; he slammed it up and down. He did it so violently that one of the photographs shook loose from the front of his iron lung and drifted in zigzags to the floor. "Quit it!" he said in an angry voice.

Right away, the others stopped.

"Okay," he said, more quietly now. "I want to hear Laurie tell her story."

"Me too," said Dickie.

"But no splints on the baby."

◆ ◆ ◆

Fingal wouldn't think of harming his baby. Jimmy was now the most precious thing he owned, as good as a golden goose.

In the basement, Fingal had barrels full of money. He had coins of silver and coins of gold. He had round coins, square coins, coins with six or eight sides. He loved to pour them like grains of sand through his fingers. His only fear was that his new wealth wouldn't last, because Jimmy was growing bigger.

On the day of the first snowfall, when it was bitterly cold, a stranger arrived at the inn. He was older than any traveler who had ever come before, older than the inn itself. He looked like an ancient oak in a woolen cloak, twisted and wrinkled and gnarled, his skin as rough as bark, his fingers like so many twigs.

He pushed the door with all his weight, and a frigid gust set Jimmy's cradle rocking on the bar. It woke the embers in the fireplace and made them gleam and crackle. The last traveler had departed for the south an hour earlier, so the fire was near its end. The Woman was upstairs, cleaning the emptied rooms.

Fingal looked up from the bar. "Are you going north, sir?" he asked.

The old man didn't speak. The cloak covered him from

head to toe, while his face was hidden in the shadows of his hood. He came into the parlor with a heavy step that sounded like the clopping of a horse.

There was snow on his shoulders, on the top of his hood, and it fell away as he crossed the parlor with that curious sound: *clop, clop, clop.* He walked right up to the bar and lifted a foot to the brass rail. He was wearing leather boots with wooden soles.

"You'll want to tip the babby now," said Fingal, nodding toward the cradle. He gave it a poke that set the coins sloshing inside. Jimmy made happy, muttering sounds. "It brings fortune, you see. The more you give, the more you receive, if I can offer some advice."

"I do not seek advice," said the old traveler. "I want only a fire, a drink, and a bowl of soup, all three as hot as you can make them."

"Yes, sir," said Fingal, peering into the dark shadows of the traveler's hood. He could see a chin that was bristled with white hairs, an eyebrow as thick as rope. "You do have the means of payment?" he said.

Above them, the Woman was moving from room to room, carrying her bucket with a clatter and creak. The old traveler shook the last bits of snow from his shoulders. He reached into his sleeve and pulled out a small leather pouch. "Here is the means of my payment," he said.

The pouch made no sound when it touched the bar. There was no jingle of silver, no rattle of gold. "Why, it's empty!" said Fingal.

"Not at all."

"Then what's inside it?"

"The answer to your dreams."

"Bah!" Fingal snatched up the little bag before the man could say another word. He crushed it in his fist. "Look there, you old fool," he said. "I can see there's nothing in it."

"Your eyes deceive you," said the traveler. The shadows moved in his hood as he shifted his head. There was a hint of hooked nose, of pox-scarred cheeks, of blackened lips. "That pouch contains anything you can imagine. Unless, of course, you imagine too much."

"Bah!" said Fingal again. "What do you mean by that?"

"It's a matter of fair exchange," said the traveler patiently. "I will pay well for my meal. But if you ask too much, you get nothing."

Fingal laughed. It seemed that no matter what he did he was going to get nothing. But as he pushed the purse across the bar, a phrase came into his mind, words spoken by his mother fifty years before. *Flat as a Wishman's pouch.* He could hear her saying it, and the memory suddenly triggered another. *Never wish for a Wishman.* He had thought, then, that it was nonsense. And in all the time gone by, he hadn't changed his mind.

Now he frowned. "Are you a Wishman?"

"I am," said the traveler.

"You bestow wishes?"

"I do."

Fingal leaned on the bar, nearly overcome by surprise. "I didn't know that Wishmen existed," he said.

"Once, you didn't doubt it," said the Wishman.

"I was a child." Fingal looked suspiciously at the old

man, at his worn cloak and warty hands. "Can you bestow wishes on yourself?" he asked.

"Of course."

"Aha!" Fingal held up a finger, as though he had bettered the traveler. "Then why do you walk in such rags?"

"I choose to," said the Wishman.

"Why are you not young and handsome?"

"If you cannot explain that yourself, then your wishes are wasted, my friend." The traveler leaned forward. "Now, please, I would like my brandy."

There was a keg right behind the bar, but Fingal didn't want to serve watery brandy to a Wishman. He went down to the basement instead, and brought up a glass as yellow as amber. He warmed it over the red eyes of the embers in his fireplace while the Wishman took his pouch to a chair beside the hearth. Fingal served him the brandy, then fetched an armload of wood and lit the biggest fire that he'd ever lit. The flames reached up and stroked the wood, then stretched again high into the chimney. Air roared through the fireplace. On the bar, Jimmy's little cradle began to rock in the draft. The boy giggled and laughed.

Fingal brought soup from the kitchen. He brought a spoon, but the Wishman didn't use it, choosing instead to drink right from the bowl, lapping it out like a dog.

When he was fed and warm, the Wishman at last pulled back his hood. Fingal watched with interest, then turned away, disgusted. The old man's face was as ugly as a troll's, the skin all pitted and scarred.

The traveler drank his brandy and sat for a moment staring

into the fire. Then a smile came to that terrible face. "I'll make my payment now," he said. "What is it you wish for?"

The question made Fingal's heart beat faster. He could imagine a thousand wishes, but not how to choose between them. Should he ask for riches? For happiness? Should he ask for the Woman to be young and lovely? Should he ask for youth for himself?

*If you ask too much, you get nothing.* But how much was too much? Was he meant to ask only for fair value, for nothing worth more than a splash of soup and watery brandy?

"Please," said the traveler. He held up his pouch. "I would like to settle my account."

In the fireplace, the flames shifted. On the bar, the cradle rocked. Jimmy laughed, delighted.

"Ah, the babby!" cried Fingal. He looked into the eyes of the old Wishman. "Would it be too much if I asked for the babby to stay the size that he is?"

"To grow no bigger?"

"Not an inch."

"That is fair," said the Wishman.

"Then do it." Fingal looked up at the ceiling, trying to tell where the Woman was working. "Do it now."

"I should warn you first," said the Wishman. "It's been my experience in this business that a wish may not always manifest itself in the manner the wisher intended."

"What the devil do you mean?" asked Fingal.

"If you wish the boy not to grow another inch, he may not live another day. You could bring about his death."

"Ah." Fingal nodded.

The Wishman studied him closely.

"Well, everybody dies," said Fingal. "Not that that's what I'm after, mind you. If he grows up, that's fine; that's well and dandy, as long as he doesn't grow big. I want him to be the size of an infant forever."

The Wishman fiddled with his pouch. "Once done, this cannot be *un*done," he said. "Not without a terrible price."

"Fine. That's fine," said Fingal. "If you can do it, do it now."

The Wishman opened his purse. A draft of frigid air came out, so cold that it rimmed the leather with frost. Crystals of ice formed on the Wishman's fingers, on the tip of his nose, on his eyebrows and lashes. His breath came out in a steamy cloud that rose, swirling, to the ceiling. Then the Wishman closed his purse again and tucked it up his sleeve.

"That's all?" said Fingal.

"It is done." The Wishman stood up and lifted his hood. Then out he went, under the dragon's tooth and through the door, into the cold and the snow. He turned to the north and, head down, trudged along his way.

Fingal watched the tooth swinging in its chains. Then he looked at the empty brandy glass, at the soup bowl beside it, and wondered who had cheated whom. Anyone could open an empty bag and claim it was full of wishes. Even a fool could move his hand about mysteriously, then say, "There, it's done." Perhaps Fingal's mother was right. *There's nothing flatter than a Wishman's pouch.*

◆ ◆ ◆

"You mean the Wishman was a cheat?" asked Chip. "He did a dine and dash?"

"No. I think he was real," said Dickie. "He got frost on his fingers. 'Cause wishes are cold."

"I guess there was no way to know," said Chip.

"That's what Fingal thought," said Laurie. "At that moment, Jimmy was about this tall." She held her hand above the floor, a little lower than her waist. Chip and Dickie and Carolyn turned their heads to see for themselves, and their faces tilted in the mirrors.

Dickie smiled, then closed his eyes. "Boy, I wish there was a Wishman," he said.

"What would you wish for?" asked Laurie.

"Gee, I wonder," said Carolyn. "What on earth could he want? A kid in an iron lung."

Laurie blushed. She'd known right away it was a silly question. What else would he wish for, but to be healthy and happy again?

But Dickie was always surprising.

"Disneyland," said Dickie. "Boy, I'd wish I could get to Disneyland."

# CHAPTER FIVE

## THE SADDEST WISH OF ALL

The sun was as high now as it would get that day. On the grass below the window, the shadow of the hospital was a dark slab on the green. The radio antenna on the roof cast a thin arrow pointing straight at Piper's Pond.

Laurie stared out, saddened that another argument was under way behind her.

"Dickie, you're a dope," said Carolyn.

"I am not," he said. "Quit saying that."

"You are if that's your wish," she said.

"Oh, yeah? What would you wish for, Carolyn?"

"That I never had to come here."

"Why?" asked Dickie. "It's not so bad."

"What's to like?"

"I got to meet Chip. And you," he said. "And Miss Freeman. And all the others. Boy, we have fun sometimes. It's like being at camp. But you never have to go home. Like we're lying in bunk beds talking."

"Aw, shut up, Dumbo."

"Don't call me that."

He was nearly crying now, and Laurie hated to hear that. If he had to spend his days in an iron lung, it didn't seem right that he had be sad. "I guess it *is* a bit like camp," she said. "If you think about it. Isn't it, Chip?"

"I don't know," he said.

"But you've been to camp."

He shook his head. "No, I haven't."

"But there's a picture." She pointed at his iron lung, and then went up beside it. She ran her hand across the crazy mat of photographs. "I saw it here."

It had shown the boy holding a little tomahawk like Dickie's, trying to look fierce in a headdress made of paper feathers and a cardboard band. Above him was a wooden arch that said *Camp Hiawatha* in letters made from nailed-together sticks. Laurie was certain that she'd seen it, but there were so many pictures half covered by others that she couldn't find it again.

Chip seemed annoyed that she was looking. If he could have reached out of the iron lung and pushed her away, he would have done it—she was sure of that. She pretended not to notice, but soon took her hand from the pictures and wandered off.

Dickie had a funny half smile now. He was looking up at

his comic but not reading it. "What would *you* wish for, Chip?" he asked. "If there were Wishmen."

"I dunno," said Chip. "I guess maybe to be somebody else."

"Oh, who?" asked Laurie, pleased to change the subject.

"I dunno," he said again.

"Like someone famous, you mean?" She was already back at the window, a sentry at her post. "Like Elvis Presley?"

Chip shook his head. "Just anybody else. It doesn't matter who."

That seemed the saddest wish of all to Laurie. The boy in the pictures was so happy, so busy. When he went into hospital he must have left a dozen things unfinished, like that strange car in the garage. Laurie could imagine skeletons of balsa airplanes waiting for their skin, roofless wooden birdhouses, go-carts without wheels. Didn't he ache to get home and finish those things? Why didn't he wish, like Carolyn, just to be the child he'd been before?

"Let's forget it," he said now. "What about the Wishman? Was he real? Or was he fake?"

◆ ◆ ◆

Fingal wasn't certain at first if the Wishman had kept his promise. His son looked just the same, of course; that was the point of the wish. Every morning, as he popped Jimmy into the cradle, he looked anxiously at the boy's small feet. He stretched out the little legs, like the tax man's folding ruler, to see how close they came to the end of the barrel.

There were days when he was certain that Jimmy was still growing, and others when he swore the boy was *shrinking*.

And then the Woman, pausing in her work one day, rocked the infant in the cradle. She rubbed his stomach, something that always made his feet kick crazily, his fists swing as wildly as a fighter's. He writhed and laughed. Then the Woman turned to Fingal.

"There's something wrong with him," she said. "He used to grow like a bean sprout. But not anymore. He's no bigger than he was a month ago."

If hearts could sing, Fingal's surely did that day. He was so happy that he poured himself a small nubbin of brandy and drank a toast to the Wishman. "Here's to you, my friend, wherever you may be," he said. And he meant it so sincerely that he brought a tear to his own eye.

Soon even Fingal could see that it was true. Jimmy the giant-slayer was stuck at thirty-one and three-quarters inches high. He grew older; he grew smarter and stronger. But he grew no bigger, not even by a smidgen.

On his sixth birthday, he was exactly the same. And he still spent his days in the cradle.

◆ ◆ ◆

At nine years of age Jimmy the giant-slayer could read and write and do his numbers better than his father. "You're a little man now, with little jobs to do," said Fingal.

Every night, Jimmy emptied his cradle and the offering box. He carried the coins down to the basement, though it sometimes took three trips. He sorted and counted the money, then entered the totals into the ledger, making sure that he carried the sum to the next day's page.

"You'll be running the inn before long," Fingal told him proudly. "I'll spend my last years sitting by the fire—me and the Woman—and you'll tend to us, you will, and a fine job you'll do."

Fingal was beaming at his boy. It was very early in the morning, and the four travelers who had taken rooms were still in their beds. Jimmy had already carried in the day's wood and got the fire started. Now he was taking a moment with his father, who had hoisted him up to the top of the bar, where he sat at the edge, drumming his feet on its front.

"I'm proud of you, Jimmy," said Fingal. "You're doing so well that I think it's time to reward you with another trust."

"What is it, Father?" asked Jimmy.

"The dragon's tooth," said Fingal. "From now on, that great old tooth will be in your care, yours to dust and polish."

"Really?" asked Jimmy. He kicked his small feet happily against the bar.

"Now you will learn the secret. And mind it *stays* a secret, understand? It's only for me and you to know."

Jimmy nodded solemnly. "What's the secret, Father?"

"Look at the tooth."

Little Jimmy peered across the parlor at the huge dragon's tooth hanging in its chains. It was white at the tip, mushroom-colored higher up, streaked down its length with stains of brown and yellow. It reminded him of smiling Smoky Jack, the minstrel who was never without a pipe.

Though the room was empty, Fingal still spoke in a whisper. "I made it myself, Jimmy. That tooth is only wood. It's just a bit of pine."

Jimmy stopped swinging his feet. All his life that tooth had hung there. He had watched a thousand travelers reach up to touch it. He had heard some of them saying they had seen the dragon that had grown it. There was one who'd claimed he'd killed the beast himself. They all, every one, swore by the luck in that dragon's tooth, and believed that a touch had kept them safe on the Great North Road. They had filled barrels and barrels and barrels of coins in trade for that safety. And now he was told that all of them were fools? The great tooth was only wood?

Jimmy giggled. Then he laughed, and soon he was doubled over, his head nearly touching his knees. Fingal was roaring beside him, father and son laughing together at the foolishness of travelers.

They nearly laughed themselves into ruin, for neither heard the blacksmith coming down the stairs until it was nearly too late.

"Quick!" cried Fingal. "Into your cradle!"

Jimmy squirmed through the mouth of the barrel. Fingal had to give his heels a push, and the boy vanished just as the wandering blacksmith came through the doorway.

"Good morning, sir," said Fingal loudly. "Before you get on your way today, mind you tip the babby." He gave the cradle a push that set it rocking.

In the barrel, Jimmy sloshed the coins to make them jingle. He let out a babyish laugh, then settled back, smiling. He had a book to read, and a sandwich for later, and thought he was a very lucky boy.

The blacksmith came to the bar in his big boots. He was an enormous man, with a beard that was nearly the size of a blanket. He looked into the cradle, and Jimmy looked back, making silly faces, shaking his tiny fists.

This usually charmed the travelers. But the blacksmith looked disgusted. He made a horrible face, then turned away, shouting, "This is no baby. A small boy in a barrel, that's all he is!"

So the Wishman was right in the end. Fingal had got what he wanted, only to learn that he didn't really want it at all.

The blacksmith was livid. "I'm not putting coins in your blasted crib," he said. "I'm not tipping your baby or touching your tooth; I'm not even paying for my room."

He stomped upstairs and fetched his things; he stomped back down again. On his heels came the other three travelers. But they stopped at the foot of the stairs as the blacksmith blocked their way. Red-faced, holding his anvil, his hammers and tongs, the smithy shouted at the innkeep. "You're a cheat and a liar, Fingal," he said. "I've half a mind to take the boy with me."

"If you had the other half, I'd give him to you," said Fingal. "He's no good to me now, is he?"

◆ ◆ ◆

"Boy, that's mean," said Dickie. "Did Jimmy hear him say that?"

"Yes, he did," said Laurie. "He had been so happy, remember? Laughing with his dad. Now he felt just terrible. He lay in his cradle and cried."

"Did the blacksmith take him away?"

"No." Laurie could see him in her mind, as broad as an ox, so tall that he couldn't stand upright in the parlor. The huge anvil under one arm, the tools under the other, he stood wondering what he would do with a tiny boy.

"Then the Woman came in," said Laurie. "She heard all the noise and the shouting, and she ran into the parlor."

◆ ◆ ◆

"Fingal, what's wrong?" the Woman said. "A body can't hear herself think."

"It's him." Fingal pointed at the blacksmith. "He won't pay for his room."

"Oh, is that so?" She turned to the smithy, putting her hands on her hips. "Now you listen to me, you big oaf."

"No, you listen to *me*," said the blacksmith. His voice was like booming thunder. "That boy's got a curse on him. Or he's a changeling or something."

"Here, that's enough," said Fingal. But no one heard him, because the Woman was shrieking. "How dare you?" she cried. "There's nothing wrong with my baby."

She ran to the bar. She snatched little Jimmy from the cradle and held him in her arms.

"He's not quite plumb," said the blacksmith. "He's not on the right lines."

Even in her fury, the Woman could see that the smithy was right. Jimmy was nine years old but no bigger than an infant. He couldn't reach up to the top of the bar.

"He may be cursed or he may not," said the blacksmith.

"But there's one thing for certain. If he was mine, I'd be consulting a witch."

"Get out!" said the Woman.

"All right, I'm going." The blacksmith moved toward the door, stooped below the big beams of the parlor. With his arms full of tools, he couldn't work the latch. Another traveler, a pieman, squeezed past and opened the door.

"I'd go to the swamp," said the blacksmith. "If he was mine, that's what I'd do."

"Get out!" she cried. And he did.

Fingal waited until the door closed, then slapped his hands together. "Well, I'm glad to see the back of *him*. That's the end of that, isn't it? Now, let's put wee Jimmy into his cradle and —"

The Woman held on to her son. "Is he a changeling?" she asked.

Fingal was left standing there with his arms out. The three travelers were watching.

"Is he?" she said. "Tell me!"

"Don't be daft, Woman. Does he look like a changeling?"

Well, he *did*, in a way. His ears were maybe a little too big to be normal, his nose a touch too long.

"Bah!" said Fingal. "You took precautions. I remember that. You had your coat hanging inside out for day after day, so he can't be a changeling, can he?"

"Then we have to go the swamp," she said.

Jimmy looked up at her face. "Mother, what's at the swamp?"

"It's where the Swamp Witch lives," she said.

Jimmy cried, "I don't want to see a witch."

"And you won't," said Fingal. "No son of mine is going anywhere near the swamp."

"I'll go myself," said the Woman.

"It's bottomless," warned Fingal.

"I don't care."

The Woman was determined. That very day she put on her good shoes and her lipstick and set off for the swamp. She didn't know exactly where it was, nor what she'd find when she got there. But she went on her way nonetheless, following the sun down the High Road, with the thought of striking north when she met the first river.

◆ ◆ ◆

The Woman was gone a week. She was gone a month. She was gone a year and a half. When the first snow of another winter fell over the inn, there was still no sign of the Woman.

In the morning the snow covered the ground three feet deep, and Jimmy looked out in despair. "Father, how far away is that swamp?" he asked.

"Now why do you want to know that?" said Fingal.

The travelers were in their beds. The fire was burning, but the parlor was still cold. Jimmy was standing at the top of a ladder, polishing the wooden dragon's tooth, while Fingal swept the floor. The boy could see out the window to the Great North Road, its white coating as smooth as plaster, not broken yet by tracks.

"I just want to know," he said. "Is the swamp beyond the mountains?"

# CHAPTER SIX

## THE MAN WHO HUNTED UNICORNS

Early on Sunday morning, with breakfast just over, Miss Freeman stood outside the respirator room, listening with a smile. She had heard the children talk of many things—mostly of rockets and cars and candy—but never of unicorns. She doubted if unicorns had ever been discussed in there before.

There was another nurse beside her—Mrs. Glass with red and curly hair—and they stood by the open door, just listening. Dickie was saying that unicorns were huge animals, bigger than plow horses, and then Carolyn—without being rude at all—said she didn't think that he was right.

"They're small," she said. "Like little lambs."

Miss Freeman hurried into the room as though she had just arrived. Mrs. Glass came behind her, pulling a metal cart laden with supplies.

"What's everyone talking about?" Miss Freeman asked.

"Unicorns, Miss Freeman," said Dickie. "Do you think they're big or little?"

"Oh, in between, I guess," said Miss Freeman. She always tried to please everybody. "Now, it's time to get you cleaned up."

"Aw, gee," said Dickie.

"It's not so bad as that, is it?" Miss Freeman didn't wait for an answer. "Laurie should be here in an hour, so we'd better hurry."

The nurses started with Carolyn. They stood at each side of her iron lung. "Ready?" asked Miss Freeman.

"Okay," said Carolyn.

Miss Freeman turned off the iron lung. Her hand was resting on the big curve of metal, and she felt the thing go dead as the bellows stopped moving, as the machine stopped breathing. She unfastened the clasps around the front of the respirator.

Carolyn started gulping. Her mouth opened and closed like that of a fish. Her tongue moved forward and back, trapping air that she forced down her throat and into her paralyzed lungs. She made a ticking, smacking noise.

"Good for you, Carolyn. You'll be an expert at frog-breathing soon," said Miss Freeman. She and Mrs. Glass slid the girl from the respirator, drawing her backward on the moving cot, as though pulling a drawer from a filing cabinet. The whole front of the machine came away, a huge metal collar fixed to the cot. Carolyn kept forcing air down her throat.

Mrs. Glass wrinkled her nose and held her breath for a moment. But Miss Freeman pretended not to notice the stench that came out of the machine, the reek of waste and urine. Sometimes it was nearly more than she could bear, but she never let on. She didn't even grimace at the awful sores on Carolyn's hips or at the pathetic sight of limbs as skinny as pipe cleaners. She worked quickly and steadily, talking happily all the time.

"I used to wish I could ride away on a unicorn," she said. "Other girls wanted ponies, but I wanted my own unicorn. I wanted to ride it bareback."

"See?" said Dickie. "Boy, they have to be bigger than lambs."

"I was just a little girl," said Miss Freeman.

One on each side, the nurses pulled away the soiled sheets, cleaned and scrubbed the girl, then stretched new bedding into place. On top of the stench came the new tickling smells of soap and antiseptic.

"I dreamed about him," said Dickie.

"Who?" asked Miss Freeman.

"Oh, the hunter. In the story." Dickie gazed straight up at his mirror, through it to the window. He wouldn't look at Carolyn, hoping she wouldn't look at him when his turn came around. "He hunts unicorns, Miss Freeman."

"Really? Is that what Laurie's telling you about?"

"Yes. And you know what else?" said Dickie. "In my dream I was him. I was the hunter."

Carolyn forced her lungs full of air. "You're just saying that," she said. Her tongue started ticking again.

"It's true," said Dickie. "I was Khan the hunter. I had a white horse. And a bow and arrow. I killed unicorns."

"My goodness!" said Miss Freeman.

"It's like I rode into the story." said Dickie. "I don't know. But boy, it was neat." The coonskin cap dangled in front of him, like a pelt that Khan had collected. "I was in the mountains, in the snow. I killed a unicorn with an arrow."

"Oh, that's sad," said Miss Freeman.

"It sure was," said Dickie. "I hit it in the heart. It fell in the snow and I ran to get it. I kept falling down. 'Cause the snow was so deep."

He closed his eyes as he remembered the dream, the soft, tumbling way that he'd fallen. He could feel the coldness as his hands had plunged into the snow.

"The unicorn was dying," he said. "It was kind of singing when it breathed. It kept trying to lift its head. But its big horn was so heavy. Then it looked at me and died. Boy, it was so beautiful. I felt kind of sick."

"No wonder. Poor Dickie." Miss Freeman was helping Mrs. Glass arrange the new sheet over Carolyn's withered legs. "There, you're done," she said. "Good work, Carolyn." They returned the girl to the iron lung, fastened the seals at the front, and started the bellows again.

Chip was next. He began breathing on his own before Miss Freeman had even opened the iron lung. He was proud of his frog-breathing, eager to show it off.

The nurses threw off the catches and pulled out the bed, and the mirror shimmied and jiggled as the front of the machine rolled along. The smell was awful, but again they said nothing.

Carolyn was watching. "You'd better hurry, Miss Freeman," she said. "I think he's turning blue."

He wasn't turning blue at all. "I think he's doing just fine," said Miss Freeman.

But Chip didn't talk, as Carolyn had. He was so intent on breathing that he did it almost frantically, and a shine of sweat appeared on his face. It was obvious that he was frightened. He looked all around, like a rabbit caught out of its hole. Miss Freeman hurried to finish, clattering bedpans and bottles. Dickie kept talking about his dream, but no one was listening.

♦ ♦ ♦

In his dream, Dickie could walk; that was the thing. Boy, he could *run*, though the snow was up to his knees. He could see his feet, in their boots of dragon skin, kicking the snow as they sank into it. He could hear his charms of bone and shell rattling together as they swayed inside his shirt. It was a dream so real that he *lived* it.

Dickie had never been up in the mountains. But in the dream he saw the trees shrunken by the altitude, spaced wider apart the higher they were on the slope. He saw the pine boughs bent with snow, and heard the whoosh and thud as great clods fell to the ground. He saw the sun in a million sparkles all around him, and the clouds of blown snow, like spray on the ocean, where the wind tore at the drifts along ridges and crests.

He heard the snort of the unicorn, and turned to see it stepping from the trees with its breath like smoke, its fur all frost and shimmer.

He felt the numbness in his hands as he pulled an arrow from the quiver and notched it on his string. When he drew the bow it hurt, the string cutting into his frozen fingers. He knew just how to aim and just how to shoot, because he'd done it countless times. He heard the shush of the arrow flying and the twang of the string, and saw the red blur of phoenix feathers ripping past his wrist.

The arrow bedded in the unicorn's chest. The animal fell to its knees. It tried to get up again but stumbled forward. Then it crumpled into the snow in a puff of white crystals, slowly somersaulting until it sprawled out in a heap.

He didn't like to think of the unicorn dying, of the trickle of red that came from the wound and the scarlet drips on the snow. He could hear the little song of its breath, and saw the scared whiteness of its eyes.

In the dream he put his hand on its cheek to calm it. The sleeve of his coat pushed up, and he saw on his skin a tattoo, the sun and the moon on the back of his wrist. He could feel the coarse hair of the unicorn, and the pulse of its heart slowly stopping.

He didn't like to think of the skinning either, of the sound of the knife going in, or the pelt tearing away, or the rasp of his saw at the base of the horn. But he was comforted by the offering he made. He liked the smell of the dried leaves and twigs that he shook from a pouch and tucked into the mouth of the unicorn. He felt the spirit of the animal around him, made happy by the taste of its favorite food.

He stood up then, as Khan. He stood up in his long coat, in his hat of a hydra head, and looked far across the valley, across a river half frozen, to a line of peaks as sharp and cold as icicles. He was heading there, down to the river and up to the pass, over the mountains to the Great North Road.

Already there was a gryphon above him, circling so high that it was just a dot of dirty yellow on the clouds. Soon there would be two, then three, and they would fall in a fury onto the corpse of the unicorn.

The hide was still warm on the inside. It made a bundle that steamed in the cold. He lashed it among the others on the back of his horse, took the reins in his fist, and started down through the forest.

◆ ◆ ◆

Dickie thought about the dream as the nurses finished with Chip. When they had the machine sealed and locked, its bellows breathing, they came over to him.

"I think I can frog-breathe now," he said.

"No, you can't," said Miss Freeman. "You're too young for that, Dickie."

She didn't open the front of his iron lung. She never pulled him out as she did with the others. She stood on the left side of his machine, while Mrs. Glass stood on the right. They opened the hatches and pulled out his bedpan. They pulled out his sheets and slipped new ones inside. Then they closed the hatches and opened the access ports, round as a ship's portholes. They thrust their arms through those, into gloves attached to the machine. They did their work leaning forward, peering through the little windows.

Dickie hated to watch them working, to feel their hands prodding, to see their eyes staring at his body. They cleaned him like a baby.

But he wasn't really there. He was in the mountains in the winter, watching bighorn sheep pawing through the snow to reach the grass. He could hear the huffs of their breaths, so sharp in the cold that it sounded like hammering.

Then Miss Freeman jarred him back, though she didn't mean to. She took away the comic book of the Two-Gun Kid, because he wasn't reading it anyway, and she swung the mirror round so that he could see out the window instead. But it turned too far, and suddenly he was looking up at himself, at a white face and weird, spiky hair.

He wasn't Khan. He wasn't hunting unicorns. That was just a stupid idea, the whole thing.

The face in the mirror looked down at him as though it was somebody else's. Dickie could hardly believe that he was seeing himself. And just then, he could hardly believe that he would ever get better.

How many doctors had come to see him? He couldn't remember. One after the other, they had come and bent his legs like a rubber doll's, and said in loud jolly voices that he would be up and around in no time. Even when his lungs had stopped working and he was put into the respirator, they'd said that it wouldn't be for long.

He believed that doctors never lied. There had always been that day in the future when he would get out of the iron lung and breathe on his own again. And on that day he would march right out of the hospital, strutting along like the boy he had seen in a poster somewhere.

It was thinking of that day that had kept him happy. He had thought of it often, especially at night as he fell asleep. It would be a wonderful day, but a terrible day—happy and sad together. He would say goodbye to Chip and Carolyn, and promise to come and visit. Then he would pick up his box of comic books and stuff, put on his coonskin cap, and walk out with Miss Freeman. At the door he would look back and see the bellows moving, Chip and Carolyn watching. "See ya soon," he'd say, and wave. He and Miss Freeman would stop at the other rooms, and he would say goodbye to all the others he'd met: Jennifer and Ruth and Peter and Steve, Mark and Kathy and the three Susans. And then he would ride down on the elevator with Miss Freeman and walk toward the big glass doors. He would see his parents on the other side, waiting in the sunshine. They would be holding each other and smiling at him. Miss Freeman would shake their hands, then get down on her knees, in her white skirt and white stockings, and give him a hug. She would smell a bit of perfume. "Oh, Dickie, I'll miss you," she'd say. "I'll miss you so very much."

But now, for the first time, Dickie wondered if that day would come at all. It was hard to believe the boy in the mirror could *ever* get up and walk away.

He thought of all this in a moment. Then Miss Freeman raised the mirror again, to aim it at the window, and the boy vanished as it tilted. She went to work on his withered body, changing his sheet.

Dickie closed his eyes and counted days. In his mind he

used his fingers, and he decided that it was four nights until his parents came again. He wished it weren't quite that long, but he didn't doubt they would come—no matter what Carolyn said. In the beginning they had visited every day, and on the first day they missed, Carolyn had laughed about it. She could be so mean sometimes.

"You know, they'll never be back," she'd said.

"Don't say that!" Dickie had told her. "It's just one day. They promised."

But Carolyn had laughed again. "That's always how it starts," she'd said, "with 'just one day.'"

Dickie counted the days again. His parents would bring him candy or cookies, because they always did that, and they would have enough for Carolyn and Chip as well. They would bring a new comic book, and maybe something about Davy Crockett, but probably not the bowie knife that he always *hoped* they'd bring. They would have a funny story of something that had happened, and his father would tell it in a way that would make everybody laugh—even Carolyn. But after that they would both get very sad, and Dickie would have to cheer them up.

They would leave slowly, saying goodbye a dozen times before they reached the door, and then a couple more as they moved down the hall. They would keep waving until the last moment. Then the whole room would be sad. The bellows of the respirators would hum and puff, and through the doorway would come the muffled chime of the elevator. Then maybe Chip would laugh again at Mr. Espinosa's story. "You sure got swell folks," he'd say. He said it every

time. "You sure got swell folks, Dickie; you're pretty lucky."
And Dickie would lie there with his head turned aside, feeling the tickly itch of a tear that he couldn't even hope to wipe away.

In his mind, he was counting on his fingers.

◆ ◆ ◆

When Laurie arrived that Sunday, Miss Freeman had gone.
The room smelled of Lysol and soap, and even the faces of the polios seemed freshly scrubbed.

Dickie cried out, "What kept ya?" But he didn't sound so cheerful now, as if his happiness had been sponged away too. "Hurry, I want to hear about Khan," he said.

So Laurie settled at her place by the window and started the story again. Jimmy the giant-slayer was watching the hunter arrive.

"He had never seen a man so wild," she said. Khan was covered in furs and skin, as much an animal as the horse that he led. The two of them walked the same way, looking warily around them, alert to every sound, snorting cloudy breaths together.

Then the horse stopped in its tracks. It lifted its head, and its ears twitched nervously. Khan stopped too. He looked up, just as the horse had done, and stared straight through the window at Jimmy.

"Boy. Was Jimmy scared?" asked Dickie.

"For a moment, yes," said Laurie. "Then Khan held up a hand. He just held it in the air with his fingers spread apart like this, as flakes of snow fell from his arm. And he smiled, and his teeth were as white as a wolf's.

"In the parlor, Jimmy called out to Fingal. 'Come and see!' he said. 'Father, look!'

"Well, Fingal looked. He thought it was the Woman coming home, and he ran to the window. When all he saw was a man and a horse, he got angry. 'Why did you call me?' he asked. 'Do you think I've never seen a hunter before?'

"'Not like *him*,' said Jimmy. 'Isn't he wonderful, Father? That's what I want to be when I grow up.'

"Fingal laughed. 'When you grow up? You're *not* growing up, you little fool,' he said. 'Jimmy, you'll never grow up.'"

"Gee, that was a mean thing to say," said Dickie. "I hope he's sorry."

"Oh, he'll be sorry," Laurie said. "Later on he'll be very sorry."

◆ ◆ ◆

In a whirl of white, the hunter came into the parlor. He stomped his feet on the floor and pulled off his hat, and the snow fell away in clumps.

Fingal was adding wood to the fire. "Come sit by the hearth, sir. You'll want a hot meal inside you."

"That I surely do," said the hunter.

But he would neither sit nor eat until his horse was taken care of. And because the snow was nearly as deep as Jimmy was tall, Fingal had to go himself. "The boy will look after you," he said.

Khan beat his arms against his sides, shedding snow from

his coat. "What's that?" he asked, tilting his chin toward the ceiling.

Jimmy looked up. "That's the dragon's tooth, sir." It was right above them, shining with its fresh coat of polish.

"I heard tell of this," said Khan. "A tooth the size of a man. Never believed it myself." He set down his bow and quiver. The feathers on his arrows were orange, yellow, and red. "They say you ought to touch it for luck. Put a coin in the box." He made another motion with his head. "In that box there, I reckon. Is that so?"

Jimmy nodded. He had shown countless travelers exactly where to put the coins, but for some reason he couldn't do it for Khan.

The hunter loosened his coat. He was wearing deerskins underneath, and a dozen necklaces of different lengths: a jumble of shells and bones, claws and teeth, skeins of hair like woven scalps. He dug through his pockets until he found a coin, an eight-sided silver Marcus. "Is this enough?" he asked.

Anyone else, Jimmy would have plied for more. *A Marcus?* he would have said, looking doubtful. *Well, if it's all you've got . . .* Now he watched the hunter reaching out toward the money box, and he found no pleasure at all in the glint of light on the silver coin. It made him queasy inside to think he was robbing Khan for the touch of a wooden tooth, that he was making a fool of the man.

"Wait!" Jimmy leapt up and grabbed the hunter's arm. "There's no luck in this," he said. "It's a wooden tooth."

The hunter looked at him, then slowly smiled. "Reckon any fool could see that, once he's gone hand to claw with a dragon," he said. "But I'm tickled you told me." He pressed the coin into the boy's small palm.

"Thank you," said Jimmy.

Khan took up his arrows and his bow and chose a seat near the fire. Jimmy hovered round him, as close as he could be. He couldn't look anywhere except at the hunter's face. The wrinkles round the man's eyes fascinated him. He could picture Khan always squinting into sun and snow and ice.

Khan put up his feet on the fire grate, inches from the flames.

"Sir?" said Jimmy. "Have you ever been to the swamp?"

"The bottomless swamp? Never seen it, but I know of it," said the hunter.

"Do you know the witch who lives there?"

"Not personally. Can't say I've had the pleasure." Khan hooked his long bow onto an empty chair to draw it closer. "But take a seat and I'll tell you what I know."

Story followed story. The other travelers came down from their rooms and joined the pair at the fire. Jimmy sat with his tiny legs jutting straight out from the chair until Fingal came in and set him to work.

Warmed by the flames, Khan took off his necklaces. He called Jimmy to his side and put around the boy's neck one of his own charms—a delicate sphere of tiny bones, enclosing the claw of a dragon. "Now, *that* will bring you luck," he said. "It's an old Gypsy charm. I got it myself from an old Gypsy."

The hunter had pushed up his sleeves. Jimmy could see on each arm a blue tattoo that might have been carved with a knife: on his left a fiery dragon, on his right a moon and two stars that seemed to twinkle as his muscles twitched.

◆ ◆ ◆

"See?" said Dickie. "See, I told you so."

◆ ◆ ◆

That night in the basement, when the travelers had gone to
their rooms, Fingal gaped as Jimmy emptied his pockets.
Out came coin after coin, more than the boy had ever collected in one day in his cradle. A greedy look came to
Fingal's face in the candlelight.

"Where'd you get all that?" he asked. "Did you nick it,
boy?"

"No, it's from the travelers," said Jimmy. "Khan gave me
this one; the mule skinner gave me that one; that tall shepherd, he—"

"For what?"

"For nothing, Father. Just for listening."

Fingal cackled. He rubbed Jimmy's hair. "That's my boy,"
he said. "Why, you're made of money, aren't you? Keep listening like that and I'll tell you what: we'll start your own
cache. Why, we'll start it right now."

Fingal went into the shadows and rolled out an empty
barrel. It was just a two-gallon keg, the smallest there was,
but to Jimmy it seemed quite huge. Fingal knocked off the
top and stood it upright. He picked up the silver Marcus
that Khan had given Jimmy and, with a flick of his thumb,
sent it tumbling it into the barrel. It made a lovely, hollow
sound as it bounced around the staves.

"That's for you, boy. Just for you," he said. "From now

{103}

on, every night, you'll get a share like that. You might say we're partners now, me and you."

So Jimmy the giant-slayer grew up in the parlor of the Dragon's Tooth, hearing the tales of travelers. He tottered from table to table, his eyes just peering over the tops. He carried glasses back and forth, kept the lamps and candles burning, and made himself useful in every way he could.

The travelers would cry out to him: "Jimmy! Over here!" and "Jimmy! Come and have a word!" Round and round he'd go, hoisted now to a minstrel's lap, now to a woodsman's massive thigh, and at each stop another coin was pressed into his hand, until he jingled like a Gypsy with every step he took. Fingal was astounded; he began to believe that he had, after all, got the better of the Wishman.

Jimmy loved the parlor when it was full of travelers—full of smoke and talk and laughter. He never tired of the stories, even when he'd heard them six or seven times. At night he'd repeat them, word for word, in his little bed in the room that he'd shared with his mother.

When he was twelve years old, Jimmy knew the lay of the land better than most of the travelers. While each of them had seen only a part of it, Jimmy felt as though he had seen every acre—from the depths of the deepest valley to the tip of the tallest mountain. He knew the weakness of the hydra and the manticore, how to hide from a giant or go hand to hand with a troll. He knew where the swamp was—or at least where it started.

He had even heard tell of Collosso.

# CHAPTER SEVEN

## THE TAX MAN RETURNS

On Monday, after school, Laurie stopped at Woolworth's. She had found long ago that the less money she had, the longer it took to spend it, and today she had very little. For nearly an hour she wandered through the store, up and down the aisles, past the lunch counter with its row of red-topped stools.

Chip was no problem. She got him the newest *Hot Rod* magazine. And Dickie wasn't much harder; one whole aisle was full of Davy Crockett stuff. There were Davy Crockett lunch boxes, Davy Crockett puzzles, Davy Crockett drinking glasses, Davy Crockett this and that and everything. Two little boys in coonskin caps kept pushing her aside to get at the flintlock rifles, the knives and powder horns. It made Laurie sad to watch them, and to think of Dickie lying just then in his iron lung. She chose a set of decals with pictures of Davy Crockett in black and red, fighting a bear on the first one and an Indian on the other.

But Carolyn was hard. Laurie trekked round and round the store, past displays of five-cent earrings, through the pet section with the budgies and turtles and goldfish. But in the end she was back at the magazines, choosing the latest *Silver Screen* with Debbie Reynolds on the cover, and the teasing promise of "The Inside Story of the Ty Powers Breakup!"

Laurie took these things to the hospital on her next visit. She didn't ask for Miss Freeman but went straight past the desk and up to the room. No one even asked where she was going.

On the fourth floor, she met the boy on the little wheeled platform, the one who had raced the wheelchair girl through the hall. This time he was alone, pushing himself in circles at the first bend in the hall.

He twisted his neck to look up as she walked toward him. "Where are you going?" he asked.

"To the respirator room," said Laurie.

"I'll show you the way."

"I know where it is," she told him. "I've been there."

But that didn't matter to the boy. He paddled along with his hands, rumbling down the hall more quickly than Laurie could walk. When she lagged too far behind, he waited for her to catch up, swiveling round to watch her, then swiveling back again. His hands made slapping sounds on the floor.

"What's your name?" he asked.

"Laurie," she told him. "What's yours?"

"James," he said. "James Miner." He turned his platform around and pushed himself backward ahead of her. "Are you the one telling the story?"

"Yes."

"Can I listen?"

"I guess so." It made her uncomfortable to look down at the boy. She kept wanting to crouch at his level, and couldn't understand why he didn't seem at all embarrassed. She couldn't imagine scuttling along the floor like a cockroach, with everyone staring down at her.

The boy knew every turn so well that he passed round the corners without looking, swinging out to the wall like a race car. His hands paddled quickly to straighten himself.

At the respirator room, Laurie stood aside while James wheeled himself through the doorway. He called hello to Dickie and the others, who greeted him as happily. "I came to hear the story," he said.

Laurie self-consciously produced her little purchases. "I brought you stuff," she said.

"Oh, boy!" cried Dickie.

He loved his decals. Laurie had to hold them above his head for nearly five minutes while he told the story behind each picture, how Davy Crockett had beaten the Indian, and how he'd come to be fighting a bear. Dickie called it "rasslin' a bar."

Chip was just as fond of his car magazine, though he wouldn't let Laurie turn through the pages. "I want to save it for later," he said.

But Carolyn didn't even pretend to be pleased with the

*Silver Screen.* "I guess you can't return a magazine," she said. "At least you didn't spend too much. So *that's* good."

Laurie felt creepy inside but didn't want to give up too easily. "It's got a story about Debbie Reynolds," she said.

"Big hairy deal. Why should I care?"

"You look kind of like her," said Laurie.

It was true, but Carolyn didn't think so. "More like Heidi Doody," she said, which wasn't true at all. Both had long blond hair, but Howdy Doody's puppet sister was a bizarre-looking thing.

"I weigh sixty-five pounds," said Carolyn. "Like a ten-year-old."

"You still look pretty," said Laurie.

"Yeah. Pretty ugly."

Laurie poked her glasses higher on her nose. She didn't know what to do with the magazine. She couldn't very well put it on top of the iron lung, as though on a great big coffee table. So it pleased her very much when James Miner asked, "Can I have it?" She said, "Sure," and bent down to pass it to him.

"Gee, thanks!" He tucked the magazine under his chest, then rolled himself out of the way, into a corner of the room. He spread it open on the floor and looked through the pictures.

"Can we hear the story now?" said Dickie.

"It's a free country," said Carolyn. "Go ahead."

That was fine with Laurie.

◆ ◆ ◆

When Jimmy was twelve, the tax man returned to the inn. His carriage was even finer than before. Every inch of it was covered in gold, and half of the gold was covered again by emeralds, diamonds, and pearls. Six horses pulled it now, in a billowing cloud of dust, while a crew of four attended.

At the front were the footman, thin and lean, and the driver in his scarlet clothes. On top rode a trumpet man with a silver horn that he blew at every bend and building, and on the back rode a wiper in a tall black hat.

The carriage came swaying up the road with the harnesses jingling. Dust boiled from the wheels and the hooves of the horses. It clung to the sweat on the animals' ribs, outlining every bone and muscle in smears of gray, so that it looked like a team of skeleton horses galloping down the road. The dust swirled so thickly round the carriage that only the heads of the driver and the footman rose above it. They seemed to ride in a bubble of smoke that moved along with a thundering, hammering sound. From its midst, the trumpet man blew a shrill and tingling blast.

Jimmy stood at the door, watching. He could not even dimly remember the last time that the tax man had come, when he had lain gurgling in his cradle on top of the bar. But he knew from Fingal's stories that the man had measured him and gone away with barrels of gold. And he certainly knew that his father had been furious that day.

Jimmy called to him now, shouting through the door. "Father!"

Fingal came in his apron, wiping his hands. He looked down the road and squinted. All he could make out were the heads of two black horses and a ball of dust that seemed to follow them down the road, as though the animals were trying to outrun a tiny, vicious storm.

◆ ◆ ◆

The carriage came right to the inn. The footman jumped down from his seat and opened the door. The wiper hopped from his perch, straightened his hat, and went to work with a cloth. He wiped down the carriage, turning a gray lump— one streak at a time—into a gleaming wonder.

When everything was clean and bright, the tax man stepped out of the carriage in buckled shoes and white stockings. He carried his big black book into the parlor, to a table near the bar where the footman was arranging an ink pot and paper. He turned through the pages of his book, stopping where it said,

One Fingal
One Woman
One baby, twenty-two inches

The tax man dipped his quill in the ink. "Where's the Woman?"

"Gone to the village," said Fingal, as though she might be back at any moment.

"Where's the baby?"

"Right at your elbow," said Fingal. Under his breath he muttered, "Are you blind?"

The tax man looked at Jimmy. "Oh, no," he said, shaking his head. "No, no. This won't do."

"What do you mean, it won't do?" asked Fingal.

"This won't do at all." The tax man set his quill back in the ink pot. He brought out his folding ruler, snapped it open, and measured the height of Jimmy the giant-slayer.

"Thirty-two inches." The tax man squinted. "Minus a quarter." Then he folded the ruler again, picked up the quill, and made a note in his book. "I'm sorry to say that this will cost you rather dearly," he said, though he didn't sound sorry at all.

"I don't understand," said Fingal.

"A child has to grow." The tax man tapped the tabletop. "That's the law." He quoted a paragraph of a section of a chapter of an act. "I'm afraid the fine is rather hefty."

"Ah, well, that's a problem now," said Fingal, his little eyes narrowing like a rat's. "You see, I have nothing. I've given it all to the boy."

"Everything?" said the tax man.

"Lock, stock, and barrel," said Fingal.

Jimmy grinned at his father. They exchanged a wink. It was a wonderful feeling to be rich, if only temporarily.

"So you have nothing?" The tax man looked suspicious. "Your son is wealthy, while you are penniless?"

Fingal cackled. "That appears to be the state of it."

"Highly unusual," said the tax man. "And, for you, some-what unfortunate. You see, it's the boy who pays the fine, as he's the one in contravention."

"What?" said Fingal.

"Well, it's hardly your fault that he hasn't grown," said the tax man. "Is it?"

Fingal sighed. He certainly wouldn't admit that he'd brought a curse upon his own son. There was an enormous tax on curses.

The tax man snapped his fingers to summon the driver and footman, the trumpet man and the wiper. All five went down to the basement, where the tax man began to levy his fine in barrels of coins. He stood aside, watching, as the men carted the barrels up the stairs and rolled them across the parlor floor. The wiper kept knocking his tall hat against the ceiling beams, so he was forever setting it straight.

The tax man took every barrel but one. He took the knives and forks and spoons, four of Fingal's shirts, and one stick of firewood. He even took the wooden dragon's tooth that had hung twenty-three years in its chains.

The carriage was loaded inside and out. Then the men climbed aboard and, with a snap of his whip, the driver pulled away. He cried out to the horses: "Gee up!" And the trumpet man blew his horn. "Gee up! Gee up!" shouted the driver.

The carriage gathered speed, and the dust whirled up from the wheels. Then a thin arm poked out through a window, and a white hand waved goodbye.

Fingal could hear his money jingling in the barrels. As soon as the carriage was out of sight he looked down at Jimmy and gave him a clout on the head.

"This is your fault," he said. "You little squirm, do you see what you've done?" His face was purple, his voice full of fury. "You've put me in the poorhouse!"

"I'm sorry, Father," said Jimmy.

"Sorry? Why, you certainly are," said Fingal. "You're a sorry excuse, that's what you are." He was shouting now. "You're a ruination. And a runt to boot. You're a horrible runt of a ruination."

Jimmy shrank even smaller than he was. He looked as withered and bowed as a trampled sapling, and the words seem to fall like weights on his shoulders. Fingal was actually screaming, hopping up and down on the road.

Jimmy started crying. "I am sorry, Father," he said.

"There's no use blubbering," shouted Fingal. "You great babby."

"I'm not a baby," said Jimmy the giant-slayer.

"Oh, yes you are," roared Fingal. "A babby you were born, and a babby you'll always be. I wish the gryphons had got you." He spat on the road at Jimmy's feet, then turned and stalked away.

◆ ◆ ◆

"He's so mean," said Dickie. "How can he say things like that?"

"He's a bit like my dad," said James Miner. He was crammed in the corner, all but forgotten. On the floor in front of him, the magazine was still open. "Where's that little boy's mother?"

"She went away," said Chip.

James nodded. "That's like *my* mom."

To look at him, Laurie had to lean from the chair and peer under the curve of the respirators. "Why don't you come closer?" she said.

"Okay." The boy tucked the magazine onto his platform and pushed himself across the floor.

Carolyn watched him too. The boy skidded sideways on his platform.

"That's keen, that thing," said Laurie. "It's like that deal a mechanic uses, when he slides under a car."

"A creeper," said Chip.

Laurie laughed. "That's what they're called? Creepers?"

"For mechanics," Chip said. "For polios, they're treatment boards."

James maneuvered into place. "It's supposed to exercise my arms and legs," he said.

"It's your mouth that gets the exercise," said Carolyn.

"Shut up. You're as mean as Fingal," said James Miner. But he was smiling. "So what happened next?"

◆ ◆ ◆

Jimmy stayed where he was for a long while. He watched the glob of his father's spit melt away into the dust, a dark stain like a black sunburst on the Great North Road. Then he went up to his room, drew the shutters on his window, and sat all alone in the gloomy shadows.

That night, when it was dark, Jimmy the giant-slayer filled a small bag. He put in a few clothes, and a locket that had belonged to his mother. He made certain that the hunter's charm was round his neck, though he had never tried to take it off. Then he crept down the stairs and out through the parlor, under the dangling chains where the wooden tooth had been.

The moon was half full. Jimmy walked out to the meeting of the roads and stood right in the middle. To the east and the west were hamlets and towns, markets and shops. To the north were the woods, the mountains and swamp, the giants, the dragons, the gnomes.

It seemed to Jimmy that if he was really a baby he would go east or go west. But if he was a man, or bound to become one, he had to go north instead. So that was the way he went, up the very middle of the Great North Road. In a few minutes he was among the trees, and in a few minutes more he could no longer see his own feet. The moon was hidden, the road invisible.

Just half an hour of walking took Jimmy farther from the inn than he had ever been before. For the first time in his life he was alone in the woods at night. And every sound scared him.

He heard shrieks and groans. He heard the snapping of twigs, the rustle of branches. He turned to the left; to the right. He looked up and down and all around.

Every story that the travelers had told him came to his mind in terrible fragments. "They found his head in a tree, his feet in a river." "The dragon turned him to ash as quick as a wink." "They say his ghost sits by the road, holding his own bloody head." Jimmy heard the voices of the travelers in his mind, and saw their faces loom before him. "Gryphons go for the eyes." "A hydra can smell you a mile away." "If a manticore comes after you, play dead. But if it's a troll, run for your life."

An owl hooted nearby. Something swooped past Jimmy's head with a rush of air.

"There's a dead man for every mile of forest." "Trolls lie by the road and grab your ankles." "Burned him alive, the poor devil."

Jimmy ran. He scampered along the road with his little bag thumping against him. But in the darkness he blundered into the bushes. He screamed, thinking that the many heads of a hydra had taken hold of him. In the dark, he wrestled with the bush. Twigs lashed at his face, as though trying to pluck out his eyes. Thorns stuck into his skin like teeth. Jimmy kicked and punched; he tore away fistfuls of leaves.

When he realized that it was only a bush that had him, Jimmy let himself fall to the ground. Snared in the branches, frightened and lonely, he shivered and waited for dawn.

At first light he untangled himself and went along on his way.

His little feet made little tracks along the Great North Road. The woods that had terrified him in the night seemed quite pleasant in the daytime. Squirrels chattered from tree branches. Small lizards, green and orange, crouched on rocks at the roadside, blinking as he passed.

At noon, Jimmy rounded a bend and saw a sight that he knew very well from the tales of the travelers. So many had spoken of it that seemed familiar right away. It was an enormous tree fallen right across the road, its trunk so massive that a tunnel had been chopped right through it.

◆ ◆ ◆

"Oh, yeah," said Dickie. "Boy, that was a big old tree."

Chip frowned. "I don't remember that."

"'Cause we never heard of it," said Carolyn. "It was never in the story, you stupe."

"I know that," said Dickie. "I remember from my dream."

◆ ◆ ◆

The tunnel tree was a landmark on the Great North Road. The hole through its trunk was wide enough to fit a double team of oxen, high enough that a knight could ride through it on horseback. The sides had been smoothed by adzes, then covered with strange symbols and messages in many languages. Some were painted with charcoal, others with vermilion, but many had been carved into the wood with knives.

◆ ◆ ◆

"Don't forget the coins," said Dickie.

"What coins?" said Laurie.

"All over the tunnel," he said. "Travelers nailed coins to the wood on their way north. They used those silver ones, those Aggies, they called them."

"Why was that?" asked Laurie, prodding him on. She always liked it when Dickie added to her stories. Just like old times. "What was special about Aggies?"

"They had holes in the middle," said Dickie. "Aggies were easy to nail to the wood."

"But why would they nail them there?" said Chip.

"In case they came back poor. At least they'd have something," said Dickie. He was smiling, as though at an old memory. "But boy, most of 'em never came back."

"Oh, yes, that's right," said Laurie. She said now that there were so many coins in that hollowed tree that they covered the wood like stucco.

◆ ◆ ◆

As though he'd been given the eyes of an eagle, Jimmy could look down on the whole world and see exactly where he was. The tales of the travelers had put a map in his mind, a picture of the land. He could see how far he had come from the inn, and how very much farther he had to go.

He passed through the tunnel and went on to the north. On either side of the road were trees as big as the one that had fallen, with buttressed roots that made them look like churches. He tried to see their tops, but it only made him dizzy.

Toward evening, as the shadows deepened, Jimmy began to worry about the night. Long before darkness fell, he was scouting for a place to sleep. He saw comfortable hollows and little round wallows but passed them by, remembering the advice of travelers: "Never sleep where something's slept before; you never know what creature made the bed." "You want to be safe, get off the ground."

But the trees were too big for Jimmy to climb. So he kept walking, and his worry mounted. The wolves began to howl and sing, and a manticore roared in the distance. The shadows deepened around him as the night settled over the forest. When Jimmy saw a light ahead, a small fire at the roadside, his heart lifted at the thought of company. He imagined that he would surely know the traveler.

Soon the fire was the only thing that Jimmy could see, and he groped his way toward it. Then a figure appeared in the light of the flames. It looked like a bear at first, and it gave Jimmy a terrible fright until he realized it was only a man wrapped in a bearskin. He thought what a laugh the fellow would have when he told him that.

Jimmy was at the very edge of the firelight before he remembered the words of a minstrel: *The woods is full of murderers.* What if he had stumbled on a cutthroat? A garrotter? A butcher or strangler?

Across the fire, the man turned toward him. He stared through the flames, then shifted his head from side to side. Blinded by his own fire, he called out, "Who's there?"

Jimmy didn't answer right away. The man bent down and snatched a burning stick from the fire. He held it up like a torch and advanced toward Jimmy.

Too frightened to move, Jimmy just stood there. The man came out of the flames, still in his bearskin, holding the stick as far out as he could reach. It made a red glow along the road and in the bushes at its sides. The light swept over ruts, over branches, and fell onto Jimmy the giant-slayer.

The man screamed. He dropped his stick and shrieked the old expression that Jimmy had learned as a child. "Gnome, gnome, leave me alone!"

Jimmy looked back, amazed. The man, all a-tremble, made a sign with his fingers, a shaky little diamond. "Gnome, gnome, leave me alone," he cried again.

"I'm not a gnome," said Jimmy.

The man pulled his bearskin tighter. He took a step backward. "You have the look of one."

"But I'm not. Cross my heart," said Jimmy.

"Stand in the light," said the man. "Let me see your face."

On the road lay the smoldering branch, invisible in the

darkness except for the glow at its tip. Jimmy picked it up and swished it round to bring the embers into flames. He held it so the light flickered on his skin.

"Why, you're merely a boy," said the man. "Diminutive, but human."

"I live at the end of the road. At the Dragon's Tooth," said Jimmy. He lowered the branch, because the light was stinging his eyes. "Yesterday I ran away. I'm trying to reach the swamp."

"But it's bottomless."

"It doesn't matter. I have to find the witch," said Jimmy. "She lives in the mud, with the lizards and alligators. She's old and she's ugly, and she smells like cabbage weed. She's half woman, half frog, and—"

"Yes, I have heard of the witch. I believe her name is Jessamine."

◆ ◆ ◆

James Miner laughed on his treatment board. Then Chip laughed too, though not as brightly.

"Very funny," said Carolyn. Her voice sounded cold as ice. "You think you're so clever."

"What's bugging you now?" asked Laurie.

"Like you don't know," said Carolyn.

"I *don't* know." Laurie was getting angry, annoyed by the girl in the iron lung. "I thought you didn't care about the story. You said—"

James interrupted. "That's her middle name."

"Jessamine?"

"Yes." He nodded on his treatment board. "Carolyn Jessamine Jewels."

The girl lay perfectly still. Her long hair was unbraided, and it spread across the pillow like a halo round her face. She looked up at her mirror, out through the window.

Laurie asked, "How would I know your middle name?"

"Gee, I wonder," said Carolyn. "It's only right in front of you." She gestured with her chin toward the medical records held in the frame of the mirror. "You probably heard about frog-breathing. So you made me half frog. You made me ugly and mean."

"I wasn't even thinking of you. It's a flower," said Laurie. "That's where I got it. Jessamine grows in swamps."

"Wow. News flash," said Carolyn. "I know that, four-eyes."

Laurie squeezed her fingers into fists. She felt like screaming, but kept her voice quiet. "I thought it was a pretty name, that's all."

In his iron lung, Dickie was watching. "An ugly witch with a pretty name?"

"Why not?" said Laurie. "She's old and ugly and mean, but once she was a girl with a mom who loved her, who gave her a pretty name."

"Boy, that's kinda neat," said Dickie.

"It wasn't even my mom who named me," said Carolyn. "It was my dad."

"Who cares?" said Chip. "Let's just hear the story."

# CHAPTER EIGHT

## THE LAST WORDS OF SMOKY JACK

The traveler roasted a rabbit and shared it with Jimmy. Then he held a hand in front of his mouth and, behind it, picked his teeth.

"You sure you don't have any gnome in you, boy?" he asked.

"No, sir," said Jimmy. "I told you, I just never grew big."

"Huh." The man spat a scrap of meat into the flames, then went back to his picking. "It's a striking resemblance. You could pass for a gnome anywhere."

Jimmy shrugged.

The man picked and chewed and spat.

Somewhere in the woods, an animal shrieked. Branches rustled nearby.

"You say you grew up in the Dragon's Tooth, boy?" asked the man.

"Yes, sir," said Jimmy.

"Been past it a hundred times. Never been inside. Don't believe in paying for a bed." He hooked his finger round to the back of his mouth. "Most Tellsmen feel the same. Not that we're poor; we're just frugal."

"What are Tellsmen?" asked Jimmy.

"Put simply, we make tells. We're charmers, boy."

An owl hooted among the trees. A wolf howled, and another answered.

"What's a tell?" asked Jimmy. He would rather talk than listen to the sounds of the forest.

"Anything with magic in it, boy. We manufacture charms, is what we do."

"What kind of charms?" asked Jimmy.

"Any kind at all. Charms for good luck, charms for bad. Charms that would make you as noble as a king, or as a happy as a jester. That's what I like the most about the profession, boy. It's always different. Can never tell from day to day what sort of charm you'll be crafting next."

"Could you craft me one that would make me bigger?" asked Jimmy.

"Sorry, boy, there's not a chance."

"Why not?" asked Jimmy.

"A Tellsman's charms work within the mind. Only Wishmen deal with tangibles."

Disappointed, Jimmy sat back in silence. But the darkness and the sounds of the night pressed around him. He put his hand to his neck, feeling the string. "If I showed you a charm, could you tell me what it does?" he asked.

"I'd give it a darned good try," said the Tellsman.

Jimmy pulled out the ball of bones. The dragon claw rattled inside. "It's supposed to keep me safe," he said. "I don't know how it works."

The hollow sphere swung from Jimmy's hand. As the firelight caught the edges of the bones, it made strange patterns of black and white.

"Who gave you that?" asked the Tellsman.

"Khan. The hunter."

"Would you care to part with it?"

"No, sir," said Jimmy. "It's going to help me, I think." He let the charm turn on its string. "What does it do?"

"I don't know. I didn't make it," said the Tellsman. He spat into the fire and sat brooding for a while. Then suddenly he laughed. "I've known at least a thousand men. Perhaps ten thousand more. The smallest of them all would be five times as big as you. But did even one of all those men go up the Great North Road with just a single charm, and not an inkling of its purpose? Jimmy, you dwarf them all."

He got up then, and moved to the edge of the firelight. In the shadows he had a square barrow on wooden wheels. It unfolded to become a workbench, with a grindstone in the middle, a treadle underneath. There were cubbyholes and narrow drawers that, one by one, the Tellsman sorted through.

Jimmy watched from his place as the man brought out charms and amulets of all sizes. Some were new and shiny, others chipped or broken, brown with dirt and rust.

"Here's the very thing." The man held up a tarnished

bracelet, thin as a blade of grass, with a tiny disc of oyster shell suspended by a ring. "I'll throw a shine on it for you," he said and spat twice on his grindstone. He gave the stone a push to get it going, then pumped away on the treadle. The barrow rocked and shook. When the man touched the bracelet to the stone, sparks flew away in a blizzard.

Jimmy liked the rumbling sound of the wheel and the sizzle and whirr that came from the metal. In the darkness the sparks made a spray like fiery water.

The bracelet was still hot when the Tellsman gave it to Jimmy, as though the spirit of the sparks had passed into the metal. Jimmy slipped it over his wrist and watched the bit of shell turn and shimmer in the firelight.

"What does it do?" he asked.

"I'm not exactly sure, as I've forgotten how I came upon it," said the Tellsman. "Oh, of course it has something to do with water. The piece of shell attests to that. And the thinness of the metal suggests the effect is temporary. It's bound to help in a swamp, but I wouldn't trust it in the sea."

"Well, thank you," said Jimmy.

He fell asleep with the bracelet on his arm, a smile on his face. He thought that he was well on his way already, and that the kindness of travelers would see him through to the end. Happy and contented, Jimmy slept so well that he didn't stir until late in the morning. When he woke, the Tellsman was gone, the fire was out, the barrow hauled away.

Jimmy was sorry that he wouldn't have a chance to thank the man—until he sat up and looked properly around.

His pockets had been turned inside out. His bag had been torn open, its few sad contents strewn right across the

Great North Road. Frantically, he reached for the string around his neck.

Jimmy found with relief that he still had his charm, his ball of bones. But it dangled now against his shirt, as though the Tellsman had tried—but failed—to pull it away. He tucked it back into place and crawled in the dust to collect his things. He found his socks, his shirts, and his underwear, but not the locket that had been his mother's.

At first, Jimmy felt more disappointed than ever. He wanted to give up right then and go home to Fingal. But at the edge of the old fire, he found a leg of the rabbit placed politely on a flat stone that had been cleared of dirt. And beside the stone was a message. It was scraped into the ashes:

*Has lightning inside.*

◆ ◆ ◆

Jimmy ate the rabbit leg for breakfast as he stared at the writing. What did it mean? he wondered: *Has lightning inside?* He poked the ground gingerly but found it cold.

From the edge of the woods he took a stick, and with that he dug through the ashes and the bits of black charcoal, half believing that he might find lightning down in the ground. But when he didn't, he wasn't surprised. Then, puzzled, he tossed his bundle onto his shoulder and walked north up the road, tapping the stick before him.

He tapped all morning. He tapped into the afternoon, over a hill and into a valley, past Unicorn Rock with its white spire thrusting straight in the air. He knew it at once, though he had never seen it before. Toward evening he came to a field of flat brown stones, each as perfect as a brick. "Ah, the Devil's Courtyard," he said aloud, as though he'd passed it a hundred times.

Again he saw the world as if through eagle's eyes. A few miles ahead, the road would fork. The better path would lead to the east, around a small lake with red water, where Gypsies liked to camp. The other fork would go on to the north, but soon it would dwindle into a narrow trail, then disappear altogether. That was the way to the swamp.

There was only an hour of daylight left when Jimmy reached the fork. He thought he should press on for as long as he could. But the music of Gypsies was coming faintly from the east, and he believed he'd be welcome there. So he trudged round the lake, still tapping his stick, and it was the Gypsy King himself who came out of the camp to meet him. The King flung his arms wide open. "My boy!" he cried.

Jimmy had met the Gypsy King only once, years before, when a long train of caravans had stopped outside the inn. It was the King who had knocked on the door, asking for water for his horses. Fingal had said that no Gypsy horse would ever drink from *his* well. But Jimmy, in secret, had carried bucket after bucket, until the horses were sated. The King had said then that he would never forget Jimmy's kindness. And now his teeth flashed with gold fillings as he grinned at the boy. "You long way from home, Jimmy. You come eat now. Come eat," he said.

There were thirty Gypsies, in seven caravans, camped beside the red lake. They treated Jimmy like one of their own, making sure that he had food and water and a place to sit before they let him say a word. Then, when he was ready, they peppered him with questions: Where was he heading? Why was he going? Was something wrong with Fingal? Jimmy told them about the tax man and the terrible things his father had said.

"I'm going to the swamp," he told them. "Bottomless or not, I don't care; I'll swim if I have to," he said. "My mother went in there, and so will I. I have to speak to the Swamp Witch."

A hush fell over the Gypsies. They looked away from Jimmy, down at the ground or off across the water that was now as dark as blood. Far out on the lake, a loon whistled crazily.

The Gypsy King said, "We never speak of the Swamp Witch."

"Why not?" asked little Jimmy.

The King made a sweeping motion with his arm. His clothes were black, and in the gathering night he looked like a bird taking wing. "She's a devil woman. It was a witch who stole my heart, and all witches are the same," said the Gypsy King. "When the moon is dark the Swamp Witch comes close to the camp. The dogs, they smell her."

◆ ◆ ◆

Jimmy learned no more than that. True to his word, the King wouldn't speak of Jessamine, the Swamp Witch. And Jimmy, anxious to please, didn't press him. There was an uncomfortable moment, until someone plucked quietly at fiddle strings. Then someone else joined in with tambourines, and soon the camp was loud with music, wild with Gypsy dancing.

All the women, all the girls, had a dance with Jimmy. They twirled him round the fire circle, round the wagons and the horses. They flung him here and flung him there, and everyone was laughing.

Jimmy had never been so happy. He had never imagined that such happiness was even possible. In fact, he felt more loved by the Gypsies than ever by his father.

They gave him a bed in the King's wagon, on a pile of woolen blankets. A Gypsy princess, with hair as black as a raven's feathers, bent down to kiss his forehead. But when she saw the ball of bones at his neck, she pulled away.

"What's the matter?" asked Jimmy.

"I don't like that," she said.

"It's a charm," he told her.

"No, it is more." She crawled into her own bed at the foot of the wagon and pulled a red blanket around her. "It is two charms. One protects the other."

"Why?" asked Jimmy.

"So that no one can remove it but the owner."

"But won't it keep me safe?" asked Jimmy, up on one elbow now.

"Yes. It is a good charm," said the Gypsy girl.

"Then why don't you like it?" asked Jimmy.

"Because it has evil in it. Your charm brings death."

It was a mystery to Jimmy how a good charm could be full of evil. He asked the Gypsy to explain, but she wouldn't. She blew out the candle beside her bed and lay in silence as the King and all the others laughed and talked outside.

Jimmy dreamed of nothing. His sleep was long and safe,

and in the morning he bathed with the Gypsies in the cool scarlet water. He ate again, and drank again, then took his stick and bundle and sadly said he had to go.

The King followed him out to the road. "My boy, you stay with us, why not?" he said. "From now on you live with Gypsy, yes?"

"I wish I could," said Jimmy. "But I have to go to the swamp."

"Why?" said the King. "Why must you see this witch so badly?"

He thought he'd explained it. He had to see the witch to set things straight. He had to learn what had happened to his mother, and he hoped to grow to be big. He had to show his father that he wasn't a runt or a squirm.

"So many things you have to do," said the King. "So much on your little shoulders. But one day, when you have done them all, you come home and live with Gypsy. Promise me, my boy."

"I would like that very much," said Jimmy.

◆ ◆ ◆

Jimmy followed his tracks down the Great North Road, tapping a Gypsy tune with his stick. When he reached the fork he turned right, toward the swamp and the home of the witch.

The road soon ended, just as the travelers had said it would. The trail that snaked into the forest was easy to follow for the first seven miles. Fresh blazes, bright as yellow paint, marked the route over three hills, each higher than the next. The trail was trodden to bare dirt, and bridges of logs had been built over rivers and creeks.

In the eighth mile, Jimmy found a traveler's pack abandoned beside the trail. It had been torn open, by men or animals, and nothing worth having was left. Half a mile farther on, he found an empty barrel, tossed aside, and a pair of boots with the soles worn off. He passed a thrown-away compass with no needle, an abandoned cart with one wheel shattered, a chest of drawers, the handle from an axe. There was more and more as he went along, as the trail faded slowly into the forest. It had all been left behind, he supposed: abandoned by weary travelers willing to give up their all to carry on.

Beside a creek was the skeleton of a horse, now as flat as a white drawing on the grass, crushed by its own pack saddle. On the other bank there was no trail to follow, no mark or blaze at all. So Jimmy made his own path into the wilderness, and four hours later it brought him to another creek, where he was surprised to find the bones of another dead horse squashed below its pack. Only when he crossed the creek for a second time did he realize that he'd gone in a circle.

The forest was too thick to let Jimmy see the sun. He stumbled along in what he hoped was a straight line, toward what he hoped was north. But every cliff and fallen tree made him veer to one side. And he knew that he was lost again when he came across a trail.

It was a smooth rut through the forest, so deep that a woodsman might have made it by dragging a heavy log. For half a mile Jimmy followed it, until he found a patch of scaly skin snagged on a tree, and realized that he was walking down a hydra's trail. He stood still and listened. Very faintly, he could hear it coming: the hiss of its many tongues, the slithering of its body along the rut toward him.

Jimmy turned off the trail and fled into the forest. He bounded through clearings and smashed through the bushes. He ran and he crawled and he crept. It was chance that took him east, down a stony slope, through a grove of cottonwoods, right to the bones of a dead man.

He was in a little meadow then, where the grass was brown and yellow. The bones made a heap at the base of a white cross, where the man had sat—long ago—to die. The legs were straight out, the arms folded across the hips. The head must have rolled away, because it was nowhere to be seen. But a clay-stemmed pipe had fallen through the bony cage of ribs and lay now on the grass. Propped against the cross—to make a backrest for the skeleton—was a slab of bark that bore a few words carved into its inner surface:

**HERE WILL LIE POOR SMOKY JACK**
**BURIED HIS PARTNER TODAY**
**DIED OF THIRST TOMORROW**
**LOST NOW AND FOREVER MORE**
**POOR OLD SMOKY JACK**

It made Jimmy feel cold and creepy to see the skeleton sitting there, the remains of a man he could remember very well, laughing in the old Dragon's Tooth. He hurried past and ran across the meadow, only to find himself enclosed by a wall of bushes. It rose high above him, too thick for any man—or any army—to hack a way through it. He could see a few broken branches where someone had tried to carve out a path but had barely made a dent.

Jimmy nearly lost heart. Far behind him was the last blaze of the trail, the last footprint of any man. Ahead was a black tangle that seemed to have stopped every traveler who had tried to get through.

The little giant-slayer sank to the ground. He tapped his stick on the toes of his boots, making a sound like a heartbeat.

Among the cottonwoods where he had run, a twig snapped with a quiet click. Jimmy was used to the woods now, and not every noise startled him. But this one made him freeze. He didn't breathe; he didn't blink. The stick was in his hand, hovering in the air.

Another twig snapped. Leaves rubbed against leaves. An odor of animals came drifting through the meadow.

Jimmy watched for movement on the ground. He knew beyond doubt that a creature was coming toward him. He could sense it and smell it and hear it. But he saw nothing until a spidery knot of old twigs sailed down from the tree-tops, somersaulting from one branch to another. Then he looked up and saw the manticores.

There were five of them, skulking from tree to tree, between the forest and the sky. They had the bodies of lions, the wings of bats, the faces and minds of men. They were the most frightening things that Jimmy had ever seen. As he watched, they crept to the ends of the cottonwood limbs, crouched with the branches swaying, then opened their leathery wings and soared to the next tree.

Jimmy stayed absolutely still. He knew from the travelers'

tales that manticores had the eyesight of old men and that they couldn't see him if he didn't move. They were so close now that he could watch their ears twitch as they listened, their faces wrinkle as they sniffed. Then they stalked along the branches, in toward the trunk.

From behind Jimmy's back, a rabbit hopped into view. It sat close to his side, its nose and ears quivering nervously. Jimmy hissed at it: "Stay still!"

The rabbit bent its ears. It hunched down, ready to flee.

"Don't move," said Jimmy in a whisper.

But the rabbit turned and bounded off, and the manticores—with terrible cries—all looked down from the tree.

The rabbit vanished into the bushes, its white tail bobbing like a bouncing ball. A manticore shrieked, and all five of the beasts came swooping from the tree, plunging through the branches.

In a flash, Jimmy whirled around and scrambled after the rabbit. He dove among the tangled bushes, the stick in his hand, but his bundle forgotten.

The manticores landed heavily. Their tails swished, and their wingtips flailed, and they snarled at the bushes with their sharp fangs showing. Then all five threw themselves at Jimmy's bundle, roaring at each other as they tore it apart with their claws.

Jimmy squirmed along the ground. He used the stick to poke ahead of him and find a route. The bushes seemed to close in behind him, and the manticores disappeared. For an hour or more, Jimmy slithered and crawled and crept. Then the tangle of bushes suddenly ended, and he came out into a clearing.

He was afraid to look up, certain that he had blundered back to the same meadow, to the terrible company of Smoky Jack and the manticores. But he heard the sound of running water and the cheerful chirp of many birds, and when at last he raised his head it was to see a sight that no traveler had ever talked about. Jimmy thought that he was maybe the only person alive who had ever seen it.

Set into the forest floor were enormous slabs of stone. They made the Devil's Courtyard seem tiny and silly, for they were laid end to end to form a road that stretched to the east and the west for as far as Jimmy could see. It hadn't been used for eons. Whole trees grew up through the cracks, and the stones were half hidden by moss and dirt. But once the road had carried enormous wagons. Jimmy had no doubt of that at all, because one of them was still there.

It was that wagon, not the road, that astounded the little giant-slayer. All he saw at first was a wheel. It was twenty feet high, the spokes as thick as trees. The bed of the wagon was so high above him that Jimmy toppled backward as he tried to look up at it. Then he just lay on his back, stunned by the size of this thing. It could have carried the whole of the Dragon's Tooth, along with the stable and garden. It could have carried all of that and the Gypsy camp with all the caravans and horses, and every traveler that Jimmy had ever met, and there would still be room enough for no one to be crowded. The driver's seat was at the top of a tower made of struts and bars, reached by a ladder with so many rungs that Jimmy couldn't count them. When he reached three hundred and couldn't tell them apart anymore, he wasn't even close to the top.

At the front of the wagon were the tongues and bars of a harness, and yokes for a hundred oxen. The reins had rotted away so badly that they looked like old spiderwebs. But every other part of the wagon—from yokes to spokes—was made of bronze. The years had turned the metal green, but wherever Jimmy rubbed, a shine came back as bright as ever.

Behind a rear wheel, a bit of chain dangled to the ground. Each link was longer than Jimmy was tall, but he managed to scramble up the chain to the enormous bed of the wagon. All along the edge were massive rings, threaded with miles of chain and cable. With one look around, Jimmy figured out what the wagon was for. It was big enough to carry, all at once, any of the massive trees he had seen in the forest. He could imagine a hundred woodsmen chopping away, the chips flying everywhere, and the great tree finally falling, toppling so gracefully—to land right onto the bed of the wagon. Now, with the forest cleared, the wagon was useless—abandoned.

He couldn't leave before he'd climbed to the driver's seat. Though he was out of breath before he'd even reached the first platform, he kept going up the hundreds of rungs, from level to level, like a sailor up the rigging of a ship.

When he reached the very top, Jimmy was surprised to find that the seat was just a tiny thing. He fell onto it, exhausted, and for the first time in his life his feet touched the floor. In every other chair where he'd ever sat, his legs had stuck out as straight as sticks. But this seat might have been made just for him. He lolled on it comfortably, looking out at what he thought were the ends of the earth. For mile after mile was the forest, then a range of spiky mountains that looked like the jaws of a shark. The sun was setting behind them, turning the sky to the color of oranges and plums. And to the east, not far away at all, were the pools and grasses of the swamp.

He was pleased by the sunset, and awed by the stars. They appeared by the thousands, so bright and gleaming that they reminded him of the spangles on the Gypsies' black clothes, and then of the twinkle of coins deep in a barrel, and that made him think of the inn, of Fingal and his mother.

Jimmy used his belt to tie himself to the seat. He slept there, higher than an eagle in its aerie, and when the sun came up he woke to see a yellow sky, and the last of the stars disappearing. The watery channels that threaded through the swamp looked like rivers of gold, and he picked out a route to follow. Then, with this new picture in his mind, he started down as the sun was still rising. With his charms and his stick, he set off for the swamp.

Before noon he was splashing through marsh grass, with the brown tips of bulrushes waving in a breeze high above his head. He felt as small as a bug on a lawn. At every step he thought he would find no solid ground underneath him, that he would plunge through the mud and the water. But though the bottom was soft, it was there.

He climbed over hummocks and waded through water. Mosquitoes whined in clouds around him. Flies nipped at his skin. Huge dragonflies darted past on wings that clattered and clicked, while water beetles the size of rats scurried across the water. Jimmy clambered up to another grassy hummock, over its summit, and down to the water.

In his path lay a dark log. He began to run, hoping to hurdle it. But his feet slipped in the mud, and he fell face first across the log. He groaned.

And so did the log.

It shifted underneath him. It rose onto four short legs. At one end, a pair of yellow eyes cracked open.

It was an alligator, and Jimmy lay right across its back, just in front of the hind legs. Its mouth opened, showing yellow teeth with strings of meat snarled between them. Then it snapped its jaws and lunged at Jimmy, but only wheeled around in a circle as the giant-slayer clung to the knobby skin. It took another lunge that carried it again in a circle, so fast that Jimmy was nearly hurled from its back. Then it slowly turned its head nearly all the way around and looked right at him, as though trying to figure out what to do.

# CHAPTER NINE

## THE MAGIC IN THE CHARM

"Gee, what happened next?" asked Dickie.

Laurie had stopped talking. She was looking out the window.

"What's wrong?" asked Chip.

In the shadow of the hospital, on a bench at Piper's Pond, sat a man who looked just like Mr. Valentine. In a gray hat that hid his face, he sat with his hands on his knees, just patiently waiting, it seemed.

Chip asked again, "What's the matter?" When he got no answer he said, "Lawdy, Miss Laurie."

Laurie smiled at the twisted lyric. "Sorry," she said. "I think my dad's out there."

"So what?" said Carolyn.

It was Chip who answered. It took him two sentences to say it. "Bet her old man . . . doesn't want her coming here."

"Boy, is that true?" asked Dickie.

"Yes, I guess so," said Laurie. "But I hope he isn't spying on me." She was still looking at the pond, at the man on the bench. She tried to make him lift his head by sending him thoughts: *Look up. Look up.* He seemed so much like her father, yet it was hardly possible. Mr. Valentine had never left work early, and he'd never gone anywhere except straight home. Why would he go to Bishop's and sit at Piper's Pond? But Laurie had a terrible feeling in her heart that the man really was her father, and that he had already seen her in the window as clearly as she had seen the prince in the tower.

Dickie was twisting his head, trying to look outside through his mirror. "What will he do if he knows you're here?" he asked.

"I don't know," said Laurie. "He'll be sore, that's for sure."

Chip laughed. "So will you."

"No, he wouldn't hit me," said Laurie. "He'd never do that."

"No kidding?"

"Of course not. He's my dad."

She looked at Chip's iron lung, at all the pictures there. She was too far away to see them clearly, and the many faces of the boy and the man made a blur in her glasses. She couldn't imagine the smiling man in front of the garage ever raising his hand to hit the boy. But he was nearly as

changeable as the boy, and the pictures showed only in-
stants of time, the flash of a camera's shutter. There was no
way of knowing what had happened before the shutter
opened, or what had followed when it closed.

Laurie saw Chip's face then in the mirror, floating above
the iron lung, watching her watch him. Embarrassed, she
turned back toward the window.

The benches were empty around Piper's Pond, and it took
a moment for Laurie to spot the man with the gray hat. He
was walking down the path, nearly at the gate already.
When he reached the street he turned to the right and vanished behind the wall.

"You know what Davy Crockett would have done with
that old gator?" asked Dickie. He hadn't stopped thinking
of the story. "He would have stuck his arm right down its
throat. Then he would have grabbed its tail and turned that
old gator inside out. That's what Davy would have done.
Stuck his arm right down its throat."

"Well, that's funny," said Laurie. "Because that's just
what happened."

"Gosh, I knew it," said Dickie.

"Except not quite that way."

◆ ◆ ◆

The alligator dragged Jimmy into the bulrushes. It was all
the boy could do just to hold on. The charm around his neck
swayed and bounced so violently that he was afraid he
would lose it. His belt snagged on the reeds. It nearly yanked
him from the alligator's back before it snapped in half and

fell away behind him. The bracelet nearly went the same way. But Jimmy somehow held on.

They went crashing through a wall of bushes. A flock of ducks erupted from the other side, scattering on whirring wings. The alligator shot up a hummock and over the top, and down to a pool of black water.

It hit with a tremendous splash and carried Jimmy under. Deeper and deeper it went, trailing a stream of tiny bubbles from its nostrils. Jimmy saw the sun above him, a yellow ball that grew smaller and darker, then disappeared altogether. And down in the darkness, the gator rolled over and over in quick little turns.

Jimmy was flung aside. Half drowned, he spun through the water, and the alligator came at him. Jimmy held out his arm to fend it off, but the gator only opened its mouth and took his whole arm inside it. Jimmy kicked its neck and tried to pull free. He would have done it too, but the bit of shell on his bracelet snagged on the gator's front teeth.

The great jaws were closing. Jimmy pulled again. The bit of shell tore loose from the bracelet, and Jimmy was free.

At that instant, he felt himself buoyed up like a balloon full of air. He was rushing through the water, shooting for the surface, and he broke through it headfirst like an arrow fired from the bottom of the swamp. He flew six feet up, then plummeted down again.

Jimmy hit the water with his feet; and it was like landing on a trampoline. The whole pool sagged to take his weight, then sprang up and launched him in the air. He could feel a warm glow from the bracelet and knew that he'd found—by chance—what the Tellsman had only guessed at: the magic in the charm.

Jimmy twisted in the air to land again on his feet. The water bent and held him, and he bounded on across the swamp in giant leaps, three yards at a time, somersaulting over islets of grass and reeds.

A snake uncoiled toward him. A hydra raised its many heads. Another alligator snapped its jaws. But Jimmy leapt over them all. He ran for the middle of the swamp with the water flexing underneath him. But soon his leaps began to shrink. He bounced two yards instead of three; he had trouble hurdling a hydra. The warmth of the bracelet was fading already.

A mound of sticks and mud appeared. From a hole in the top, a thread of smoke was oozing down toward the water, where it lay like a thin blanket on the top of water black as tar. A small door opened at the bottom, and out came the Swamp Witch.

She stood knee deep in the mud, one hand still holding the door. Her throat ballooned into a big red ball. And she watched the giant-slayer bound toward her.

The bracelet gave up the last of its warmth as Jimmy neared the witch's house. It turned cool, and then so bitterly cold that he knocked it away. It snapped in two and fell from his arm, and when Jimmy landed again his foot broke through the surface. He stumbled forward, sprawling on top of the water. He could see an alligator right below him, turning now toward him.

Its legs kicked; its tail thrashed. It swam up to the surface and came right through it. It grabbed Jimmy by the waist and carried him into the air. For a moment it seemed to stand on its tail, then slowly toppled over.

In a croaking voice, the witch called out, "Don't eat him! Bring him here."

The alligator swam toward the Swamp Witch and stopped at the edge of a little garden, where bladderworts and fly catchers grew in tidy rows. It cracked its lips and whispered hisses at her.

"Put him down by the patio," said the witch. "You stupid thing."

The patio was a slab of hardened mud. In the middle was a flower box where deadly nightshade and scarlet toadstools grew. The alligator carried Jimmy to the edge and crouched in the mud to let Jimmy slide from its back.

"Now get away," said the witch, her throat bulging. "Go on!"

With a swish of its tail, the gator crept away through the shallow pool around the house. It went gliding past the witch with only its eyes above the water, and those swiveled round to watch her. At the edge of the reeds it swung its head and gave Jimmy the most sly and evil look he'd ever seen.

"Shoo!" shouted the Swamp Witch. "Scat!" She waved it away with her hands, and watched as it slithered through the reeds. "If there's anything more thick-headed than a gator, I hope I never meet it," she said.

At last, the witch turned to Jimmy. She looked at the strange boy, too old to be a child, too small to be a man, and remembered from years ago the visit of the giant. She saw the charm at his neck, and reached out to touch it with a long and knobby finger. "Where did you get this?"

"From Khan," he said. "The hunter."

Her round eyes blinked once. Her throat filled and emptied. "Did you kill him for it?"

"No, he gave it to me." Jimmy found it hard to look the witch in the face, but he didn't turn away. He said that his name was Jimmy, that he was the son of Fingal.

"Yes, I know who you are," said the witch. "In thunder and lightning you were born."

"That's true," said Jimmy.

"You will ask me the way to the castle of Collosso."

Jimmy frowned. "Why will I do that?"

"Because it is your destiny," she told him. "You were born to kill giants."

Jimmy sat down. *Born to kill giants.* The words of the witch seemed to echo in his head. All his life he had thought he was too small to be important. A runt, his father had called him. The idea that he would kill giants made him feel huge inside. But it scared him too.

He asked, "How big is Collosso?"

"He has the height of twenty men," said the witch. "The girth of seven horses."

"Gosh." Jimmy tried to picture a person that size, but it was impossible. It was more than he could imagine. "Do you think . . . ?" He had to stop and start again. "All I wanted was to be more important," he said. "Do you think you could make me a little bit bigger?"

"Without doubt, you are big enough already," said the witch. "Collosso lives in terror of the day that you will come for him. When you have killed the giant you will become a giant yourself. In the hearts of the people, you will be the biggest man that ever lived."

"Could I be the tallest?" asked Jimmy.

"Enough talk," said the witch. "You must go now or never."

"But how do I get there?" said Jimmy. "Show me the way to the castle."

"Aha!" cried the witch in her croaking voice. She looked to the north and pointed at the line of blue peaks in the distance. "Below that highest mountain you will find a pass. As you reach the other side, Collosso's castle will be above you."

"How do I kill him?"

"There are many ways," said the witch. "You could clip him like a flower, or strike him with a lash. You could do him in an hour or—"

"I will do him in a flash," said Jimmy very fiercely.

The witch smiled her froggy smile, that thin line of lips and gums. "I believe you are ready," she said. "Come, I will take you myself to the edge of the swamp."

◆ ◆ ◆

"That witch is a phony," said Chip. "Isn't she?"

"What do you mean?" asked Laurie.

"She's giving him the business." Chip sounded a bit angry about it. "She's making the giant's dream come true."

"I guess she is," said Laurie.

"Poor Jimmy."

♦ ♦ ♦

The witch led the boy into her house.

A small fire was burning with a sweet smell in the middle of the floor, in a circle of red stones. A chair and a table, both built of sticks, made up the only furniture. But there were a great number of baskets woven from grasses, and beside the chair stood a spinning wheel, where the witch had been turning rushes into thread. On the wall hung a picture she'd drawn with red and black mud, showing Gypsy caravans drawn up in a circle.

"That picture. Is it the red lake?" he asked.

"It's nothing," she told him.

"I stayed there with the Gypsies," he said. "The King told me that a witch stole his heart. What do you think he meant?"

She smiled at this, but only briefly. Then she waved her froglike hand, as though to dismiss the King. "Bah!" she said. "Who knows what Gypsies think?"

With that, the witch turned away and led Jimmy across the room, to a door even smaller than the first one. A smell of dirt and worms came out when she opened it. "Stay close behind me," she said, and went through.

Beyond the door was a tunnel that dropped steeply through the ground. When it leveled off Jimmy was far beneath the swamp, in utter darkness, following the witch only by the slithery sounds of her walking or the wheezing of her breath.

For an hour they walked and crawled through the tunnel. Then it started sloping up again, and at the top Jimmy bumped heavily into the witch's back, not knowing that she'd come to the end of the tunnel. She grunted, and a crack of light appeared as she pushed against a door.

"Come this way," she said.

She led Jimmy out of the tunnel, into the hollow trunk of a burned-out tree. At one time it might have stood hundreds of feet high, for the trunk was wide enough that the witch had set up a little summer cottage inside it. Even now, with the top shattered off, it was the highest thing around. Like a black rock on a green sea, it rose all alone from a rolling field of heather.

Jimmy looked back toward the swamp. He could hear the dragonflies clattering over the reeds. "Years ago," he said, "my mother set out for the swamp. Did she find you?"

"No," said the witch.

"Are you sure?"

"Since Collosso, you are the first to come. Now your destiny is over there." The witch pointed again to the far-off mountain. "The giant swore that he will crush you like a nit. But I do not believe it is so. He lives in fear of the day that you will find him."

She put a webbed hand on Jimmy's shoulder. "Good luck, giant-slayer. When I see you next, I will have to look way up to recognize you."

◆ ◆ ◆

Mr. Valentine was sleeping when Laurie came home. Flat on his back on the sofa, he had a book in his hands. He did this every now and then, but always denied it. He would wake embarrassed and tell anyone who'd seen him, "I wasn't asleep. I was resting my eyes."

Mrs. Strawberry was still there, though dinner was set out on the table. She was sitting at a chair in her coat and gloves, as though chilled by her own frosty glare.

"Where have you been?" she asked as Laurie came into the room. "You're very late."

"I was at school," said Laurie.

"Oh, really. Until this time of day?" Mrs. Strawberry tapped her watch three times. "Your father was very upset when he came home and you weren't here."

In the living room, Mr. Valentine shifted on the sofa. He spluttered and coughed, half awake.

"He went looking for you." Mrs. Strawberry stood up. "He looked *everywhere*."

Laurie was surprised to find that Nanna could still put a fright inside her. A little tingle ran up her back like a slithering snake.

"He waited dinner for you too," said Mrs. Strawberry, heading for the hall. "Of course it's stone cold now." She shouted goodbye to Mr. Valentine, then slipped out the door.

If Mr. Valentine knew where Laurie had been, he didn't say so. He greeted his daughter with only half a smile and told her that he was glad she was home. But he didn't ask why she was late or where she had been. He didn't even look at her as he tucked his tie into his trousers and sat at his place for dinner. He opened the paper and started reading, and didn't say another word.

He didn't mention Bishop's that evening, nor any day for the rest of the week.

On Saturday morning the sky was gray and bleak. "Feels like thunder," said Mr. Valentine as he poured his morning coffee.

He was right. An hour later it had rained and stopped, and a hot wind was gusting through the trees. From far away came the rumbling tremor of a thunderclap. Laurie put on her green coat, though she hated wearing it. It had a big hood that she thought made her look like an enormous newt when she had it pulled up, with her glasses on. She didn't say where was off to, but just shouted from the door, "Dad, I'm going out!"

She could feel the thunder coming closer as she walked to Bishop's and in through the gate. The sky was darker. The wind pushed against her. At Piper's Pond it made the branches of the willows rustle. A duck floated in the middle of the pond, thrusting its head into the water again and again.

Laurie rode the elevator to the fourth floor. As she passed the big room with the television and the building blocks, James Miner called for her to wait. He came trundling out on his treatment board, his hands paddling madly, like an alligator running.

He went ahead of her along the hall, now sideways, now backward. Outside, the thunder rolled more loudly.

The lightning started as they reached the respirator room. Dickie and Chip and Carolyn were all watching the storm in their mirrors. Great clouds were building in the sky, toppling over each other. The lightning made bright flashes that filled the window. The glass rattled with the thunderclaps.

"Boy, it's real close," said Dickie. He seemed weaker than he had before. He sounded nervous too.

But Chip and Carolyn both were smiling. "It's kinda neat," said Chip. "Isn't it, Laurie?"

It *was* kinda neat. It was keen, she said. "But what if the power goes out?"

She imagined the iron lungs shutting down, the thick silence that would fill the room when the bellows stopped wheezing and huffing.

"It's okay," said Chip. "There's a generator."

Then Carolyn spoke. And for once she sounded friendly. "That gave out too," she said. "One time."

"What happened?" asked Laurie.

"It was the middle of the night," said Carolyn. "In the middle of winter." A snowstorm had knocked out the power. "There were eight people in iron lungs that year," she said. In the respirator room they were listening to the rumble of the generator down in the basement.

The sound was a steady, comforting hum—until someone made a mistake while transferring fuel. Then the generator suddenly faltered.

"We heard it sputter," said Carolyn. "The lights went dim." In that moment, she said, the respirators stalled, as though catching their breath. But in the next instant the lights were bright again, and the sound was surging. "I turned to the girl beside me, and just as we grinned at each other, the power went off."

Carolyn described how the bellows on the respirators wheezed to a stop. The silence, she said, was eerie, almost frightening. "Then the alarms on the tops of the respirators started ringing. From all through the hospital we heard chimes and buzzers and people shouting."

Just telling the story made her seem frightened all over again. Her face turned more pale than ever; her eyes grew wider. "I wasn't very good at frog-breathing then," she said. "I thought I was going to suffocate." In the dark, she had struggled for every breath, her muscles almost useless. The girl beside her could still move her arms, though she was paralyzed from the waist down. She started tapping her knuckles on the iron lung—*tap, tap, tap.* "It was ghostly," said Carolyn, "in the dark like that. It made me think of a story I'd read, about a deep-sea diver and a haunted shipwreck." From the other respirators had come a frantic ticking and clucking of tongues, the sound that riders made to hurry their horses, but that polios made to call for help.

The beams of flashlights had swished through the corridors. Into the room had come nurses, invisible in the dark, nearly as frightened as the polios themselves. They'd shone their lights here and there, so that the beams swung through the room, glaring now and then in the tilted mirrors.

"It was getting cold," said Carolyn. There had been frost on the windows. The nurses had tried to calm the polios as they struggled with the iron lungs, and at last they started pumping with the hand bellows, grunting as they heaved on the handles. When Carolyn had felt air being drawn through her throat, her lungs filling, she thought it couldn't possibly come hard enough or fast enough.

"It was really scary," she said.

"I bet," said Laurie.

Carolyn's face was drawn and weary. She lay looking straight up, blinking her eyes.

"That girl beside you: was she Penny Nolan?" asked Chip.

"No. Way before her."

"Who?"

"I forget her name." The bellows wheezed on the iron lungs. "She died the next week."

Laurie whispered. "She *died*?"

"Sure," said Carolyn.

"How old was she?"

"Nine?" said Carolyn, unsure. "It wasn't because of the power failure. She was dying already. We knew she was going, 'cause the nurses closed a curtain around her."

"That must have been horrible," said Laurie. "You were right next to her?"

"I heard her kind of gurgling," said Carolyn. "It went on for ages. Then they turned off her machine. Everyone came out from behind the curtain. A nurse walked by and tilted my mirror. She tilted all the mirrors so we couldn't see behind us. But we heard the iron lung rolling through the room. I can still hear that. At night sometimes. That poor girl rolling out."

There was a rumble of thunder just then. It wasn't horribly loud, but it went on for a long time, almost stopping then starting again. It made everyone look at each other and laugh in a nervous way.

Down on the floor, little James Miner hadn't spoken for a long time. Laurie leaned down and asked him, "You okay?"

"Uh-huh," he said, nodding happily. He was even reading his magazine; the storm meant nothing to him.

"You're not scared of thunder?" asked Laurie.

"No way," said James. "I was born in a thunderstorm."

The window brightened with a flash of lightning. The thunder followed soon after, booming through the sky.

"That's weird you were born in a thunderstorm," said Dickie. And Carolyn, at the end of the row, added, "It's unlucky, you know."

"No fooling," said James. "My dad says it blew a big hole in the roof and burnt up the wires like crazy. He says it pushed all the nails out of the walls, and the pictures fell down in every room. He says being born in a storm means you can see the future."

The window glared with lightning; it shook with thunder. And the rain started then, so heavy that it seemed they were looking out through a waterfall, at a world as dark as night. Water swept down the glass in waves and ripples, and the wind made a howling noise round the drain spouts and the eaves. And the ivy clung on as it rustled and heaved, shedding leaves that whirled away on the wind.

# CHAPTER TEN

## THE GNOME RUNNERS

Behind the storm, the sky was clear and bright. A white swan came down on whistling wings and landed on Piper's Pond. All around, the grass was strewn with twigs and leaves.

Laurie watched the rain steaming away from the ledge and the windowpane. She heard the sound of someone coming, and turned to see a boy in a wheelchair. He looked like a hillbilly farmer, with big ears and a missing tooth, his hair like a snarl of copper wires. Behind him, a girl appeared, peeking shyly into the room.

"We've heard about the story," said the boy. "Can we listen?"

"Sure, I guess," said Laurie.

They came trundling in and wheeled their chairs behind the iron lungs. The boy was Peter; the girl was Ruth. Peter wore leg braces under his trousers, and his black shoes were built right into them. Ruth had a gray blanket over her lap, covering her legs and feet. Her face was spotted with pimples, and she looked everywhere except at people's faces.

"We sort of know what's going on," said the boy, " 'cause everybody's talking about it. But where's Jimmy now? He's the giant-slayer, right?"

It was Carolyn who answered, turning her head on the pillow to look. "He's come out of the stupid swamp, and now he's heading for the mountains."

"He's crossing a field of heather," said Chip. And Laurie took it up from there.

◆ ◆ ◆

The heather was as high as Jimmy's knees. It was tough and springy, so that he felt as though he was walking across an enormous hairbrush, snagging his feet in the bristles. Creepy little bugs shaped like triangles kept leaping around him, pinching his legs.

At first he staggered and struggled, every step such an effort that he thought he would never get out of the fields and into the woods again. He stumbled many times.

At dusk Jimmy could still see the witch's burned-out tree behind him. He spent a night in the heather, hiding as well as he could from the bugs. With his shirt pulled over his head, his hands turtled inside it, he slept in a curled-up ball, a tiny thing all by himself in an endless stretch of heather. In the dark a herd of deer went bounding past him, their white tails bobbing among the stars. Then a flight of gryphons flapped overhead, and soon the deer were shrieking.

Jimmy forged on. It was late in the morning when he reached the forest again and found a trail beside a tumbling river. He trudged upstream, round rapids and waterfalls, until he looked up and saw a bridge ahead, and the ramshackle home of a troll underneath it.

Jimmy had been taught to never trust a troll, so he took to the woods and struggled on. An hour later he came to a road that cleaved through the forest. He turned to his left, walking up the middle of the road toward the mountains of the giants.

At a beaver pond that afternoon, he came across an old cart pulled up on a strip of grass, and an old gray donkey in the harness. The cart was nothing more than a big box with a tiny door and window in the back and another window in the front, meshed with iron bars. It was the sort of cart that was driven by beaver hunters, but lashed to the side was an enormous bundle of pipes and rope, and a leather ball that looked like the head of a snake.

Jimmy looked up and down the road, then out across the pond in the hope of seeing a fellow traveler. Instead, he saw two.

They were swimming in the pond. One was fat and round, the other as skinny as an eel. They floated on their backs, the fat one blowing water from his mouth like a fountain. Jimmy sat down in the shade of the wagon and watched the old donkey graze in the grass.

The men had piled their clothes on the beaver dam.

They clambered out, dressed, and came along the shore together.

It was the fat one who was the first to see Jimmy leaning against a cart wheel. "Zounds!" he cried, stopping in his tracks.

The thin man looked just as surprised. "Where did that one come from?" he said.

Jimmy smiled at the men. He raised his tiny hand as a greeting. "Hello," he said. "I've come from the swamp."

The men seemed amazed. They looked at him and then at each other with expressions of utter disbelief. The thin one scratched his head. "Am I hearing right, Meezle?" he said.

"Yes, it's true; I came out of the swamp," said Jimmy proudly. "I even met the Swamp Witch there." He stood up as tall and straight as he could. "She sent me to kill Collosso."

The fat man laughed. He didn't have the jolly, booming sort of laugh that Jimmy would have expected, but a schoolgirl's timid giggle. *Tee-hee-heeeee. Tee-hee-heeee.*

"It's not funny," said Jimmy, offended. "The Swamp Witch said I'm born to kill giants."

The men exchanged glances. The fat one said, "You're a lingo, aren't you? Tell the truth now."

"I don't even know what a lingo is," said Jimmy, a bit annoyed. "I'm the son of Fingal, from the Dragon's Tooth. And I don't see why you're laughing at me."

"Oh, I'm not laughing *at* you," said the fat man. He wiped a hand across his face and put on a solemn look. "It's just . . . well, a little fellow like you taking on Collosso?" He shook his head. "You've got spunk, all right. Jiggs, wouldn't you say the boy has spunk?"

"Piles of it," said the thin man.

"Oodles, even." The fat one grinned. "We're Meezle and Jiggs. I'm Meezle."

"I'm Jiggs," said the thin man.

"I think we can help you," said Meezle. *Tee-hee-heeeeee.*

The fat man pulled his partner aside. They went a few yards down the road and stood talking in low voices, with Meezle doing most of the talking. Both glanced now and then at Jimmy, and went on with their whispers. Finally they nodded and came back, each with a huge, friendly grin.

"We've decided to throw in with you," said Meezle. "We'll help you take on Collosso. If you'll have us, of course."

"That would be terrific," said Jimmy.

"But first there's a little job needs doing," said Jiggs.

*Tee-hee-heeeee.* Meezle laughed. "It's not that you *have* to do it. We thought maybe you'd want to, that's all. Scratch our backs, we scratch yours."

"What sort of job?" asked Jimmy.

"Come up on the cart and I'll tell you."

The seat wasn't big enough for the three of them, so Jiggs climbed aboard the poor old donkey. Meezle took the reins and gave them a shake. "Get up, Dinkey!" he shouted.

The donkey brayed and stretched, then pulled against the harness, and off they went along the road. There was one wheel that squeaked with every turn, a shrill sound that grated inside Jimmy's head. But he was glad to be riding instead of walking.

Meezle got right to business. "We're gnome runners," he said. "We catch the little fellas."

"Why?" asked Jimmy.

"Profit, mostly." Meezle shifted on the seat, and the whole cart leaned sideways. "Would you care to give it a try?"

"Well, I'd like to," said Jimmy. The wheel squeaked below him. "But I've got a giant to kill, and—"

"Won't take long," said Meezle. "What do you say? Do you really fancy taking on that giant by yourself?"

"I don't know how to run gnomes," said Jimmy. "I never met a runner."

"Nothing to it. If you can fall off a log, you can run gnomes," said Meezle. "Usually, we run them with the snake. One of us shoves the snake into the house and shouts through the pipe, and the other does the netting. But you could fit right inside a gnome house. You herd them; we trap them. Simple as that, my little friend. We run the gnomes and head on to the castle."

"Well, all right," said Jimmy.

"Good for you." Meezle clapped the giant-slayer on the back. "You'll go in by the top when I give the word, and—"

"The top of what?" asked Jimmy.

"The cave! By golly, you think gnomes live in trees?"

"I don't know where they live," said Jimmy. "I've never seen a gnome."

*Tee-hee-hee.* "Gnomes are everywhere," said Meezle. "I've seen six in the last mile."

"Really?"

"Ask Jiggs if it isn't so."

"It's so," said Jiggs.

"When you're walking down the road and you hear something in the bushes but you can't see a soul, that's a gnome," said Meezle. "When no one's looking at you but you feel

that someone is, that's a gnome. When you catch a movement in your eye, then turn and nothing's there, that's a
gnome. They're quick as foxes, sly as all get-out. Gnomes is
everywhere, as they say."

The cart rumbled along so slowly that it raised barely a
feather of dust. The wheel squeaked, and the box rocked
side to side. "How far is the cave?" asked Jimmy.

*Tee-hee-heeee*. "We've just passed it."

Jiggs patted Dinkey's neck, a friendly little gesture. "You
never go straight at a gnome house," he said. "You always
circle round it. Otherwise, you find it empty."

Meezle drove half a mile farther before he brought the cart
to a stop. "Whoa, Dinkey," he said as he pulled on the reins.

Jiggs stayed with the donkey while the fat man took
Jimmy into the woods. The ground was steep and rocky,
with enormous boulders strewn along the slope.

"Keep quiet now," said Meezle. He went at an angle up the
hill, puffing with every step. Jimmy followed close behind,
round boulders and trees, climbing from ledge to ledge.

At the top of the slope, Meezle squeezed between two
boulders. He had to suck in his stomach and push himself
through, like a cork trying to press itself into a bottle. In
the space behind them was a hole in the cliff, a black tunnel.
"Here's where you go in," said Meezle.

The tunnel was just the right height for Jimmy to stand
upright at the entrance. He smelled peppermint and laven-
der on the cool draft that came from inside. He heard a
strange sound, a sort of coo and mutter that reminded him
of home. It was the same happy noise that the chickens had
made in his hen house as they settled into the nesting boxes.

Suddenly, in his mind, he was standing with his mother at the doorway there, smelling the straw of the chickens' nests.

"Stop gawking and listen," said Meezle. "Me and Jiggs will go down to the entrance, over there by that tree. When we're ready we'll signal with a red flag. Soon as you see it drop, in you go."

"What do I do?"

"You run. Fast as you ever ran before. You won't see a thing at first, but don't worry. The tunnel will spiral to the right and go downhill." Meezle made a circle in the air with his finger. "Gnome tunnels always spiral to the right. It will take you to the upper chamber. Understand?"

"Yes," said Jimmy.

"You keep shouting, 'Run, gnome, run!' as loud as you can. You waves your arms like this." Meezle flung his arms in all directions. He looked like a fat spider trying to feel its web. "That'll clear them out. They'll head downhill; they always do. Then you just run them, Jimmy. Keep shouting—'Run, gnome, run!' Keep waving, and run the lot of them from chamber to chamber, till they spill out the bottom. Me and Jiggs will catch them there. Understand?"

"Yes," said Jimmy again.

Meezle left the giant-slayer at the gap between the boulders. He disappeared down the slope, and a long time later the creak of the cart wheel came faintly through the woods, fading away with every turn.

Jimmy looked uneasily toward the mouth of the cave. He had never seen a gnome, and wondered what he would do if a bunch came rushing out right then. Like the Tellsman he

{162}

had met on the road, he was afraid of the creatures. What he knew of gnomes he'd been taught by Fingal. He imagined them as stupid things but cunning, little better than moles or badgers. He knew they worked in the mines, for digging was about all that a gnome was good for. Or so Fingal had told him.

The sun and the shadows moved around him. Jimmy waited for hours, it seemed, and was beginning to think that the runners were playing some cruel sort of joke when the red flag popped up below him, just where Meezle had said it would. Jimmy leaned on a boulder and stared at that dot of red in a world of green. Afraid to look away, he made his eyes hurt with the staring, until the ground and the trees seemed to shimmer and sway.

Then the flag fell. Jimmy turned and raced for the tunnel.

He went in at full speed, and in a moment was in utter darkness. His shoulder rubbed on the stone wall; his feet pattered on the ground. The smells grew stronger, the chattering louder. A crack of light appeared, widening quickly as he whirled through the spiral. He started shouting: "Run, gnome, run!"

He flew out of the tunnel and into the chamber. The ceiling soared above him in a room as big as a church, aglow in the light of a hundred lamps. A dozen gnomes were sitting on the floor, all looking up with terror in their eyes.

Jimmy hadn't expected them to look like little men. But that was just what they were: little old men with white beards and worn faces. They all looked alike, in red slippers and green trousers, in long caps with tassels on the tips.

All the stories he'd heard, the warnings about gnomes, came

back to him. More from fear than anything, Jimmy waved his arms; he screamed and shouted, "Run, gnome, run!"

Up they got, the little old men, their quiet chatter now a frightened squeal and squawk.

"Run, gnome, run!" cried Jimmy.

They bolted for a door in the opposite wall. They crowded through it, pushing each other so that some of them stumbled and fell. The fallen ones shrieked as they struggled up again.

Three more fled from the next room, and four from the one after that. Jimmy herded them on, full of excitement now. The slap of the gnomes' little slippers, the squeal of their voices, made his blood rush fast and hot. If Meezle had told him to stop at the third chamber, he couldn't have done it. He had no thought now except of herding gnomes.

They leapt up from games of dice and stones, from beds of cedar boughs, from a dinner table set with wood. The plates were wood, the goblets wood, the knives and forks were sticks. And the gnomes threw them all down and toppled their chairs as they ran for the door.

"Run, gnome, run!" cried Jimmy.

They fled through bedrooms and sitting rooms, through a kitchen with a small fire burning in a pit. They ran through a chamber stuffed with gold and silver.

For a moment, Jimmy froze. He stood there with his little arms held high and far apart, his mouth still open from shouting. He looked around at countless riches, at more than even his father had ever dared to dream about.

The gold was raw, straight from the earth. It was piled to staggering heights, more gold than had ever been seen by any king of the land. There was another pile of silver that was nearly as high, and another of diamonds, and another of rubies and opals and emeralds in a shimmering jumble of colors. Suddenly and completely, Jimmy felt the greed of Fingal.

In the door, a gnome had stopped. He was looking right at Jimmy, and Jimmy was the taller by nearly a quarter of a cubit. Somewhere down the hill, past the lower chambers, Meezle and Jiggs were shouting, and all the gnomes were shrieking. But the one old gnome didn't seem frightened: only sad, and maybe a bit angry.

In little more than an instant, Jimmy had passed from excitement to greed. And now he wasn't sure how he felt at all. He was partly ashamed and partly angry, as though he'd been caught doing something shameful. He couldn't stand to see the gnome looking at him, so he waved his arms and shouted again, "Run, gnome, run!"

The gnome didn't move.

"Run, gnome, run!" Jimmy raced toward the little man, waving and shouting. But the gnome didn't budge even then. So Jimmy ran right past and left him standing there alone.

He ran through a chamber full of shovels and picks, another stuffed with gnome-size overalls and tiny helmets with lanterns on their fronts. And then he was outside, out on the slope of jumbled boulders, and Meezle and Jiggs were there, laughing as they bundled all the screaming gnomes into a ragged cargo net.

"Ah, Jimmy," said Meezle. "Good work, boy. Good running."

Meezle and Jiggs dragged the gnomes in a kicking, squirming

ball over the rocks to the wagon. Jimmy watched the red shoes and red caps tumbling along; he saw the beards and the faces and the eyes of the gnomes. The little men reached out through the net and jabbered away in their frightened squeals.

"Shut up! Shut up!" cried Meezle as he stuffed them in the cart. Jiggs slammed the door and threw the latch in place. He put away the net.

*Tee-hee-heeee.* "Off we go," said Meezle.

Jiggs took his place on Dinkey's back. Meezle helped Jimmy into the seat, then climbed up beside him. He got the cart moving. "So," he said casually. "Did you see any gold in the gnome house? Hmmm?"

Jimmy looked up at Meezle. Behind rolls of flesh, his eyes seemed small and rat-like.

"You've heard it said, I'm sure," said Meezle. "Gnomes and gold is like bees and honey. Their homes are full of the stuff."

"It was pretty dark in there," said Jimmy. "I was busy running."

"But if you saw gold you'd tell me, wouldn't you?" Meezle was squinting greedily. "You wouldn't think of keeping it for yourself, or anything like that? We're partners, after all. Aren't we?"

"Sure, Meezle," said Jimmy.

It was a miserable ride for Jimmy along the Great North Road that day. As well as the creak of the cart's wooden wheel came the moaning and crying of the gnomes. But Meezle and Jiggs never stopped to look after them.

"Maybe they're thirsty," said Jimmy.

"Maybe so," said Meezle, as though the idea were only an interesting theory. When the sounds grew too loud, he banged his fist on the roof and shouted, "Shut up in there, you blithering gnomes."

◆ ◆ ◆

They traveled through the night. Though the wheel kept creaking and the gnomes kept wailing, Jimmy fell asleep. He swayed back and forth like a doll made of rags and didn't wake up until the cart stopped at dawn.

The sky was yellow and orange. Blocking the road in front of the cart was a wooden gate in a wall made of logs. A man was coming out of a little booth, shuffling his feet in the dust. He unfastened his locks and latches.

"Where are we?" asked Jimmy, rubbing his eyes.

"The end of the road," said Meezle. *Tee-hee-heeeee.*

Jimmy expected to see the castle of Collosso on the other side of the wall. But when Meezle drove the cart through the gate, they entered a dusty compound that looked more like a prison than anything. There was a row of pretty houses, with flowers in window boxes, but most of the buildings were stark and square, with locks on the doors and bars on the windows.

Jimmy looked warily at Meezle. "What sort of place is this?"

"It's the mines, of course," said Meezle. "Gold, mostly. Bit of silver." He steered the cart toward the row of houses, then cleared his throat and called out in a voice that was loud and deep, like the hoot of a foghorn: "Gnomes for sale!"

Out from the houses came men in fine clothes, and women in dresses, and boys and girls who didn't pause on the porches but came running across the compound with dust flying from their heels.

"Gnomes for sale!" shouted Meezle.

In the cart the gnomes were wailing louder than ever. They pressed against the window, reaching their fingers between the bars.

Meezle stopped the cart. "Gnomes for sale!" he cried again.

A man in white clothes, with bushy whiskers on his cheeks, came over with a walking stick. "How much?" he asked.

Meezle named a price that was, per gnome, what Fingal would have earned in an afternoon. The man nodded. He climbed up on the back of the cart and peered in through the window. Then he stood below the driver's seat and pointed at Jimmy. "Why's that one riding with you?"

"Me? Oh, I'm not a gnome," said Jimmy. "I'm not for sale, sir."

The man looked delighted. He grinned at the boys who stood around him, watching from a distance. "Why, he's a lingo."

"Yes," said Meezle. "He speaks very well for a gnome."

"What do you mean?" said Jimmy. "We're partners."

The boys and girls hooted with laughter. The man stroked his whiskers happily. "Will a gnome never speak a word of truth?" he said. "I'll give you a thousand Royals for the lot."

"Two thousand if you want the lingo," said Meezle.

The man looked into his purse. "Fifteen hundred."

"Done."

They shook hands, and that was it. Jimmy was sold as a slave.

◆ ◆ ◆

A gang of men came to unload the cart. They brought a cage on wheels and pitched the gnomes into it like so many bags of potatoes. Jimmy argued and pleaded, but they pitched *him* too, tossing him feet first.

He grabbed onto the bars of the cage and reached through them. "Please," he said. "Somebody save me." But nobody moved to help poor Jimmy. A boy looked around with a stupid grin. "I never seen a funnier gnome," he said.

It was the gnomes who comforted the giant-slayer. They closed around him, patting his shoulders, rubbing his back. They talked in their jabbering voices as the cage was wheeled across the compound, and although Jimmy couldn't understand a word they were saying, he felt less wretched and abandoned.

Jimmy and the gnomes were hauled high into the mountains, above all but the scrawniest trees. They were taken to a camp that was ringed by a stone wall, guarded by hounds with no tails, by burly men from Hooliga, armed with blackjacks and bludgeons. They were put to work in a silver mine, where they labored in darkness with hammer and chisel. They went down before dawn and came up after dark, never seeing the sun.

◆ ◆ ◆

"Boy, why didn't Jimmy know about gnomes?" said Dickie. "The travelers at the inn should have told him."

"They didn't know," said Laurie. "The runners and the miners were the only ones who knew what was going on, and *they* didn't talk to anyone. Everyone else was afraid of gnomes. Why, most were scared to death. Jimmy had no idea what a gnome was like until he met the runners."

"How long did he work at the mine?" asked Chip.

"A long time," said Laurie. "A very long time."

◆ ◆ ◆

Jimmy was kept so long at the mine that he learned the language of the Gnomes. He became friends with many, even with those he had herded from the cave, because they were the ones that he lived with, all crammed in a windowless hut barely bigger than a Hooligan dog house.

He told them about Fingal and the Dragon's Tooth, and they sometimes laughed when he mixed up the strange gnome words—but never in a cruel way. He told them that he was born to kill giants, and that—somehow—he was going to slay Collosso.

That made the gnomes excited. Gnomes were always excited, but then more than ever. In the dark little hut, with Jimmy the giant-slayer sitting in the middle of a circle, they began to talk of giant killing. It soon would be all they ever talked about.

"Killing giants is easy. It's child's play," said one, named Felix. "I've killed three of them myself."

"I've killed four," said another.

Jimmy smiled. It seemed wonderful that a turn of bad luck had brought him into the company of giant-slayers. "Tell me," he said. "How do I do it?"

Felix pulled at his long beard. "Knock him down, that's what. Let physics do the rest."

"But how do I knock him down?" said Jimmy.

"Trip him up," said Felix. "Trip him up and knock him down. That's all there is to killing giants."

"But how do I trip him up?" asked Jimmy.

"Put his shoes on the wrong feet!" cried a different gnome.

"Tie the laces together," shouted another.

"Yes, I invented that method," said Felix.

It seemed there were many ways to kill a giant, and the gnomes rattled them off for hours, until one of the Hooligans bashed on the hut with his bludgeon and told them all to be quiet. The gnomes only lowered their voices and in excited whispers described their many adventures, each more thrilling than the last.

# CHAPTER ELEVEN

## THE RETURN OF THE HUNTER

Jimmy stood out among the gnomes, and not only because he was the tallest. He didn't have a beard like the others, nor a voice that was old and manly. His ears were too big; he had longer legs, so he didn't run in the staggering way of a gnome. But most obvious of all, Jimmy couldn't dig and chisel like a gnome. As a miner, he was useless.

To the Hooligan guards, Jimmy was "that big one," which pleased him, or "that funny-looking one," which didn't. They knew he was a lingo, but they treated him like a fool. "Diggy here!" they said, thrusting a shovel in his hand. "Diggy, diggy! You savvy?"

When they saw what a poor miner he was, the guards

made Jimmy "boss gnome" and put him in charge of the woodcutting party. They taught him how to drive the wagon with its team of four horses, and every morning Jimmy headed off across the mountainside, instead of down into the mine. A Hooligan guard was always with him, a slathering dog in hand.

Jimmy drove the wagon back and forth. He did that in the autumn and all through the winter, when the air was so cold that he wrapped himself in seven furs and still shivered every minute.

But the woodcutting was easy in the winter. There was no need to limb the trees, because the branches broke away as the great pines came crashing down. They shattered so cleanly that they might have been made of glass, and the sound was clear and sharp—echoing forever through the mountains. At the end of the day, the beards of the gnomes were solid with frost, and icicles dripped from their eyebrows. But they sang their old gnome songs, with that wonderful echo, as they rode the wagon back to camp.

It was on a day toward the end of winter when the unicorns came over the ridge and down across the mountain. There were six of them running, with the snow in a cloud around them, their snorting breaths—in white puffs—the only sound in the world. The gnomes just stood and watched, and the Hooligans didn't order them back to work because *they* were watching too.

Long manes flowing, horns sparkling with sunlight, the unicorns went plowing through the snow, past the woodlot, down the hill, into the thickness of the forest.

And behind them came a hunter.

◆ ◆ ◆

"Was it Khan?" asked Dickie.

"Yes, it was Khan," said Laurie.

Dickie smiled. "I knew he would come."

Peter in his wheelchair, and Ruth beside him, hadn't heard of the hunter. "Who is Khan?" they asked. Chip said that he was a hunter, that he followed the unicorns, and that he had given a mysterious charm to Jimmy the giant-slayer. And then Carolyn said, "Dickie thinks it's him."

Ruth hid her smile by looking suddenly at the floor. But Peter laughed out loud. So did Chip, though he'd already heard the idea.

"It's true," said Dickie. "I'm Khan. Every night I ride across the mountains in the snow."

"You dream about him every night?" asked Peter.

"It's not dreaming, really. I *am* Khan," said Dickie. "At night I live in the story. It's like I've always been there, kind of."

Chip looked across from his pillow. "Are you giving us the business?"

"No way," said Dickie. "It's hard to explain, but it's true." The coonskin cap dangled in front of his face. "I'm Khan the hunter. And I think James is Jimmy." The machine took a whirring, wheezing breath. "And Carolyn's the Swamp Witch."

"Then who am I?" said Chip.

"I don't think you're in it."

"What about Laurie?" asked Carolyn. "If it's her story, she oughta be in it."

Dickie frowned at his mirror. "Maybe she's the Woman," he said at last. "That kind of makes sense, 'cause she made the giant-slayer. You know? Like he was born on account of her?"

"But the Woman vanished," said Carolyn. "Probably the giant got her. So Laurie should be squashed or something. She should disappear."

"Well, I can't figure all of it out. Not yet," said Dickie. "All I know is that I'm the hunter."

James Miner wheeled himself sideways on the treatment board. He looked up at Dickie. "At night do you travel on the road? The Great North Road?"

"Sometimes," said Dickie.

"Do you know where it goes?"

"No."

"I do." James looked up at all the faces, but nobody asked him where he thought the road went. So he said, "I think it goes to Piper's Pond."

Laurie smiled to herself; she liked that idea. But Chip snorted. "Piper's Pond is a real place, you dummy," he said. "How can a fake road go to a real place?"

"I don't know," said James. "But it's still what I think. If you go far enough along the road, you get to the pond. First, you hear the piper way in the distance, and that's how you know you're getting close, 'cause you hear the bagpipes when there's no one around to play them."

"Aw, cut it out, you goof," said Carolyn.

James ignored her. "And you know what? Not all of us are going to get there. I think one of us is going to die."

"Cut the gas, will you?" Chip turned away. "Let's just hear the story."

◆ ◆ ◆

Khan was riding the big white horse that Jimmy had seen long ago from the window of the Dragon's Tooth. A pony trailed behind it, walking with weary steps. On its back was a bundle of furs.

The hunter swayed with his horse. He wore his coat of unicorn hide, while his legs were bundled in wooly wrappings that might have come from a mastodon. He held the reins but let the horse find its own way as it stepped through the snow.

Jimmy was up on the wagon, helping the woodcutters load their timbers. Felix was beside him, and the rest of the gnomes were just standing at their places, leaning on their axes. They and the Hooligan guards, and even the hounds, were watching the hunter ride steadily toward them.

One of the Hooligans waved his bludgeon above his head and shouted Khan's name. It boomed through the mountains, back and forth between the peaks. "Khan! Khan! Khan!"

As the hunter rode into the woodlot, the hounds tugged madly at their leashes. They snarled and barked, and the horse shied away until Khan spoke to it calmly. "Steady, girl. Steady."

The Hooligans pulled on the leashes. They bashed at the

hounds with their bludgeons, but nothing would quiet the dogs. High on his horse, Khan looked down at the gnomes and the toppled trees, at Jimmy on the wagon's bench. If he recognized the boy, there was no sign of it.

The biggest of the Hooligans spoke to the hunter. "You come early," he said.

"So does spring." Khan pulled the pony up to his side and started unlashing the bundle. "In the valley, the daffodils grow."

The Hooligans didn't care about daffodils. They wanted to buy furs and pelts, and especially the yellow skins of manticores. They crowded round the little horse as Khan spread open the bundle. On the instant, and as though he had loosed a magical power, the hounds suddenly lay flat in the snow, whining like puppies.

Jimmy turned to the grinder, the gnome who sharpened axes. "What happened?" he asked.

"They smell gryphon," said the gnome.

From his bundle, Khan pulled a clutch of talons and feathers, the remains of seven gryphons. The hounds yelped as though they'd been whipped, and buried their faces deep in the snow.

"You see?" said the grinder. "Just the whiff of a gryphon will cower the hounds."

The Hooligans took all of the manticore hides, a unicorn pelt, and a long strip of hydra skin that glistened like oily water. They pulled coins from their pockets, but Khan only waved them away. "Give me one of them gnomes," he said.

The Hooligans looked at each other as though trying not to laugh. It would cost them nothing to give away a gnome.

Khan still sat on his horse; he hadn't budged from its back. He raised an arm and pointed at Jimmy. "Give me that one there. The funny-looking fella."

"That's the boss gnome. He's a lingo," said one of the Hooligans. "He's worth three times the others."

Khan kept the feathers and talons, and rolled the rest of his bundle onto the snow. It tumbled from the horse's back, spilling horns and pelts and furs of every kind. There was enough to buy a dozen gnomes, but Khan took only the one. A Hooligan grabbed Jimmy by the arm and pitched him up to the hunter, and the guards fell on the furs like a pack of wolves.

The hunter shoved Jimmy down in front of him. "Don't talk to me, gnome," he said. "Just sit and be quiet." He nudged his heels at the horse and set off at a gallop, straight up the hill the way he had come, plowing along in his own tracks. The gnomes called out with the most pathetic cries, and Jimmy twisted round to look back. He called farewell in their language, and they shouted back, "Goodbye! Good luck! Good living!"

◆ ◆ ◆

Khan stormed across the ridge on the big white horse, in a cloud of kicked-up snow. The pony ran at his left side, bounding like a deer. Jimmy clung to the horse's mane and leaned out, looking back behind Khan, watching until the woodlot vanished behind the hill. Some of the gnomes were waving their hats, others reaching out with their little arms. Then it was only snow behind him, and the voices of the gnomes echoing all around.

Khan let the horse slow to a walk. He looked down at Jimmy and said, "Mistook you for a gnome, did they?"

Jimmy grinned back at the hunter's red and frosty face. "You knew it was me?"

"Soon as I seen you." Khan opened his coat and pulled Jimmy into its warm folds. He closed it tight around the two of them. "I'll take you down to the valley and turn you loose. You can make your way home from there."

"I don't want to go home," said Jimmy. "There's something I have to do before I ever go to the Dragon's Tooth again."

"Now what would that be, Jimmy?"

"I have to kill Collosso. The Swamp Witch told me so."

Khan grunted. He rode across the slope and came among the trees. Then he let the reins go slack, leaving the horse to find the way downhill. The snow grew thinner, then faded away altogether, and at the bank of a tumbling river, Khan stopped to make camp.

Below a pine, he built a fire. He kept it small and free of smoke, and above the flames he roasted strips of rabbit. There was tea to follow, sweet with honey, before the hunter settled back and looked at Jimmy.

"You haven't a hope," he said.

"Of what?" asked Jimmy.

"Of killing that giant."

Khan kept feeding twigs to the flames. The day turned to twilight and then to darkness, and in the woods below them little specks of light appeared—the lamps and candles of the mining camp. Jimmy talked and talked, and the hunter didn't say a word until the story was finished, and he didn't waste them even then. "Maybe you should look for a Wishman," he said. "Let the giant be."

"Why?" asked Jimmy.

"Could be that you are what you are because of a Wishman. A Wishman can give you what you want, if you pay the price. A giant can only get you killed."

But Jimmy said that he was determined. "If I'm born to kill giants, I have to kill giants," he said.

"Now you're plum crazy," said Khan. "That Swamp Witch is filling your head with sawdust. She's not a real witch, you know. She's not much of anything: half woman, half baloney."

"What do you mean?" asked Jimmy.

"She's a changeling."

Jimmy remembered that word. His mother, long ago, had asked if *he* was a changeling. He hadn't understood it then, and didn't understand it now, but Khan gave him no chance to ask.

"You listen to me, Jimmy," he said. Down in the mining camp, a hound was baying. "A Wishman's fortune doesn't come from giving wishes. It comes from taking them back. No one was ever satisfied by getting what he wished for, and the Wishman counts on that."

It took a while for Jimmy to understand. But at last he saw the truth. If a Wishman had made him small, it must have been his father who had wished for it. Fingal had never been satisfied with anything. He wondered if the rage of his father was because of the Wishman and not really because of him.

In silence, Khan was adding more sticks into the fire. Flames leapt along them, crackling. Then the hunter got up and slipped away into the darkness. His horse whinnied, and in a moment Khan was back, carrying a small bundle in his hands.

"Here," said Khan. He set down for Jimmy the bundle of gryphon talons and feathers. They glowed yellow in the light of the flames. "That's worth more than enough to pay for a Wishman," he said. "Come morning I'll show you where to find one."

They bedded down near the fire side by side, the hunter and the giant-slayer. They heard an owl hoot, and a large animal clatter its way over the rocks and splash across the river. Then up from the camp came the slow singing of gnomes. The sadness of it kept Jimmy awake. He cried in the darkness, and his tears sparkled in the firelight.

"I got *two* things to do now," he said, and sniffed. "Before I go home again."

"What's that? Besides killing giants," said Khan.

"I have to free the gnomes."

Khan laughed. "Reckon you can do what you want," he said. "Ain't up to me to save gnomes."

◆ ◆ ◆

Jimmy slept for just an hour. When he got up Khan was lying bundled by the fire, eyes closed, breathing softly. Jimmy looked down at him.

"I know you're awake," he said. "You don't like saying goodbye; that's all right."

Jimmy turned away and started trudging through the snow, toward the lights of the camp. He called back to Khan: "Thank you for setting me free."

The night was very cold. A crust had frozen on the snow, just hard enough and thick enough to hold the weight of the giant-slayer. He soon came within sight of the camp, and by the glow of its lights he could see the hounds that guarded the gate, and a Hooligan guard inside. Jimmy went forward on his hands and knees.

The Hounds stood up. They growled, they snarled, and the guard turned around to look. Jimmy lay flat.

"What is it?" said the guard. "What's out there?" The hounds kept snarling, a sound that made Jimmy's hair stand up on his neck.

"Go look," said the guard.

He sent the hounds out into the night. They came across the snow in leaps and bounds, smashing through the crust. Jimmy rolled to his side and pulled out the talons and feathers. The hounds fell instantly silent. They hung their heads, tucked their tails, and crept away toward the trees.

It must have seemed to the guard that his dogs had vanished. He heaved such a sigh that Jimmy could hear it clearly. Then he opened the gate, hitched up his trousers, and went crunching across the snow.

Jimmy circled round him in the dark and came to the open gate. There were other hounds inside, and every one lay down like the others and covered its eyes with its paws.

Jimmy scattered the talons and feathers as he crept from hut to hut. At each one he called quietly through the door, warning the gnomes not to make noise. He led them through the camp, past the cowering dogs, out through the gate. He had one talon left when he reached the woods.

He heard a snorting breath and a stamping in the snow. A man rode out from the blackness.

"Going into the gnome business?" he asked.

It was Khan. He was high on his horse, leading the pony.

"I came back to help you, but I see there ain't no need," said Khan. "Started eating at me, that them gnomes are all slaves. Never really saw it till you showed me. But everything ought to be free, even a gnome."

Jimmy gave his last talon to Felix and sent him down to the valley, leading the gnomes. All were in a terrible hurry to be away from the camp, but most were so thin and frightened that they could manage no more than a shuffling step.

"Ain't you going with them?" asked Khan.

"No," said Jimmy. "I have to kill Collosso."

"Thought as much," said the hunter. He leaned down from the horse, reaching a hand toward Jimmy. "Reckon I'll go with you, seein' you're so dead set on it. If that's all right with you, of course."

Jimmy smiled. "Reckon it is."

The two rode away on the big horse, with the pony trailing behind. Again the hunter wrapped his coat around the two of them. He fastened the toggles down the front, and his hands brushed against the charm at Jimmy's neck. "So you've kept that," he said.

Jimmy nodded. "What does it do?"

"Wondered that myself," said Khan. "Never seemed much useful to me."

◆ ◆ ◆

As Khan had said, it was springtime already in the valley. Women were planting in the fields, scattering seeds by the handful from baskets at their hips. Men were plowing here, painting there, fixing fences flattened by snow.

The road ran straight as a ruler, past farm and orchard, and faded away in the distance, into a cloud of gray dust.

It was the same sort of cloud that the taxman had raised with his carriage, but ten times bigger, swirling as high as a thunderhead. It came with a rumble that shook the earth, and now and then with a low, unearthly moan.

"What is it?" asked Jimmy.

"I don't rightly know," said Khan.

The hunter rode north, the cloud came south, and they met near an orchard of apples. A man on a horse was riding in front of the cloud, holding a long rope that snaked behind him into that gray. He seemed to be towing the dust, hauling that great cloud to the south. He was dressed as a drover, in a long coat that seemed to be made of dust.

From the cloud came another deep and bellowing moan. The drover tipped his hat to Khan. "Mister, if I were you, I'd get off the road," he said.

"Ain't it a free road?" said Khan.

"It is that. I know it, and you know it," said the drover. "But the beasties don't."

He tugged on his rope, and the "beasties" began to emerge from the cloud of dust. They were oxen, shaggy and brown, with long horns that reached six feet across. The drover's rope went to the first one, to a brass ring in its nose.

And the others followed, in a huge bellowing mass that filled the road from side to side.

Khan nudged his horse through the ditch and up to the fence. The gray cloud closed around them, and the oxen kept passing. From the backs of the beasts hung coils of rope and lengths of chain, yokes and whips and harnesses. In the tips of their horns, passing just inches from Jimmy and Khan, were little rings of brass and gold.

The big horse grew frightened, but Khan kept it quiet. The pony scampered and whinnied until the last of the oxen went plodding on by. Far behind was another horseman, coming along in the clear.

"He sure don't ride like a drover," said Khan. "Not one with half his senses."

The rider came in darts and circles, surging forward, falling back, wheeling in little circles. His horse reared with its front legs kicking, then shot forward like a charger, only to be brought up short again. With a feather in his hat and fringed gauntlets on his hands, the man looked as dashing as a cavalry officer, and he rode like a whole brigade.

Khan urged the white horse onto the road. The rider was just then circling around, as though regrouping for a fresh attack. When he saw Jimmy and the hunter there in front of him he made his horse kneel down on the road. He shouted loudly from its back—as though he were a mile away—"Hi ho! Hi ho, my friend."

Khan barely nodded.

The rider stared at Jimmy. "Are you the son of Fingal?"

"Yes, I am," said Jimmy.

"I knew it!" cried the rider. He sat straight as a statue. "I stopped long ago at the Dragon's Tooth. You sat on my knee and I regaled you with stories of the road. Of course, you may not remember."

"Sorry. I don't," said Jimmy.

The man looked very disappointed. "Well, you were young. But never mind, for you'll remember me now." He cocked his head and grinned.

"Well, who are you, then?" asked Khan.

"Finnegan Flanders," said the rider, as though it were something to boast of. "The best teamster on the Great North Road." Again he made the horse bow down. "I'm driving a hundred oxen."

"Why?" asked Jimmy.

"To keep them safe, of course." His grin fell away. "Haven't you heard the news from the north?"

"What news is that?" asked Khan.

"Collosso is out."

The rider shivered as he said it, and Jimmy felt a chill himself. Khan only frowned. "What do you mean, he's out?"

"He's marauding. He's rampaging," said Flanders. "For years Collosso has kept to his castle, but not anymore. He flattened a farm the other night. Squashed the cows like bugs. Took the farmer for a toy."

The rider looked back, north up the road. "Everyone is fleeing." For a moment he didn't seem so brave and dashing.

"Where's Collosso now?" asked Khan.

The rider shrugged. "Every day he goes farther from the castle. But every night he returns."

"A giant shouldn't be hard to find," said Jimmy, looking up at Khan. "You can track him, can't you?"

Flanders gawked. "Don't tell me you're going looking for him?"

"We're going to kill him," said Jimmy.

"Go on!" Flanders laughed loudly. "You're pulling my leg, aren't you?"

But Khan said that it was true. "Jimmy's bound to try," he said. "And so I'm bound to help him. That's the duty of a man, ain't it? What kind of fella would let a boy go alone against a giant?"

"The sensible kind," said Flanders. "The kind that grows old. Not that I wouldn't love to have a crack at Collosso myself. That giant squashed my best dog, you know."

"Did he?"

"Oh, yes!" The rider nodded furiously. "Skippy, that was his name. If you had need of a teamster, I'd go right now. There's a hundred oxen going down the road there, each as stupid as a brick, but say the word and they're yours."

"I could use them," said Jimmy.

"Go on!" said Flanders.

"It's true," said Jimmy. "They could pull a wagon."

Flanders laughed. "That would be some wagon!"

"There's one in the woods," said Jimmy. "It has wheels as high as houses, and a bed as big as a field—"

"Now, that's just a tall tale," said Khan. "Like the vanishing army and the bottomless swamp. Ain't no credibility to them things."

"But I saw it," said Jimmy. "It's just sitting there, on a road made of huge stones."

"The old hauling road?" asked Khan. "Could that story be true?"

"They say it's how Collosso built his castle," said the teamster. "Great wagons hauling a whole tree at a time; half a mountain all at once."

"I can take you there," said Jimmy.

"Well, let's be going," said Khan.

"Tally ho!" cried the rider. He spun his horse and galloped down the road, into the cloud of dust.

Khan and Jimmy followed him. They squeezed past the oxen, between the tips of their horns and the fence. In the gray fog, the animals were coming to a stop, and at the front of the herd, in the middle of the road, Flanders was arguing with the drover.

"I don't care. I'm not going," said the drover.

They sat on their horses, yelling at the tops of their voices, while the oxen moaned and bellowed. Khan rode up beside them.

"Your own mother!" shouted Flanders. "That giant squished your own mother!"

"I know it," said the drover. "I was there. I remember her last words, uttered while she lay flat as a leaf, breathing her last. She took my hand; she told me, 'Listen, deary, run for your life.' That's what she told me, my poor old mother. 'Save yourself, Tim,' she said, and every day I live up to that. Take on a giant? What's the use of trying when you know you're going to fail?"

"I won't fail. I can do it," said Jimmy. "The Swamp Witch said I can."

"Good luck to you, then." The drover passed the end of his rope into Jimmy's hands. He turned his horse's head and put his heels to its ribs. He went off down the road at a run, and when he was just a speck in a ball of dust he shouted back: "I will tell Fingal that his boy died bravely."

◆ ◆ ◆

It seemed wrong to Jimmy to be heading south, with the morning sun on his left. He felt he was going backward, while the hundred oxen made such a bellowing noise that he was half deaf by the time they reached the great wagon, nearly four days later.

Khan grinned when he saw it. "Well, fancy that," was all he said. But Finnegan Flanders was so awed by the size of the wagon that he got down from his horse and fell to his knees, as if he'd come to a holy ark. "My granddad used to speak of this," he said. "I thought he was an old coot telling stories."

It took more than a day to harness the hundred oxen. As Khan pointed out, the work might have gone more quickly if Flanders hadn't been there. "That fella, he's plum useless," said the hunter. "He just gets himself in the way."

It was as though Flanders had no idea how to harness oxen. He bullied them here and there, like a farmwife chasing chickens, but it was Khan who got them into place, who attached the yokes and harnesses. It was the giant-slayer who sat down to untangle the pile of reins.

"That don't look like enough leather you've got there," said Khan. "Half of them critters ain't going to have reins on them."

"They don't have to," said Jimmy. "It's only the front ones you have to steer. The rest just follow along."

"Is that right?" cried Flanders. "They just follow along? Just like that?"

Khan squinted at the teamster. "Now, exactly how much do you know about driving?" he asked.

"Why, I know it all," said Flanders. "I read every book that's ever been written about it."

Jimmy looked at Khan, who was looking back at him. "And how long have you been doing it now?" he said.

"Well, let's see." Flanders stroked his chin. "Bought the oxen up north. Hired a drover. Came down south. Must be— oh—a week now." He grinned his dashing grin. "Pretty near."

He got back on his horse and dashed here and there as Jimmy and Khan rigged up the reins. They attached them to the front oxen, to the rings at the ends of their horns. Then they threaded them back through the rings of the others.

◆ ◆ ◆

"How come you only put in two reins?" asked Chip.

"I don't know," said Laurie. "It's probably all wrong."

"No. It's true," he told her. "You only need two reins for a team of oxen."

Carolyn said, "How would *you* know?"

" 'Cause I used to drive one." Chip was looking right into his mirror, straight at Laurie. He had been watching her for the last hour. "We only had four oxen. But it's the same thing. Most people lead them. But we used to drive ours like horses."

"When was that?" asked Carolyn.

"When I lived at the farm."

"You never lived on a farm."

"I did too."

In their wheelchairs, on the treatment board, the children turned now to Carolyn and Chip. The two were facing each other, their heads tilted on their pillows.

To Laurie, it hardly seemed worth arguing if you had to do it in time with the iron lung. Their breaths were measured, timed to the pumping of the bellows.

"It was just when I was small," said Chip. "Then my dad went to college on the GI Bill. And we moved into town so he could work."

"At what?"

"The garage. He was a mechanic."

"You said he was a fireman."

"No, I never."

"Boy, it doesn't matter," said Dickie. "Maybe he was both."

That was good enough for Laurie, and good enough for Peter and Ruth, for James Miner on the floor. They all nodded and shrugged and looked away uncomfortably. But Carolyn kept at it.

"You did so say he was a fireman," said Carolyn. "You said it lots." The bellows wheezed below. "Ask Miss Freeman."

"Oh, buzz off," said Chip. "Why would I ask Miss Freeman . . . where my dad used to work?"

"'Cause I guess you forgot." Carolyn turned her head toward the mirror. "Or you lied."

"I did not!"

"Then ask Miss Freeman."

As though summoned by a genie, the nurse was suddenly there, coming through the open doorway. It could have been that Carolyn saw her shadow in the hall or heard her footsteps coming nearer. But no one seemed more surprised than Carolyn when Miss Freeman breezed into the room with a newspaper in her hands.

"Ask me what?" she said, smiling as though she had brought the light in with her. Her eyes sparkled; her mouth shone with lipstick. No one answered, but she kept smiling. "Did you hear?" she said. "They've done it."

She opened the newspaper and held up the front page. The headline was huge:

### POLIO BEATEN
### VACCINE A SUCCESS

"Isn't that swell?" said Miss Freeman.

From their iron lungs, from their wheelchairs and the treatment board, the children looked and smiled. All except for Carolyn. And all except for Carolyn, they let out a little cheer, as though they themselves had beaten the disease.

For Laurie, it seemed very sad. She looked at Dickie's face hovering in the mirror, and wondered how he could be so happy for something that had come too late for him. She suddenly heard the words her father had spoken on a day that seemed long ago: *Can you imagine how it haunts them that they got polio just because they went to a swimming pool, or something as frivolous as that?* She wished harder than she had ever wished for anything that she could turn back the clock to that afternoon at the creek and tell Dickie not to drink the water, or slap it from his hands as he cupped them to his lips. If they had never gone to the creek that day, he would be reading the headline at home, not caring about it at all.

Miss Freeman was still holding the newspaper. But her smile was fading. "Aren't you happy, Carolyn?" she asked.

"Sure. Whoop-de-doo," said Carolyn. "Doesn't do me any good."

"No, not directly." Miss Freeman folded the paper. "But think of all the children who won't go through what you've been through. All the parents who won't have to worry anymore. Can't you be happy for them?"

The girl's head didn't move on the pillow. Her body lay still in the iron lung. But, somehow, it seemed that she shrugged. "Were they sorry for me?"

"I'm sure a lot of them were," said Miss Freeman. "We'll talk about it later, if you like. For now I just wanted to pass on the news."

She put the paper under her arm and turned toward the door. "Oh, and Laurie, your father's on his way up. He just asked downstairs if you were here, so we told him to come to the fourth floor. He seems such a nice man."

# CHAPTER TWELVE

## THE CASTLE AT THE EDGE
## OF THE WORLD

There was a party that evening in the polio ward, but Laurie wasn't there. Nurses in white uniforms spooned cake with white icing into the mouths of the children in their iron lungs. Little girls in leg braces danced to phonograph records, tangling their crutches until everyone was laughing.

And Laurie Valentine sat in her living room, feeling as small as an ant on the big old sofa. As though she were still only six, her legs didn't reach the floor, and her father loomed above her.

He spoke in his calm and quiet way. "I was very angry, you know," he said. "I thought we had an understanding that you would stay away from Bishop's."

"I never really *promised*," said Laurie.

"So I should have made you take an oath?" Mr. Valentine paced on the carpet, his tie swinging across his chest. "You're not a little child anymore. We have to trust each other, Laurie."

"If you trust me, why did you spy on me?" She was taking a chance, not sure even now if the man at the pond had been her father. But by the way he paused in his pacing she could see that she was right. "I saw you at Piper's Pond that day," she said.

"As I recall," said Mr. Valentine, "you told me that you would be at the library."

"And you didn't trust me!" cried Laurie, as though she had won a huge victory. But even she could see that it was hollow. She didn't look up at her father.

"Laurie, it was wrong of you to go to Bishop's," he said. "But it was wrong of me as well to stop you. I see that now, and I apologize."

Laurie could hardly believe that her father was apologizing. "Oh, that's all right," she said generously.

Mr. Valentine stopped pacing, took out his pipe, and lit it. He tossed his match into the fireplace and watched the smoke curl from his pipe. "Mrs. Espinosa called me today. She wanted to say how kind it was of me to let you visit Dickie. You're the only one who does, apparently."

"I'm his only friend," said Laurie.

"It's good you have convictions," said Mr. Valentine. "I didn't want you to go, but you weighed my advice and took the high road. You took it by yourself; I'm proud of you. It's sometimes a lonely road, the high road."

Laurie thought of Dickie, who had said that she was the Woman in the story. It was strange that Jimmy's mother had also set off on the High Road.

Mr. Valentine puffed a ball of gray smoke. "So how *is* your little friend?"

The "little" stung her. "Well, he's still in an iron lung," she said, a bit snootily, "so I don't think he's all that great."

Mr. Valentine winced. "I'm sorry to hear that." He pulled a shred of tobacco from his lips. "I imagine you saw the headline today?"

She nodded.

"The vaccine's ready; it's finished. It hasn't proven to be quite the miracle the papers have made out, but it's better than expected." Mr. Valentine looked proud, as though he brewed the vaccine himself. "The Foundation intends to vaccinate nine million people before summer. I've been pulling some strings, Laurie, and I've seen to it that you'll be one of the first. If you're going to hang around polio wards, I think I owe you that."

The announcement pleased Laurie. "When will that happen?" she asked.

"As soon as possible," said Mr. Valentine. "I believe you're getting the first batch from the Cutter lab."

"Thanks, Dad," said Laurie. She stood up and hugged him, then reached a bit higher and kissed his neck.

He blushed and said, "Is it too much to ask that you stay away from Bishop's until you've had the shot?"

"No, that's okay," said Laurie. "I will."

And she did.

◆ ◆ ◆

It was nine days later when Laurie got the first of her two vaccinations. A photographer took her picture for the weekend paper. "Wince, please," he said, which made her smile. So he took another.

That was on a Tuesday. On Wednesday, she was back at Bishop's.

The front page with the polio headline was taped to the wall in the respirator room. James Miner rolled his treatment board right across the room to show it to Laurie. He had put up the page himself, so it was just six inches above the floor.

"Miss Freeman, she says I helped to beat polio," he said. "A little bit of the vaccine, that's on account of me."

"Really?" said Laurie.

"I guess so." He smiled and nodded. "I was a Polio Pioneer."

"Were you?" Laurie had wanted to be a Pioneer herself but was a year too old when the doctors and nurses had come around to her school with the test vaccine. She remembered how she had envied the little kids with their buttons and candy and membership cards.

"I got the fake vaccine," said James. "So I wasn't protected."

"That's awful," said Laurie.

"Yeah. My dad felt really cheated," said James. "Besides, he thought you got money if you were a Pioneer. That's why I was in it."

Across the room, in his iron lung, Chip laughed.

"It's true," said James. "My dad's always looking for ways to make money. In his store, he sells all this junk, like—"

"What kind of store?" asked Dickie.

"Kind of like a grocery store." James was turning his board back and forth to try to look at everybody. "Its real name is Miner's, but everyone calls it Miser's, on account of my dad's so cheap. I started working there when I was four. That's where I was when I got polio."

"What happened?" asked Laurie.

He turned toward *her*. "My job was sweeping—and stocking the bottom shelves. 'Cause I couldn't reach the ones any higher. One day I was filling up the jam shelf, and I kind of fell down, and all the jars of jam started rolling off the shelf. There was strawberry jam and blueberry jam and blackberry jam and gooseberry jam and all these different kinds of jam, and they were all bursting when they hit the floor." He laughed at the memory. "I couldn't stop them, 'cause it hurt so much to move. Oh, my dad was so angry! He made me get the mop and bucket and clean it all up. And I could hardly even stand, so he said, 'You shiftless bugger, you're not leaving till you finish.' So I just kept working until I kind of fainted in all that jam. When the doctor came and saw the red jam all over me, he thought my guts had fallen out."

James laughed again. But nobody else did. When he stopped, there was just the hum and whoosh of the iron lungs. Then Carolyn, looking straight up into her mirror, asked, "Where was your mother?"

"Oh, she was long gone by then," said James, turning his

board again. "She went away when I was little. I don't know where she went, not really."

Dickie said, "That's funny. It's just like Jimmy the giant-slayer."

"No fooling?" said James, who had missed the first part of the story.

"Cross my heart. His mother ran away from Fingal," said Dickie. "And he worked for his dad."

"I don't remember where the giant-slayer is just now," said James. "Did they get the big wagon going?"

Laurie nodded. "Yes, they did." She took her place at the window, hopping up to the broad sill. She poked her glasses on her nose and started again with the story. "But the teamster, Finnegan Flanders, he was scared to drive it."

◆ ◆ ◆

"I'm not going up there," Flanders said, pointing at the tiny seat at the top of the spindly tower. "Heights give me the jee-bies."

So Jimmy was the driver. He climbed up to the bed of the wagon, and Flanders threw the reins in a huge coil so that Jimmy could catch them. Then the giant-slayer scaled the tower, higher and higher, until he could again look out across forest and swamp, to the very edge of the world.

He had driven only the small team of horses at the mine. So looking down now, and seeing a hundred oxen ranged be-low him in their harness, made him feel a little frightened. He imagined that a flick of the reins might send them charging down the old hauling road, the great wagon out of control.

Then he saw Khan looking up at him, so tiny down there on the ground. And he grabbed the reins, hauled with his left hand, and screamed as loudly as he could, "Gee up! Gee up!"

From his hand, the leather ran down to the tongue of the wagon, then forward through the rings in the oxen's horns, through ring after ring, right to the very first animal. A tug sent the lead ox plodding forward. As it pulled up against its yoke, the next one followed, then the one after that, and with a great shuddering of wood and chain and leather, the wagon started forward. Its enormous wheels turned half a foot. The oxen heaved, planted their feet and heaved again, and the wheels creaked round in their hubs. The huge tower swayed to the right, then back to the left.

"Gee up!" screamed Jimmy, and tugged the reins again.

A hundred hooves slammed the ground with every step. The wheels turned faster, with squeals and shrieks of metal, now with small explosions as rocks and stones burst beneath the metal rims.

High above the trees, Jimmy the giant-slayer glided along on his little seat. He was so small up there, but huge and powerful too. He could carry a giant now, to wherever he wanted to take it, with just one pull on his arm. And even Collosso, he thought, couldn't manage that.

◆ ◆ ◆

The old hauling road took them straight to the north, right to Collosso's castle. In places, it was badly overgrown, so choked with bushes and young trees that often it seemed to end altogether, to go no farther than the next wall of gorse and ivy.

But from Jimmy's seat the road stretched on and on. And the oxen pulled right through the bushes, through stands of little trees, while the wheels crushed all in their path.

By the hour, the mountains seemed to come closer. The route through the pass became clear as craggy peaks loomed higher all around. At night, the hunter, the teamster, and the giant-slayer camped on the bed of the wagon, far above the forest and the beasts that roamed through it.

On the third day, when they were climbing through the foothills, Khan tethered his horse and pony to the back of the wagon and rode beside Jimmy, both squished into the small seat. It was the first time that he seemed afraid, holding on as he did to the armrest, while the seat rocked far from side to side. He licked his lips and stared down at the rows of oxen, at Finnegan Flanders galloping here and there. It was half an hour before he could even talk.

"Jimmy," he said then, "there's something on my mind. Something worrying at me in an awful way."

"What's that?" asked Jimmy.

Khan shifted on the seat. He didn't have room to straighten his legs. "Well, we're getting mighty close to the castle now. And I've been wondering just how you mean to kill the giant."

"Oh, that's easy," said Jimmy. "I'll do him in a flash. I'll knock him down."

Khan looked at Jimmy the same way he had looked at Finnegan Flanders. "And just how are you fixing to do that?"

"I'll tie his shoelaces together," said Jimmy. "Or I might put up a bit of string and trip him. I guess I'll decide when I get there."

The road had been bending to the left, but now it turned more sharply. Jimmy pulled on the rein, hauling it back. "Haw! Haw!" he yelled at the oxen. Far ahead, the team began to turn.

"So, Jimmy," said Khan. "How are you fixing to get to his shoes?"

"While he's eating," said Jimmy, as though it were too simple to need explaining. "He'll be sitting at the table, and I'll nip up and—"

"You learned this from the gnomes?" asked Khan.

"Yes, that's right," said Jimmy. He tugged on the other rein now, to straighten the team. "They should know; they've killed dozens of giants."

"Well, now, I'm not saying I'd swear to that," said Khan.

"You mean they're liars?" asked Jimmy.

"No, not exactly," said Khan. "You see, Jimmy, a gnome don't always see things the way that we see them. Take someone like Flanders down there." He pointed to the figure below them, dashing just then down the rows of oxen. "When Flanders tells you a tale, he means for you to believe it. Might even believe it himself. Flanders don't invent stories; he invents the truth as he sees it."

That made sense to Jimmy. In the parlor of the old inn he had heard thousands of stories from hundreds of travelers, and every man had sworn he was telling the truth.

"Flanders tells lies 'cause his truth ain't worth talking

about," said Khan. "But to a gnome, there ain't no difference. Truth or lies, it's all the same. Life's a story, and you can tell it any way you want."

Jimmy didn't really understand. "Well, do gnomes kill giants or not?" he asked.

"Well, it's true and it ain't," said Khan. Dust swirled below them, boiling over the bed of the wagon. "While they're telling the story, that's when it's true."

◆ ◆ ◆

As the wagon climbed to the top of the hill, Jimmy and Khan looked out on a vast plateau of farms and villages. They were nearly at the very end of the Great North Road, with nothing but the flatland between them and the mountains.

Jimmy steered straight for the pass, through little hamlets, past schoolyards and windmills. Finnegan Flanders rode ahead, his big horse prancing. He posted in the saddle, with the big plume waving on his hat, all his fringes shaking.

From every building, people ran out to watch the wagon pass. Children poured from the schools, farmers from the barns. Flanders kept shouting, "We're off to kill Collosso!" And the men cheered, and the children whistled and clapped, and the women tore off their scarlet, gold, and yellow scarves and held them up like streamers.

They all cheered for Finnegan Flanders, for each of the hundred oxen, for Jimmy and Khan and the enormous wagon, and for the white horse and pony that trailed along behind.

"Kill the giant! Kill the giant!" shouted the boys and girls.

"Kill the giant!" cried the women, waving their pretty scarves.

And the men stepped forward, shouting advice to the giant-slayer and his companions. "Go for his eye!" said a farmer. "That's his weakness."

A miller cried out, "He has a glass jaw!"

"Hit him in the stomach!" shouted a teacher. "You'll knock the wind out of him."

"He has a cauliflower ear!" yelled a sawyer.

Squished on the seat beside Jimmy, Khan waved to the crowd. "That's one frail giant," he said. "He's got so many weak points he might fall to pieces soon as we look at him."

◆ ◆ ◆

Just as the Swamp Witch had said, the pass through the mountains opened in front of Jimmy and his companions. The Great North Road curved between peaks that soared ten thousand feet in crags of snow and rock. It hugged the slope, so one side of the road was always a sheer cliff where boulders came tumbling down, and the other a vast nothing, a drop-off to a valley so distant that those tumbling boulders always disappeared before they hit the bottom.

Jimmy steered the team along this road, around its curves and bends. The wagon rumbled along with the oxen tramping, stones exploding under the wheels. From the swaying seat, Jimmy saw dragons in their high lairs on windswept cliffs. And then he saw Collosso.

It was just a glimpse he got, of the giant in the distance. Collosso was striding across a mountain slope, and his red cap bobbed along the top of a ridge where a glacier crawled. It was like a huge ball bouncing on the ice and rock, in view one moment, hidden the next. And then Collosso himself rose over that ridge and stepped across it.

Jimmy saw his enormous head with its bush of red hair, his mighty arms swinging, his great legs carrying him on. He saw his boots kicking up blizzards of snow, and with each step an avalanche went rumbling down the glacier.

The oxen picked up the scent of the giant and shied nervously in their harnesses. Jimmy had to wrench on the reins, screaming "Haw! Haw!" at the top of his voice to keep them from stampeding over the cliff.

And then the giant was gone. He trampled his way across an old, burned forest and slipped behind the crest of a mountain.

The sight left Jimmy shaken. He had never imagined the true size of the giant or the strength in his limbs. He put his hand to his shirt, feeling for the ball of bones that Khan had given him. It was all he had to fight against a giant.

◆ ◆ ◆

On the day after he sighted Collosso, Jimmy steered the wagon round a bend, looked up, and saw the castle.

It was white and shiny, a fabulous sight of towers and ramparts and spires. It clung to the top of a rocky knoll; it perched at the very edge of the world. At its front and sides were the mountains, but behind it was the void—just a terrible swirl of clouds, the beginning of infinite nothing.

Khan was riding on the seat again, and neither he nor

Jimmy said a word. They just stared at the white fortress, at the ramparts and the windows, until the road turned again, hiding the castle. It rose as steeply then as it had ever risen, so the oxen had to strain and pant. Then it turned again and followed the side of the mountain around. And it came out at the edge of the world.

Jimmy began to look down into the void. But Khan shouted, "Don't!" He held up his hand to turn Jimmy's head aside. "It drives men mad to look into there," he said.

"But what does it look like?" asked Jimmy.

"I don't know," said Khan. "I've never looked."

The clouds kept welling up from the void like smoke from a fire. They rose in billows, in spirals and bursts. Black as night, brown as the earth, they rolled over each other, carried by an endless wind that moaned and whined through the rock. And on the draft, a flight of crimson dragons soared. They circled in and out of the clouds, their leathery wings never moving, their long necks bent into red crooks.

Jimmy kept the oxen so close against the mountain that their horns scraped lines into the rocks. Finnegan Flanders was doing the same thing in front of the animals, turning his horse right into the rock, so it moved along sideways in high, prancing steps.

The road kept turning. It rounded the shoulder of the mountain, away from the edge of the world, and once again there was solid ground on either side. And there the giant-slayer and his friends stopped to spend the night.

Surrounded by a dead forest of gaunt, black trees, the three huddled in a close group. Khan said they were too close to the castle to let them light a fire. So they sat in darkness, even though dragons were prowling nearby. From the mountains came ghastly shrieking.

"Is that the sound that dragons make?" asked Jimmy.

"No," said Khan, not lifting his head. "Only men can make that sound. It comes from the castle."

"It's hideous," said Finnegan Flanders. He clapped his hands on his ears. "What goes on in there?"

"I pray we never learn," said Khan.

It was a long night: a night of no sleep, a night that unnerved them all. In the morning, the three friends looked nervously into the forest, though each tried to hide his fear from the others. When they dressed, they did it carefully and slowly. Flanders smoothed every one of the hundreds of fringes on his jacket and his gauntlets, as though he was doing it for the last time. Then he got up on his big chestnut horse and said in a very small voice, "Hi ho!"

Jimmy and Khan climbed to the seat of the wagon. Jimmy took the reins and got the oxen moving, and they plodded off along the road.

"It's not too late to change your mind," said Khan. "Ain't no use in being big and important if you got to be dead to do it. We could skirt the castle, go on and find a Wishman."

"No," said Jimmy. "The Swamp Witch said—"

"Now, just a cotton-picking moment. That's a flimflam witch. A phony." Khan was looking down at the oxen, half hidden now in dust. "She's no more witch than you or me. A Gypsy girl, that's all she is."

"What do you mean?" said Jimmy.

"She was born in a Gypsy wagon," said Khan. "When she was ten years old she was stolen by a witch. By a *real* witch,

{207}

Jimmy, who left a changeling in her place and took her away on a broomstick, to a coven in the forest. Her first night there, she killed that witch. She cut off the witch's head and escaped to the swamp. But the witch, with her dying breath, cursed the girl to be as ugly as a frog."

Jimmy kept driving the wagon. He shook the reins, though they didn't need shaking at all.

"That's the truth of it," said Khan. "She has no more power than any other girl. You're taking on a giant on the word of a Gypsy."

Jimmy looked straight ahead, down the Great North Road. "If that's true," he said, "why doesn't she go back to the Gypsies?"

"Who would have her now?" asked Khan. "A girl as ugly as a frog? A girl who's lived her life in mud?"

"Her mother wouldn't mind," said Jimmy. He cried "Gee!" to the oxen and swung them round a bend. "Could a Wishman fix her?"

"Maybe," said Khan.

"Where do you find them?"

"At the end of the road. Beyond the castle of Collosso."

◆ ◆ ◆

Laurie looked down from the window of Bishop's Memorial, down at the pond and the willows.

"What's the matter?" asked Dickie.

"I thought I heard bagpipes," said Laurie. She poked her glasses, then pressed her hands on the window pane and squinted at the trees. "Yes, there's a piper there. He's—"

"What?"

Laurie laughed. "No, it's just a lady. She's wearing a plaid skirt. I thought she was a piper, with a kilt and everything." She didn't turn from the window; she kept staring out. "But I guess not."

Carolyn spoke up from her iron lung, in the mirror of the room. "Do you think that's really true?"

"About the piper?" said Laurie.

"No. About the witch."

Laurie at last looked away from the window. Carolyn, in her slanted mirror, suddenly looked quite beautiful to her, as she had on the very first day.

"The Gypsies," said Carolyn. "Do you really think they'd take her back?"

"Of course," said Laurie.

"Even if she's mean and ugly?"

"Sure. It wouldn't matter."

"Then I hope they do," said Carolyn. She let out a little sigh and closed her eyes and lay with her face turned up at the mirror. Laurie could see that she was crying.

"Well, go on," said Dickie. "What happened next?"

◆ ◆ ◆

The giant-slayer and his friends drove right up to the castle. The road turned round the mountain, and suddenly they were there, at the edge of a moat as deep as a canyon, as wide as a field.

"Whoa!" cried Jimmy. "Whoa!" He pulled on both reins and brought the wagon to a stop.

Across the moat, on its rocky knoll, the castle loomed enormously. It was a mountain itself, its ramparts like cliffs, its keep a great crag, its spires as tall as the peaks around. Its windows were the size of whole houses, and its door was bigger than anything Jimmy had ever seen. He could have driven the wagon right through it, if the drawbridge had been open. But instead it was pulled up to the castle, and the moat yawned between them.

Jimmy and Khan scrambled down from the wagon. They joined Finnegan Flanders at the side of the road, and all three stood looking down into the moat. There was no water in there, for the ends of the ditch were open to the edge of the world. But down at the bottom were black pits of tar, and mounds of pitch, and many rows of sharpened stakes. Bears and wolves prowled back and forth, while hydras hissed and tigers roared. There seemed no way across.

"What now?" said Khan. "I reckon there's no getting at that giant in there. What do we do?"

"We taunt him," said Jimmy.

Flanders laughed. "Ho, ho!"

"No, it's true," said Jimmy. "A giant can't stand to be taunted, so he comes running out to get us. And that's when we get *him*."

"The gnomes tell you this?" asked Khan.

"Yes," said Jimmy, nodding happily. "It works every time."

The little giant-slayer bent down and picked up a stone. With all his strength, he heaved it at the castle. "Hey, giant!" he shouted.

His stone plummeted into the moat. His cry faded away

in that great gulf. As he stood with his hands on his hips, staring at the castle, he heard the tiny, tiny plop of his stone hitting the tar pits far below.

Flanders took up a stone. He too heaved with all his strength and shouted out at the giant: "You big dummy!"

His stone vanished; his cry faded. He and Jimmy turned, bewildered, to Khan.

The hunter walked away. He went to his horse, where he rummaged through the things on its back until he found his bow and arrow. Then he stood at the edge of the moat and carefully slotted onto the bowstring one of his arrows tipped with phoenix feathers. He drew the bow; he aimed and fired.

The arrow soared across the moat and—with a plink— struck the giant's window.

It hit the glass but didn't break it. Then it tumbled down into the moat, a little whirl of colored feathers.

At the window, an enormous face appeared. Up went the sash. Out came Collosso's head.

"Who's there?" roared the giant.

His voice was louder than thunder. It made the oxen bow their heads and paw nervously at the ground. At the bottom of the moat, the tigers shrieked in fright.

"Who's there?" he roared again.

Jimmy shouted back, "Come and look, you big oaf!" He shook his tiny fist. "You scared?"

Finnegan Flanders waved his sword. "Come on, curly!" he cried.

Beside him, Khan was notching another arrow to his string. The hunter yelled at the giant even as he aimed and fired. "Think fast, dopey!"

The arrow hit the giant on the tip of his nose. His great eyes blinked and his head jerked back, slamming into the window casing. Then he touched a huge hand to the back of his head and roared, for the third time, "Who's there?"

"It is I." The little giant-slayer stepped forward until his toes overhung the edge of the moat. "Jimmy, son of Fingal. I have come to slay you, Collosso."

The giant gaped, his mouth as wide as a cavern. To the amazement of Flanders and Khan, he looked truly frightened. "No. Not you!" he cried.

The head vanished from the window. A moment later, with a clank of wheels and cogs, the drawbridge began to open.

It fell slowly on ratcheting chains, and the giant-slayer—quiet now—just stood and watched it fall. It swung down toward him, an acre of wood and iron. Each link of the chains that fed from the castle was the size of an ox.

Jimmy and Flanders and Khan moved back. With a shuddering slam, the door settled on the ground right in front of them. Then the bars of the huge portcullis—with clang and clamor—went sliding up within the castle, and in the doorway stood Collosso.

He was unbelievably big. As tall as the drawbridge had been, Collosso was taller. He had to stoop to pass through the doorway, and then he strode across that enormous gulf in only three of his giant steps.

"Get ready to trip him up," said Jimmy.

They could hear Collosso breathing, like the panting of the hundred oxen. The drawbridge shook under his weight. The roadway shook, and the whole mountain shook, for with every step the giant came more quickly.

There was no more taunting; there was no time for that. The giant reached the side of the moat at a run, his feet in huge boots, his head now in its red cap, his coppery hair shaking.

With each of his steps, an avalanche broke loose from the mountains, and the sound of the hurtling rock—with the boom of footfalls—was so loud that Jimmy fell to the ground.

He saw the sole of the giant's left foot pass above him, blocking out the sun, the clouds, and then the whole vast sky. It came hammering down on top of the wagon, and the right foot swung ahead of it, squashing six of the oxen into a pulp of brown and red.

Like a child in a tantrum, Collosso stomped back and forth. He jumped up and down, crushing the oxen, smashing metal and wood.

In an instant, it was all over.

# CHAPTER THIRTEEN

## THE WITCH WHO RODE AN ALLIGATOR

"Gee, what happened? You gotta say what happened," said Dickie Espinosa.

"Maybe that's enough for today," said Laurie. She thought she was getting a headache.

"But we have to know. Did they kill him?" asked Dickie.

"No." Laurie pulled off her glasses and rubbed her eyes. "Flanders took a swipe with his sword and nicked Collosso's heel. And Khan shot another arrow. But it didn't do any good."

"The giant was scared, wasn't he?" said James. From his board, he looked up at everybody. "He didn't come out to fight. He just wanted to run away."

Laurie agreed. "That's right."

But Dickie wasn't satisfied. He twisted his head to look at Laurie in his mirror. "What about the giant-slayer?" he asked. "What happened to Jimmy?"

"He just lay on the ground, right where he'd fallen." Laurie was rubbing her neck, feeling the cords of her muscles. "By the time he got up, it was all over."

◆ ◆ ◆

Collosso went jogging up the Great North Road. He took long strides with his arms swinging, so he was wholly in the air between his steps, and when he landed the mountain shook. In moments he was hidden by the bend in the road, but for a long time they could feel him running on and on by the tremors in the earth.

Jimmy got up. Khan and Flanders were just standing there, looking round at the ruin.

The wonderful wagon was just a pile of metal and wood. Where the hundred oxen had been were ninety-nine stains on the road, like so many blotches of red ink. There was only one animal left, and it too stood gazing around, as though even an ox could be dumbfounded.

Jimmy could hardly believe that his great adventure had ended so quickly. There hadn't even been a battle: not a fight or scrap or ballyhoo. It had taken only seconds for the giant to defeat him.

Finnegan Flanders kicked at a bit of twisted metal. "What do we do now?" he asked.

"I guess we go home," said Jimmy.

Khan looked down. "I don't believe I'm hearing right," he said. "You're giving up already? You're throwing down the quiver before you even notch an arrow?"

"What else can we do?" said Jimmy.

"There's plenty else we can do," said Khan. "Why, we're wallowing in things we can do." He put his quiver on his shoulder. He bent his bow and unhooked the string. "When you go after a mountain bear and the first shot sends him running, what do you do? You go after him, that's what."

"But there's nothing left."

"Nothing?" Khan swept his arm across the ruined landscape. The tattooed stars flashed on his skin. "We still got one of them shaggy critters, don't we? We got the horses, and we got the leather and the wheels. Sure, it's less than we had this morning—no denying it—but it's a whole heap more than we had a week ago."

"Yes, I guess that's right," said Jimmy, cheering himself.

"In a way, we're darned lucky," said Khan. "We got us the best teamster on the Great North Road, don't we? Reckon he can build us a new wagon quick as you say Jack Flash."

"Well, now just a minute," said Finnegan Flanders. He didn't seem so full of dash and bravery all of a sudden. "I haven't got my tools."

"We can make new ones," said Jimmy. "We can forge them from the metal."

Khan beamed. "Now you're thinking."

"No, no, it won't work," said Flanders. He was holding up his hands, and the fringes were shaking on his gauntlets. "It's impossible."

"Why?" asked Jimmy.

"Because . . . well, because . . ." He sighed horribly. Then, turning toward the moat, he kicked a stone over the edge. "I'm not a teamster at all," he said. "I don't know how to build a wagon. I don't even know how to drive one."

Jimmy looked up at the man's sad face. "But you said —"

"A pack of lies," said Flanders. "Collosso squashed the rancher who had those oxen. He smashed the buildings and flattened the fences. I found the oxen just wandering down the road, so I thought I could herd them to town and sell them. I got that drover to help me. 'Here, you pull from the front, I'll push from behind,' I said, and the poor devil did all the work himself and didn't even know it."

Flanders kicked another stone. It rolled over the edge in a little cloud of dust. "Then you came along, the two of you, talking about killing giants and everything. I guess I got kind of swept up in it. I'm sorry."

It seemed that Khan's heap of things to do had grown smaller quite quickly. The hunter was smiling about it in a strange way, looking neither angry nor beaten. But for Jimmy, all the new hopefulness that had filled him suddenly trickled away. He sat down in the dirt, his little feet hanging over the edge of Collosso's moat.

"It's that witch's fault," he said. "She promised it would work. She had a vision."

◆ ◆ ◆

It was a strange place for Laurie to stop, with the giant-slayer and Khan disheartened, with Finnegan Flanders exposed as a fraud. She left the three in a weary group at the side of the road, and said she had to go home.

"What's wrong?" asked Carolyn.

"I'm tired," said Laurie. Her mouth was dry, and her head was really aching now. "I think I'm getting a cold. I just want to go home and sleep."

She left the room, and little Dickie smiled as she looked back from the doorway.

"See ya real soon," he said.

◆ ◆ ◆

Laurie Valentine was nearly at Piper's Pond when her legs gave out. She collapsed on the path, sprawling across the hard cement. Her cry frightened a duck, which rose from the pond with a squawk, its wings a whirl of green and brown.

She crawled toward a bench, thinking that if she could rest there a while she could make it home all right. But then the pain flashed through her, and she closed her eyes and screamed.

It was a nurse who found her, a young woman dawdling on her way to work. She knelt down and looked at Laurie's eyes. She pressed her fingers on Laurie's pulse. Then she got up and raced to the hospital doors, shouting, "Help! Somebody help!"

◆ ◆ ◆

In the respirator room, Carolyn was nearest to the door. She heard the commotion in the hall, the rumble of a gurney's wheels, the slapping sound of shoes. She could feel the urgency that was carried along through the corridors, that raced ahead of the running doctors and the nurses.

She saw the gurney hurtle into the room with white-coated figures crowded all around a small body below a sheet—a girl with dark hair. They were holding an oxygen mask over her face.

They whisked her down the row of iron lungs, past Carolyn, past Chip and Dickie. Then they opened the last one—the fourth machine—and slid the girl inside it. They started the motor; the bellows filled and emptied. The bellows whirred and hummed and whooshed.

When the girl was breathing, the doctors moved away. And Dickie, beside them, saw that the girl was Laurie Valentine.

They were all still there: Peter and Ruth in their wheelchairs, James Miner on his treatment board. They had all seen other children arrive, always in a little herd of people, always with a feel of fright and panic.

They had thought it was over now, that polio was beaten. The newspaper headline was still on the wall, saying that it was so. But now Laurie lay in the iron lung, with a tube sticking out of her throat. It was hard to say that she was asleep, but she was certainly not awake. She lay sealed in the metal, with just her head sticking out. And it seemed that that huge machine had been waiting for her all along, sitting silently and still, just waiting for its chance.

◆ ◆ ◆

On that day, and in the ones to follow, other children were being rushed into other hospitals. There was a problem at the Cutter lab.

A batch of vaccine that was supposed to be dead was really alive. It had been injected into the blood of those children who were first for the vaccination. And it multiplied there, doubling once, doubling again, attacking nerves and muscles.

For Laurie there was nothing. She floated in a void as complete as the one at the edge of her imagined world. She was not aware of darkness nor of light, not of sound, and not of time.

The air whistled through the tube in her neck, in and out, as the machine did her breathing. A nurse had to remove the foam that sometimes filled it.

For the first hour, Miss Freeman sat there, watching over Laurie.

"Where's her dad?" asked Chip.

"The police are looking for him now," said the nurse. "I guess he's a little hard to find today, but I sure wish they'd hurry."

"Is she going to die?" asked Dickie.

"Let's not think of that," said Miss Freeman. "It's far too early to tell."

"I don't want her to die," said Dickie.

"Of course you don't. Nobody does," said Miss Freeman. "And we're going to do our very best to see that she doesn't. But for now, Dickie, please think about something else."

He thought of the story, of Jimmy the giant-slayer, of Khan. It seemed they had been abandoned on the Great

North Road, that they would remain forever there. "Carolyn, you have to finish it," he said.

"Finish what?" she asked.

"The story."

"Oh, Dickie, not now," she said. And Chip, between them, said it wouldn't be right to go on with the story.

"But you have to," said Dickie. "You *have* to."

He sounded so worried, and looked so frightened, that Miss Freeman couldn't ignore him. "Dickie?" she said. "Why is that story so important to you?"

"Because it's for real," he said. "I'm Khan. I really am. And James is the giant-slayer."

He had tried to explain it all before, and still couldn't find the words to do it. How could he explain something he couldn't really understand himself? He said, rather desperately, "If we don't finish the story, Laurie's going to die."

"That's dumb," said Carolyn.

"No, it's not," said Dickie. "Everything's real. Like James was born in a lightning storm. And his dad was a miser. Just like Fingal. What about Jessamine? You're her for sure. And the way Finnegan Flanders knows about wagons. Like Chip knows about cars. He was going to rebuild it, I think."

"But he's a phony," said Carolyn. "If it's true, why's he a fake?"

"I don't know," said Dickie. He started to list again all the ways that the story had crossed into their lives. He told about his dreams, about the times when he'd known how the story would turn. He said, "She heard the piper."

Carolyn called him a stupe. But Chip said, "I think he's maybe right."

"Aw, you're nuts," said Carolyn. "You're both nuts. If Flanders is phony, so are you."

"Well, that's the weird thing," said Chip. "I—"

Miss Freeman interrupted, speaking quickly over top of him. "Chip, you don't have to tell them that."

"No, it's all right," he said. He paused for a moment, then started.

◆ ◆ ◆

The pictures were real, Chip said. But they were not of him. He was not the boy building cars with his father, nor the one with a fishing pole, nor the one flying a kite. He didn't know who they were, the boys in those pictures. He had never met any of them.

The postcards were real, but they hadn't come from his parents. It was Miss Freeman who'd sent them, because he had asked her to.

"I felt sorry for myself," he said. "Everyone got mail except for me."

Miss Freeman had found the photographs. She had bought them at flea markets and secondhand stores, picking them out from the albums of strangers. With the scraps of people's worlds, she had put together a fanciful life for the boy.

He had never built a car. All he knew of hot rods had come from his magazines. He had never been to summer camp.

◆ ◆ ◆

"There's one thing was true," said Chip. "I was born on a farm."

When he was three years old his big farmer father had sat him up on a wagon and let him drive the team of oxen.

That was the only memory he had of his father—of sitting there beside him with big green flies buzzing around them, smelling manure and sun-baked mud, seeing the wind brush the tops of long yellow grass.

He would have been three as well when his mother took him away to the city, and maybe six when she died and he went into foster homes. He could remember that, but not very clearly.

When he finished, there didn't seem very much to say. Miss Freeman fiddled with the tube in Laurie's throat, and air whistled through it. And the iron lungs kept breathing. And outside, beyond the grass and the pond, a car honked its horn.

Someone came tapping down the hall. Miss Freeman went to see who was there. She looked out and then down. "Oh, hi, James," she said, and stepped aside.

It was James Miner. He had come in braces, wearing short trousers under the metal straps. He leaned on crutches that didn't reach as high as his armpits. They had pegs for his hands to hold on to, and leather hoops that circled his arms. His face was red from the effort of walking down the hall. But still he smiled at the nurse. Then he came into the room, leaning forward on his crutches, swinging his hips to drag one foot after the other. He lurched right down the row of iron lungs and settled on the floor, leaning against one of the legs of Laurie's machine.

When he'd got his crutches beside him, his legs out stiffly, Carolyn took up the story.

◆ ◆ ◆

Jimmy, Khan, and Finnegan Flanders built a wagon from the old one, a strange-looking thing. The wheels were enormous, of course, but the wagon itself was like a battered old bucket hung between them. That didn't matter to Jimmy; he said it was a fine-looking wagon. It didn't have to haul giants, after all. It needed only to carry a witch.

Khan stayed behind to watch over the castle while Jimmy and Flanders went back along the old hauling road. They traveled for days before they reached the bottomless swamp. And then Jimmy put his fingers in his mouth and whistled for the witch, and she came riding out on an alligator.

◆ ◆ ◆

"You're telling it too fast," said Dickie.

"Tough luck," said Carolyn.

He was whining. "But it's all wrong. They were supposed to go after Collosso."

"They changed their minds," said Carolyn.

"But why do they want the witch?"

"Wait and you'll see."

"Okay. But you better end it right," said Dickie.

◆ ◆ ◆

The witch straddled the alligator like a jockey on a strange and ugly horse. She came at great speed, thrashing through the water, smashing through the reeds. Coated in mud, her throat ballooning, she stopped right beside the wagon.

She looked way up at little Jimmy, just as she had prophesied. "So you return," she said. "Did you kill the giant?"

"No, he nearly killed *us*," said Jimmy.

Her throat puffed out as she breathed. "Is he in his castle?"

"We don't know," said Jimmy.

She looked fearfully around, as if the giant might have been hiding right there in the bulrushes. "You must go back," she said. "Go back and finish the task."

"I don't know that we can do it," said the little giant-slayer.

"You must," she said. "You were born for this."

"Then come and help us," said Jimmy.

"Would that I could," she said, "but I cannot leave the swamp."

Her huge round eyes blinked slowly. She sat looking at him from the alligator's back.

"We'll take the swamp with us," said Jimmy. "A bit of it, anyway. We'll fill the wagon with mud, and you can slosh along inside it."

The witch looked at the wagon. Her throat swelled up, and shrank, and swelled again. "When it's finished, will you do something for me?" she said.

"Of course. Whatever you want."

"You promise?"

He did.

"Very well," said the witch. "Then I will come."

She didn't help fill the wagon. She left that job to Jimmy and Flanders as she dashed to her house on the alligator. When she came back it was mostly full, and she was carrying a little basket with a lid.

"What's in there?" asked Jimmy.

"None of your beeswax," she said.

♦ ♦ ♦

"Wait a minute," cried Dickie. "I don't think the Swamp Witch would say that. She wouldn't say 'beeswax.'"

"Why not?"

"It doesn't sound right."

"Who's telling the story?" said Carolyn.

♦ ♦ ♦

So the witch said "beeswax." And she held on to her basket as Flanders lifted her up and set her into the wagon full of mud. She wriggled her way to the bottom, until only her eyes were showing above the surface. There she blinked and croaked as Jimmy took his seat and started the wagon moving.

It rocked over the huge stones of the hauling road, sloshing mud over the wheels. Inside, the witch tumbled and slid through the mud. "There's nothing to hold on to," she said. "Drive more carefully."

"Oh, don't make a fuss," said Jimmy.

{226}

With Finnegan Flanders in the lead on his prancing horse and Jimmy driving the wagon, the three companions traveled toward the mountains. From fields and orchards, the farmers, wives, and children came out to cheer again. They cheered for the small wagon as loudly as they had for the big one, and they cried out to the Swamp Witch, "Hex the giant! Hex the giant!"

Jimmy drove the wagon through the valley and through the foothills, through the blackened forests to the edge of the world.

Again they hugged the mountain there, not daring to look over the edge and into that enormous nothing. And again the clouds swirled around them, black and evil, with the great-winged dragons soaring, belching fire.

At the castle, the drawbridge was closed once more. The huge wagon lay crumpled on the road, and a great many gryphons were pecking away at the flattened remains of the oxen. It was plain that Khan, in turn, had been pecking away at the gryphons, for a dozen hides were hanging in the sun to keep away the tigers and the dragons. The hides swung in the wind, the feathers tossing, fluttering. The hunter himself was resting in the shade of a broken wheel. But he came out now as the wagon stopped, and greeted Jimmy with a raised hand.

The witch poked her head from the mud and examined everything, from the giant's castle to the frayed ends of broken harnesses. When she saw Khan she made a croaking, ribbiting sound in her throat. "Why is the hunter here?" she asked.

◆ ◆ ◆

"Hey, wait," said Dickie again.

"Now what?" said Carolyn.

"If she lives in a swamp," he said, "how come she knows Khan?"

"Beats me," said Carolyn, looking sideways from her pillow.

"Besides, Khan said he never met her. Remember that? How does that work?"

"I don't know," said Carolyn. "It's a mystery, all right."

At the end of the row, Miss Freeman sat watching over Laurie, with James on the floor beside her. Dickie looked toward them, then back to Carolyn. He was frowning. "What are they going to do to Collosso?"

"What do you think?" said Carolyn. "One's a giant-slayer, isn't he?"

"But what if she's Collosso?"

"Who?" asked Carolyn. "The witch?"

"Laurie!" he said, frustrated. "Like I'm Khan, and you're the witch. What if Laurie's Collosso?"

"I thought she was supposed to be the Woman," said Carolyn. "Why would she be Collosso?"

"I don't know. But what if she is?" said Dickie. "Boy, don't you see? If they kill Collosso, she might die. She might really die."

He was quite upset now, so distraught that Miss Freeman turned away from Laurie and tried to soothe him. "Honey, no one's going to die," she said.

"In the story, Miss Freeman," said Dickie. "She might be part of the story."

He had to explain for the nurse, in his short little bursts, why he was scared of a story. He had to show her that made-up things might kill a girl. He didn't think she'd understand, but he tried his best. The machines hummed, and the bellows filled and emptied, and Dickie talked on and on until Miss Freeman made him stop.

"It's okay. I get it," she said.

"Really?" asked Dickie.

"Yes. And you know something? The doctors might say that I'm nuts," said Miss Freeman. "But I think Laurie can hear every word you're saying. I think she knows exactly what's going on here."

"You do?"

"I do," she said, smiling. "And I think she's tickled pink that you want to finish the story she started. It doesn't matter if the ending's different. It will please her a whole lot, I'm sure, if you end it any way you like."

"But if Collosso dies, it might kill her," said Dickie, nearly in tears.

"Oh, honey, I don't think so." Miss Freeman wiped his forehead with a cloth and cool water. She rubbed his cheeks and his neck, all around the rubber collar. "It's only a story."

Dickie saw that she didn't really understand at all. She probably *thought* she did, but she couldn't.

"Why don't you have a little nap, Dickie?" asked Miss Freeman. "You can rest a bit, and maybe Carolyn can go on with the story."

"No!" said Dickie. "I don't want her to tell it now."

Carolyn said, "I don't care." But she obviously did. Her long braid trembled as she shook her head. "You go ahead and tell it, Dickie."

"Well, *nobody* has to tell it just now," said Miss Freeman. "I think all of you should rest because it's therapy in the morning."

The idea of therapy in the morning made the children quiet. Even James felt a shiver inside, and he had his therapy on a different day. Just the thought of the hot packs sent cold twinges through his crippled legs.

◆ ◆ ◆

It took the police nearly two hours to find Mr. Valentine. He came into the ward at a run, coins jingling in his pocket, his gray hat crushed in his hands. At the doorway he paused for an instant, looking all around, then rushed to Laurie's side.

He stood above her, his face as gray as his hat. His lips started quivering, then his eyes filled up with tears that rolled down his cheeks and splashed onto Laurie's pillow. It seemed that he was trying to talk but couldn't, for the only sounds he made were pathetic whines and splutters.

The hat fell from his hand as he reached out and put his palm flat on the iron lung. He rubbed it over the metal, back and forth and round and round, as though he could reach right through and hold on to his daughter.

"Oh, Laurie," he said at last. "Oh, Laurie."

She lay just as she had all along: eyes closed, perfectly still, while the tube in her throat swayed with the breathing of the machine. It looked like a pale sort of worm reaching this way and that, with little bubbles of foam at its head.

Miss Freeman had come in behind him, and now moved up to his side. She seemed to hold him up as his whole body began to sag. She tried to lead him away, to guide him from the room. "There's papers you have to fill out," she said. "I'm sure you've got phone calls to make."

In his old brown suit, Mr. Valentine looked weary and ancient. He stooped down and got his hat. He brushed the crown to knock away a bit of dust. For a long time, with Miss Freeman's hand on his back, he just stood and looked at Laurie, knowing that Dickie and Chip and Carolyn were watching. As though it would give him any privacy, they turned their faces aside, so that all three looked toward the door, and none of them said a word.

Mr. Valentine bent over to speak to his daughter. He talked in whispers, with many sibilant sounds: "Oh, sweetheart, I'm sorry; so sorry," he said. "I did my best. I tried to do the right thing. I never dreamed that this would happen."

She lay perfectly still, not asleep and not awake, not even breathing on her own.

It was more than ten minutes before Mr. Valentine straightened up again, and then a minute more until he'd gathered himself enough to turn around. He put his hand on Dickie's pillow. "Hello, Richard," he said.

Dickie turned to look up at him.

"This won't sound right at all," said Mr. Valentine. "But I'm glad you're here with Laurie. When she comes around, it will be a great comfort to find you beside her. Do you know that you're the only friend she's ever had?"

"Boy, she's got lots of friends, Mr. Valentine," said Dickie. "Not just me and Chip and Carolyn, but—"

"It's true. She's really nice," said Carolyn. And Chip said, "I think she's peachy."

Mr. Valentine looked even sadder. "I had no idea," he said. "She never talked to me about this place. Or if she did, I didn't listen."

Carolyn said, "She was telling us a story."

"Yes, of course," said Mr. Valentine, with a small laugh.

"It was a neato story," said Chip.

"Boy, it sure was," said Dickie. "It had a giant-slayer. And a big white castle in the mountains. And lions with wings. And a witch like a frog. And—"

"I was the witch," said Carolyn. "'Cause I was kind of mean at first."

"And I was a hunter," said Dickie.

"And I was a teamster," said Chip. "I had a huge wagon with a hundred oxen."

Mr. Valentine shook his head sadly. "I wish I'd known," he said. "I wish I'd heard that story."

He left them then—with a slap of his hat on his leg, with one more look at Laurie. He went all bent and tired-looking, shuffling with his feet. At the door he tried to smile. "God bless you all," he said. And at last he started crying.

# CHAPTER FOURTEEN

## THE MAN WHO SHOWED THE WAY

Even at night it was never quite dark in the respirator room. There was always the glow of the city in the window, the shine from the corridor through the open door, a star-like twinkle from the tiny bulbs on the respirator motors. But that night it was as dark as it ever got, for the clouds were thick in a moonless sky.

Mrs. Strawberry had come and gone. She had screamed at the sight of Laurie, a tingling shriek that was the worst sound Dickie had ever heard in his life. She had thrown herself against the iron lung, arms spread wide, and had held on like a cat as Mr. Valentine had pulled her away. "This was a mistake," he'd said. "This was a bad mistake."

He was asleep now, out in the hall, sprawled across two chairs. His troubled snoring came in bursts.

Dickie lay staring toward Laurie, a black shadow never moving. It was most important to him that they finish the story, but he was afraid as well of ending it. He wondered again what should happen to Collosso. For at least the third time, he asked, "What if Laurie is the giant?" He couldn't get the thought out of his mind.

No one teased him about it. Carolyn didn't snap or snarl or laugh. "At first," she said, "I thought the giant was polio. But I'm not sure anymore. Maybe the giant's just a giant."

"Boy, he's more than that," said Dickie.

Chip said that he'd been thinking about the story, and he was wondering if Collosso was maybe a symbol. "A kinda symbol," he said. "I don't know. Like he stands for growing up or something, for not being a kid anymore." But the others didn't understand.

"It's like Jimmy's always a child," said Chip. "He never grows big. He never grows up."

The tiny lights on the respirator, reflected in the window, reflected in the mirror too. In a way, Chip was looking at himself. "But if Jimmy kills Collosso, he gets big. He becomes a man, 'cause the witch promised him that. So he won't be a kid anymore."

"Aw, you're nuts," said Carolyn.

They all lay quiet for a minute, then Carolyn spoke again. "If the giant is polio and Laurie's the Woman, it sort of makes sense, you know. She disappeared in a way, like the Woman did, and now the giant's got her."

◆ ◆ ◆

There were sounds all through the night—quiet little hospital sounds or the louder rumble of a city, now and then a siren.

On this night an ambulance came rushing to the hospital. The siren sound grew louder until it wailed below the window. The flashing lights shone on the ceiling above the row of iron lungs.

Dickie started the story.

◆ ◆ ◆

The northern lights were bright in the mountains. They flashed through the sky in all different colors, and the giant-slayer huddled with his friends round the little wagon that held the Witch inside it.

Across the wide moat, behind the drawbridge, Collosso was in his castle. The great rooms were lit with yellow light, and now and then the giant passed across a window. And at midnight the screaming started.

There were deathly shrieks, howls of agony, and then the laughter of the giant. It fell away, then started again.

"I can't stand it," said Finnegan Flanders. "I will go mad if I have to listen any longer."

"Every night has been like this," said Khan.

Jimmy said, "We have to kill him." He turned to Khan. "What do we do?" They all turned to Khan because he was the hunter; he knew how to kill.

The screaming started again, and at last the great hunter rose to his feet. "Enough is enough," he said. "I'm going to whup the tar out of that giant."

◆ ◆ ◆

"Don't make me puke," said Carolyn.

"What's wrong with that?" said Dickie.

"It's dumb. Khan's a unicorn hunter. He's not Davy Crockett. Besides, it has to be the giant-slayer who kills the giant."

"Then you tell it better," said Dickie.

So Carolyn took a turn at the story. Then Chip took a turn. All through the night, one after the other, they tried to end the story.

With each telling, there was a different hero. Carolyn had the Swamp Witch crafting weapons from impossible things: battle-axes out of oxen yokes; swords from the tongues of the wagon. Chip made Finnegan Flanders more dashing than ever, a man like General Custer, with tumbling yellow hair and a big moustache and a pair of hunting dogs that suddenly appeared from nowhere. At dawn they were all angry at each other, and Jimmy's companions were sitting round the wagon in a grim silence as the sun climbed up from the edge of the world.

Little James Miner came back to the room on crutches. The black shoes built onto his metal braces were so neatly laced that Miss Freeman must have done the tying.

He settled down in the same place, against one of the legs of Laurie's iron lung. And even he got a turn at the story.

In the first light of the day, Collosso came out from his castle. He appeared on the ramparts, and in his hands was a great box with a sliding lid. He set it down on the wall in front of him.

The sky was red in the dawn. The giant looked out over the edge of the world at the rising sun. The clouds that swirled around him were the color of blood and roses.

With his thumb he opened the box.

A frightful howling came out of the box, a wailing and a groan. Like a man pinching snuff from a snuff box, the giant poked his fingers inside and pulled out a squirming figure. It was a man in farming clothes, kicking and punching at the air. Collosso looked at him closely and then flicked him out over the edge of the world. The farmer flew screaming into the clouds, writhing down through the sky and into that endless void. Collosso watched, frowning slightly, then pulled out another man.

◆ ◆ ◆

While James was telling the story, a nurse arrived for therapy. She pushed a machine in front of her, a round tub on three legs, with wheels at the bottom. It looked like a washing machine on spindly stilts.

Her name was Mrs. Clyde. She had curly red hair and a mean-looking face that never smiled. She plugged in the machine, and it whirred and shook, vibrating over the floor on its small rubber wheels.

Miss Freeman arrived soon after, too busy to be cheery. She

loosened the clamps on the first iron lung and drew Carolyn out on the rolling cot. The girl started frog-breathing.

Mrs. Clyde lifted the lid on her machine. Out came a puff of steam and the smell of hot, wet wool. Dickie clenched his teeth. Carolyn was frantically forcing air into her lungs.

Mrs. Clyde used a pair of tongs to fish a hot pack from her machine. It was like a cream-colored blanket, sodden and heavy, steaming hot. She set it down on Carolyn's legs. Dickie closed his eyes as he heard the wet splat and the little groans that Carolyn made. The smell of steaming wool was strong and sickening.

There was another splat, another groan. Mrs. Clyde was bending down now to stretch Carolyn's leg, to work the paralyzed muscles.

When she'd finished with Carolyn, the nurse refilled the machine and set it whirring again. Chip was next, and then Dickie.

Miss Freeman set up a breathing bag and put the mask on Dickie's face. She squeezed the bag, pumping air, as Mrs. Clyde reached with her tongs for the wool.

Each hot pack brought an instant of pain, followed by a pleasant feeling as the heated muscles loosened. He couldn't decide if the pain was worth the pleasure, for the nice feeling never lasted all that long, but he believed that it was. He kept his eyes closed, thinking of the paddle wheeler that would carry him away to Frontierland. He didn't cry out as Mrs. Clyde slapped the wool in place. He just bit his lip inside the mask, and let a tear go sliding down his cheek.

The nurses washed the patients and changed the sheets.

When the iron lungs were sealed again, Mrs. Clyde took her machine and went trundling down the hall. Miss Freeman stayed for a while, hovering over Laurie. As soon as she left, Dickie went back to the story.

"Jimmy's got to kill Collosso," he said. "It's what the Swamp Witch saw."

"But how?" asked James. "He's such a little person, and that giant, he's so big."

It seemed there was a proper way to do it, fitting with the story, but they couldn't decide what it was. Chip reminded them that that Finnegan Flanders could set his hunting dogs onto the giant, but he had forgotten that Carolyn had sent them skulking away because she didn't want them in the story. Then Carolyn said the Swamp Witch could work some magic, but Chip reminded them that the witch wasn't really a witch at all.

"She could still make a charm," said Carolyn, a little bit miffed.

Then Dickie cried out, "Boy, it's the charm!"

◆ ◆ ◆

The little giant-slayer hauled from his shirt the ball of bones that he'd been given by the hunter. He let it turn on the string, and the sunlight shining through it made lacy shadows on the ground.

The hunter, the teamster, the witch—they all shouted at him.

"Smash it!" said Khan. "Loose the power trapped inside it."

"Set it on the ground," said Finnegan Flanders. "Let the giant think that it's an offering, like the ones the farmers set out in the valley. When he touches it he will turn to cinders."

"Keep it," said the Swamp Witch. "Make your way into the castle and trust the charm to protect you."

Jimmy watched the charm spin round and round. The others shouted, each one louder: "Smash it!" "Leave it!" "Wear it."

But he couldn't decide; how could he? Once broken, the charm could never be restored. Left for the giant, it could never be recovered. And he could scarcely imagine himself climbing down into the moat with the hydras and the tigers.

Round the turrets of the castle, the clouds welled darkly from the edge of the world. Collosso flung his shrieking slaves across the sky. The crimson dragons soared and swooped, snatching the men as they fell. The giant-slayer stared at the spinning charm.

It was too much for him to choose. "I wish someone would help me," said Jimmy.

◆ ◆ ◆

Mrs. Strawberry sat all day at Piper's Pond, looking up at the fourth-floor windows, praying to herself as she rubbed her hands together. Mr. Valentine found her there at six o'clock but couldn't tempt her to go any farther. He went on alone, up to the respirator room, carrying not only his hat but a book, as if he meant to settle down for a great long stay.

It was a huge book with a blue cover, and Mr. Valentine put

it down on the chair as he went straight to Laurie's side. He touched her cheek; he smoothed her hair. She lay unmoving, with her breaths whistling through the plastic tube.

As he'd done before, Mr. Valentine rubbed his hand over the iron lung.

"It's all right," he whispered. "Daddy's here."

For fifteen minutes he stood like that, one hand on her head, the other rubbing the metal. Then, with a sigh, he stepped away. He opened that big blue book.

Just ahead of the index, a sheet of paper was slipped between the pages, a picture done in crayon. Little smears of green and blue had come away from the paper and were stuck now to the atlas.

"Laurie drew this years ago," said Mr. Valentine. "It was Mrs. Strawberry, Laurie's nanna, who remembered."

He peeled away the map of Laurie's life, the island shaped like a potato. He looked at the mountains and the meadows, at the castle in the corner.

"I told Mrs. Strawberry about your story, about the castle and everything."

He was talking to all four of them at once, though he didn't look away from the picture.

"In the middle of the night, she remembered. She telephoned and woke me up, shouting over the phone. 'The map of her life! That's where I saw them.' I didn't know what she was talking about, but it was the lions she remembered. The lions with wings on their back."

He put his finger on them in the picture, tiny little figures that looked more like poodles than lions.

"Laurie showed me this. She sat on my lap when she was

just a little girl and showed me all these things." His finger ran across the page. "The road, the castle, the crosses. I didn't pay much attention, I'm afraid."

Dickie spoke up from his respirator. "Can I see it, Mr. Valentine?"

"Oh, sure. I'm sorry." Mr. Valentine stood at Dickie's side and held up the map for him to see.

Dickie grinned as he studied it. "Boy, there's the Great North Road," he said. "Going up the middle like a snake. There's the castle at the edge of the world. The road goes past it. To that pond where ducks are swimming. And the straight line, that's the old hauling road. But what's the red thing there?"

"This squiggle?" asked Mr. Valentine, pointing. "Near the castle?"

"Yes."

"Mrs. Strawberry said she wondered the same thing," said Mr. Valentine. "Laurie told her she didn't know what it was, but thought she'd have to fight it."

"Can I see?" said Chip.

Mr. Valentine moved down the row of respirators so Chip and Carolyn could see the map together. James came over on his crutches, held on to the legs of the iron lung, and stood looking up with his head next to Chip's. He said, "That's a dragon. Sure as spit. It's one of them big red dragons that's flying around the castle."

Dickie said, "I know how it ends!"

◆ ◆ ◆

At the edge of the moat, with the tigers roaring far below him, Jimmy the giant-slayer raised his little arms.

He shouted, "Collosso!"

Three times he shouted before the giant looked down at him. The huge head turned.

"I have come to slay you, Collosso!" cried Jimmy. "I will do you in a flash!"

From the giant came a roar. He hurled his box over the rampart. It spun toward Jimmy, a thing as big as a barn to him, and exploded into a thousand pieces against the wall of the moat.

Jimmy held up the charm as far as the string would let him. It swayed like a pendulum in front of his eyes. Then he took hold of the ball of bones, closed it in his fist, and ran along the lip of the moat, east toward the edge of the world.

High above him stood Collosso, glaring down from the tall turret. The giant grabbed a stone at the top of his rampart and tore it right out of the wall. To him, it was the size of a brandy keg; to Jimmy it was enormous. The giant swung his arm and hurled the stone, and it blasted into the mountain just inches from Jimmy.

Shards of rock flew into the air. Jimmy dodged and weaved between them, running on with the charm in his hand. "I will do you in a flash!" he shouted again. Down in the moat, the tigers loped along below him, staring up with greedy eyes. Dragons wheeled above him, swooping lower through the clouds.

Collosso hurled another stone, and another and another. He peeled away the rampart until he stood exposed on his platform, fierce and huge, grunting as he hurled the massive stones.

Khan snatched up his bow and arrow and went running after Jimmy. Finnegan Flanders leapt on his horse, drawing his sword as he kicked it into a gallop. They both raced along the edge of the moat, trying to catch the little giant-slayer. They didn't know what they would do when they reached him, but they couldn't just stand and watch.

The stones flung down from the castle smashed on the road and the ruins of the wagon, on the mountainside and the wall of the moat.

At the very edge of the world, Jimmy stopped. Again he held the charm as high as he could, and the dragon's claw in the middle glowed like a little flame in the light. "I have come to slay you, Collosso!" he shouted again.

The giant had torn down the whole rampart. Now he stooped and snatched a stone from the floor, breaking it free from the edge. He drew back his arm.

From the sky above Jimmy, a dragon pounced. It came down like a red streak with its wings drawn back, its legs extended. It came with a shriek and a roar of fire, its long neck twisted, its tail thrashing.

Collosso threw his stone.

Inches from Jimmy, the dragon flapped its great wings. The rush of air knocked the giant-slayer flat. But he held up the charm, and it swung madly from his fingers. The dragon flapped again, hovering above the giant-slayer, its face snaking round to look at him. It grabbed on to the charm with its claws.

The string that held the charm was no thicker than wool. But the magic in the bones made it stronger than steel. The dragon screamed and pulled, its huge wings now beating at the ground. Jimmy lay below its belly, kicking at the scales with his little feet. The dragon breathed a spume of fire.

Finnegan Flanders rode right in against the dragon. He pulled out his sword and slashed at its neck, at its wings. Khan leapt in to save Jimmy, his quiver of arrows on his back. He held on to the giant-slayer as the dragon tried to lift them both in the air.

With a thud, Collosso's stone hit the dragon on its spine. Its back arched and its neck straightened for a moment. Fire belched from its mouth.

Stunned, the dragon fell. It landed on Jimmy and Khan, and the arrows in the hunter's quiver pierced the scales on its belly. The wings opened again, beating furiously now. It lifted Jimmy from the ground, and Khan held onto his waist.

From the belly of the dragon came drips of black blood. They fell on Khan, on Jimmy. A drop fell on the charm, and the bones began to gleam and shine. They turned to red as a heat built up inside them, then to white and blue. With an enormous flash, that ball of bones burst open.

Khan and Jimmy tumbled together onto the ground, while the dragon shot up through the air, hurled backward into the cloud with its red neck writhing. The claw from the center of the charm fell on the road beside Jimmy. Half its length hung over the edge of the world, and slowly it tipped over. Jimmy reached out to grab it, but down the claw went, into the void.

"No!" shouted Jimmy. "No!" There seemed nothing else that could help him now, no hope of killing Collosso.

But he had forgotten the words of the Tellsman, the message scrawled in cold ashes: *Has lightning inside.*

The claw exploded with a flash that was brighter than the sun. An instant later, a clap of thunder nearly deafened the giant-slayer. Then the dark clouds of the void began to flare and flicker. They pulsed with sheets of lightning.

The giant screamed. He tore off his red cap and held it over his face as though to hide himself from the storm.

Thunder boomed again. Lightning seared in a bolt from the clouds and hit the tower where the giant stood. Another followed, crumbling the stones. A third blasted into the moat, setting the tar and pitch on fire.

Flames leapt up from below, and the lightning kept flashing above. Collosso reeled across his platform. One foot went over the edge; he tried to catch himself. For a moment he balanced there at an impossible angle, his huge arms flailing. The red cap soared from his hand. It spiraled higher on the draft of wind and fire. Then—with a scream—the giant slipped from his tower and plummeted down, past the edge of the world.

The lightning stopped. The thunder faded away in echoing booms. And the red cap fluttered down to land on the road near Jimmy and Flanders and Khan.

◆ ◆ ◆

In her iron lung, Laurie stirred. She didn't wake, exactly, but she almost did. Her eyes came open, and her head turned slightly, and then she slipped away again.

Mr. Valentine, at her side, saw it happen. He shouted her name. "She's awake!" he cried.

James called out for the nurse. He lurched toward the

door on his braces, hobbling as fast as he could. "Miss Freeman!" he shouted. "She woke up!"

The nurse came running. By the time they got into the respirator room, Laurie was back in her coma, in her own strange silence and blackness. Mr. Valentine held his hands on his daughter's face and begged her to open her eyes.

◆ ◆ ◆

Collosso was dead, but the story wasn't finished. There was not a person in the room, including Mr. Valentine, who didn't want it to carry on.

Carolyn was the one who started again.

She said that Finnegan Flanders jumped down from his horse, that he and Khan raised the little giant-slayer between them, up onto their shoulders, and paraded him down the road. They carried him to the wagon, where the Swamp Witch pulled herself from the mud and looked down from the top. And they all shouted three cheers for Jimmy.

In the castle, across the moat, a rumble of metal began. The giant-slayer and his friends had heard the sound before and knew what it meant. They looked up at the drawbridge and saw it slowly open.

The chain clanked. The drawbridge dropped into place. The iron portcullis rose from the floor.

Through the gap below it came the servants of Collosso, the giant's slaves and toys. They crawled on their bellies when the gap looked pencil thin. They came in a crouch when it was a little bigger, and then running—in a flood—as the portcullis rattled up into the castle walls.

There were hundreds of people, many holding hands, most skipping along, all laughing and cheering. They streamed across the drawbridge and onto the road, and they gathered in a huge crowd around the strange-looking wagon and the even-stranger-looking giant-slayer. They shouted out that Jimmy was a hero. They made him stand up on the wagon so that they could see him that much better, and they cheered and cheered and cheered.

It was a wonderful thing for Jimmy to have men looking up at him. He heard them praise and bless him; he heard women shout out that they loved him. And then a voice cried above all the others. "He's my boy! That's Jimmy."

The Woman was the last to leave the castle, and she was just then nearing the end of the drawbridge. Jimmy tried to get down, to run and meet her, but there wasn't enough room on the ground for Jimmy to stand. And there was no need. Men lifted the Woman high, and she came running to Jimmy on the shoulders and heads and hands of the crowd. She vaulted across to the wagon and hugged little Jimmy more tightly than he had ever been hugged before.

The crowd whistled, laughed, and cheered. A little group of men brought the giant's red hat, carrying it on long poles that they balanced on their shoulders. A mass of people closed around them in a babble of voices. For a moment it seemed the crowd would tear the hat to shreds, but instead it was hoisted up above the wagon, mounted on the poles as a sunshade for the Swamp Witch. Then all those hundreds of people stood back in a quiet group, and the men took off their hats, and they all began to clap for Jimmy the giant-slayer.

They would gladly have carried him down from the

mountain; they would gladly have carried them all. They would have carried Flanders on his horse and the Swamp Witch in her wagon all the way to the village in the valley. They would have made kings of the men, a queen of the witch.

But that wasn't fitting for Khan. It wasn't what Jimmy was after. And the witch wanted something else altogether.

Only Finnegan Flanders was happy amid the crowd. He let the people hoist him up, as he had hoisted Jimmy, and his fringes flashed as he waved his sword above them. When the cheering died down—and that took a long time— Flanders mounted his horse. He found room on its back for six young ladies, and he pranced along at the front of the crowd, leading all the hundreds of people down from the valley, free from Collosso's castle.

The Swamp Witch smiled as he rode away, her mouth in a thin red line. Khan waved once, then untied his big horse and got up on its back. "Reckon I'll be off," he said. "The unicorns will be shedding their horns soon." He backed the horse and turned it round. He looked up at the castle with its shattered tower, along the road at the ruined wagon, at the red cap of Collosso. Then he looked at Jimmy.

"Where will you go?" he asked.

"I don't know," said Jimmy. "It's up to the witch, I guess."

"If you cared to go hunting . . ." He let his voice fade away.

"Thank you," said Jimmy. He had never been so pleased, nor so torn. He would have loved to go hunting with Khan, into the mountains and the snow. "I think I have to go the other way," he said.

"Reckon you do," said Khan. "I'll watch for you, Jim, at the edge of the sky." He nodded, then dragged his horse's head around, kicked its ribs, and went loping up the road with the pony running behind. The eight hooves made a flurry of dust.

Khan never looked back. But he raised a hand, with his fingers spread, and he shouted through the mountains, "You're a mighty big man, my friend."

Jimmy watched the hunter fade away, vanishing into a world that was wild and empty. Then he helped his mother up to the seat of the wagon and settled beside her. He looked down at the Swamp Witch, who was wallowing happily in the mud. "Which way should we go?" he asked.

"North," she said, her throat bulging. "Stay on the road. We go right to the end."

Jimmy clicked his tongue. "Gee up!" he shouted, as though he were still driving a team of a hundred. The ox put its head down and plodded along the road.

Beside the giant-slayer, the Woman touched his arm. "Jimmy," she said, "you've got a lot of explaining to do."

He said it would have to wait, that the journey was nearly done. Then he shouted at the ox again, and he drove past the wreck of his glorious wagon, past the ninety-nine stains on the road. His mother looked around at the signs of his battle, at the gryphon hides blowing in the breeze. She looked pointedly at Jimmy but said nothing, happy to ride along primly with her hands on her lap, her back as straight as an arrow.

A mile beyond the castle, the road turned away from the edge of the world. It went steeply down the mountain in a series of switchbacks. Jimmy kept pulling on the handbrake, but the wagon still outran the ox, shoving it down the hill. Round the sharp bends, the mud sloshed so badly that the witch got angry. "Slow down!" she said. "Do you want a knuckle sandwich?"

◆ ◆ ◆

"It's all wrong," said Dickie. "She sounds like Popeye or something."

"Well, it doesn't matter," said Carolyn. "They drove to the end of the road."

"How long did it take?"

"Four days."

"What did they see?"

"Well, all along the way," said Carolyn, "were little piles of gold."

◆ ◆ ◆

The first pile of gold appeared in a hollow tree, a stack of small bricks very neatly arranged. The second stood beside a little pool where Jimmy stopped to water the ox. Every three or four miles was another—always a tidy stack of gold, sometimes silver as well, or little bags of emeralds.

Jimmy's mother was delighted, and the Swamp Witch gloated. They couldn't believe there was such a place in all the world where gold lay by the road for the taking. "How did it get here?" asked the Woman.

"It's from the gnomes," said Jimmy. "It's their way of saying thank you, I think."

By the fourth day, the wagon was laden down. The poor ox was struggling, breathing hard with every step. On a long hill, the wagon was barely moving when the Swamp Witch raised her head from the mud and said, "Listen."

From the distance came a strange howling, a sort of hullabaloo of hoots and whines. Jimmy frowned at the Woman, who shrugged her shoulders. "What is it?" asked the Swamp Witch.

To Jimmy it sounded like cats—like dozens of cats—in a sort of feline choir. They weren't just howling, he thought, but howling in a chorus, in a crazy sort of cat song. The sound was strangely beautiful, and it grew louder as the wagon neared the crest of the hill.

From the summit, Jimmy and the Woman and the witch looked out across a valley. Stands of trees, bright green and olive, dotted fields of yellow. Across the sky flew flocks of birds of every color, and a herd of silver unicorns grazed among the grasses. It was a beautiful, pastoral place, and in the middle was a white house and a little wooden workshop. They stood beside a quiet pond where a man was playing the bagpipes.

◆ ◆ ◆

"I knew it!" said James. He beat his little fists happily on his metal braces. "It was Piper's Pond, wasn't it?"

"Well, it wasn't Doodyville," said Carolyn.

◆ ◆ ◆

It was where the road came to an end. Jimmy guided the ox to the very last inch of the Great North Road, and on another yard, to the grassy bank of the pond. Ducks and swans were swimming there.

The man with the bagpipes came toward them, playing steadily all the time. He took steps that were small and slow, and while his arm squeezed the bag of air, his fingers played the tune. Long streamers of scarlet and gold fluttered from the pipes.

He was a very old man, the oldest that Jimmy had ever seen. His hair was long and white, his beard the same—like the tail of a unicorn glued to his cheeks. He made a last little flurry of notes, then stood smiling—panting—below the wagon as the music drained out of his bagpipes in a leaky sort of whine.

"You have done it," he said, looking up at the giant's red hat. "You have killed Collosso."

"Not just me," said Jimmy.

"I know," said the old man. "News of your deed has traveled before you."

The Swamp Witch had hauled herself up to the top of the wagon, her long fingers hooked over the edge. Just the top of her head and her eyes showed above it, and she blinked down at the old man.

"Are you a Wishman?" she asked.

"Yes," he said.

"Can you give us what we want?"

The old man put down his bagpipes. He arranged them carefully on a little round stool. Then he scratched his beard and said, "Wishes are expensive."

"Come here," said the Swamp Witch.

The man was too old to climb by himself. Jimmy had to

help him from below, and the Woman from above. They got him up to the seat, where he looked down into the tub of the wagon.

"Bah!" he said, and turned to leave, because all he saw was mud and the Swamp Witch wallowing there.

"Wait," said Jimmy.

The gold and silver and jewels had raised the level of the mud by three or four feet. The witch dug in with her webbed hands and brought up clotted mounds of gold and emeralds. Black as they were, coated with ooze, there was no mistaking the riches there. Even the Wishman had seldom seen such wealth in one place.

"Now, there's rules," he said. "One wish is all you get. One each. No changing your mind later. You're not happy, too bad." He looked sternly at all of them. "So what is it that you want? No, no. I can guess; it's so easy. I've seen this too often not to know at once."

He sat in the shade of the giant's red hat, crossed his legs, and scratched his ribs. He pointed at each of them in turn. "The witch wants her youth and her beauty restored. The Woman wants her husband to be generous and kind. The small boy wants to be big."

The three looked at each other and laughed delightedly. They laughed with such mirth that the Wishman smiled. "Am I right?" he said. "Am I right?"

"You *were*," said Jimmy.

The old man had guessed exactly what each of the three had set out to find, but what all no longer wanted.

"I think we wish for the same thing," said Jimmy the giant-slayer. "It will be one wish for us all."

"No, no." The old man shook his finger. "Shared or not, it still counts as three wishes."

"Fine with us," said Jimmy.

It was an easy wish, simply granted. "That's it?" asked the Wishman, and Jimmy said, "That's it."

The Wishman toddled into his little shop, and in a moment he was back. "There, it's done," he said with a wave of his hand.

Jimmy looked all around, but he didn't see that the wish was granted. He started to complain, but the Wishman said, "It's not like instant potatoes. You have to wait."

He pushed a little stick into the ground and laid another one flat on the thin shadow of the sun. "In a day," he said, "when the shadow comes round to that spot, the wish is granted."

They passed the time pleasantly. Jimmy and the Swamp Witch splashed in the pond, while the Wishman slept in the grass. The Woman picked flowers of clover that she fed to the ducks. But in the morning of the next day, neither Jimmy, the witch, nor the Woman strayed very far from the old man's stick.

They watched the shadow creeping round.

# CHAPTER FIFTEEN

## THE SHADOW OF THE STICK

"Laurie? Laurie!" said Mr. Valentine.

He was on his feet now, both hands on his daughter's head. One combed through her hair, again and again; the other ran softly across her cheeks, his fingers just touching her skin.

"Laurie," he said again.

Dickie tipped his head on his pillow. "What's going on, Mr. Valentine?"

"She's coming awake," he said. "Her eyes are twitching."

James went on his crutches and called for the nurse. It wasn't Miss Freeman who came, but another that Carolyn and Chip knew well. She elbowed Mr. Valentine out of the way and started prodding and poking at Laurie.

"Yes, she's coming round, I think," said the nurse. "It's a good sign, but too early to hope for too much."

Dickie was watching. Laurie looked the same to him—even worse right then for not waking with the noise and the prodding of hands. It was scary to see her like that—barely alive, but not dead, with her breath making whistles in the plastic pipe.

"But she's getting better, isn't she?" asked Mr. Valentine. "She's going to be her old self again. Isn't she?"

The nurse straightened the cotton padding on Laurie's neck, arranging it around the edge of the rubber collar. "There's a doctor on his way. A specialist," she said.

The iron lungs wheezed and whooshed. The stretching of the rubber lungs made shifting shadows on the floor.

Dickie turned away, distraught. "Boy, you better say what they wished for, Carolyn," he said.

◆ ◆ ◆

The day seemed long with waiting. The shadow of the stick crept so slowly across the grass that Jimmy the giant-slayer kept looking up at the sun, willing it to hurry.

At noon the shadow was a short little spike. Then it stretched and shifted, swinging round more quickly. Jimmy, the Woman, and the witch all crouched beside it. They watched as the shadow touched the pointer stick that the Wishman had set on the grass.

Right then, across the valley, came a jingling sound. And from the trees on its far side emerged the Gypsy wagons.

They came rolling right across the grass, pitching from side to side. The drivers, in their seats, looked like sailors tossed by stormy seas. In the wagons clattered pots and pans, bracelets, jewels, and tambourines.

Jimmy stood up and watched them. The Gypsy King was in the lead. The Woman suddenly raised her hand and waved. At the same time, the Swamp Witch dashed for the pond with her little basket in her hands. She crossed the grass in three long bounds and slipped into the water.

The Gypsies ranged their wagons like spokes on a wheel, in a circle round the pond, all facing in toward it. The boys leapt out to care for the horses; the girls stared shyly from the doors and curtains of the wagons.

The Gypsy King came in a swagger, greeting the Wishman with a loud shout across the pond. The gold in his teeth flashed in the sunlight. He came with his head tipped back, looking up at Collosso's red cap roofing the strange-looking wagon. Then he saw Jimmy and grinned.

"I never doubted you would kill the giant," he said.

"Yes, you did," said Jimmy.

The King of the Gypsies laughed. "Well, *now*, I never did," he said.

◆ ◆ ◆

"I don't get it," said Dickie. "The Wishman brought the Gypsies? What kind of wish was that?"

"It was just the first part of it," said Carolyn. "You'll see; it will all work out in the end."

"I think it will," said Chip.

The three lay hopeful and content, stretched out in their iron lungs. They slept peacefully that night.

The doctor came just after midnight, while the room was dimly lit.

He was a tall man, his black hair in a ducktail that shone with oil. He moved like a ghost in his white coat and soft-soled shoes, a gray shape that walked without sound. He passed along the row of iron lungs, looking down at the children, reaching out to softly touch their heads.

Carolyn didn't wake up, and neither did Chip. But Dickie stirred at the touch of the doctor's fingers. He opened his eyes and saw, in the mirror, the doctor passing by, moving on to Laurie.

Mr. Valentine was slumped forward in the chair. He had his chin on his chest, an arm dangling down. The map of the future had slipped from his fingers and was lying on the floor. His snoring was quiet, a pleasing sound for Dickie, who had often found comfort in the snoring of his father after waking from a nightmare.

The doctor picked up the map from the floor. He put it carefully on Mr. Valentine's lap but didn't disturb the sleeping man. Then he stood over Laurie, and with his back toward Dickie, worked away in his silent manner, making barely a sound at all.

Dickie could see nothing but the man's broad back and the shine of his hair oil. He could see his arms moving, but not what he was doing.

"Is she going to be okay?" he asked.

"Shh." The doctor looked back. "Yes, she'll be fine," he said very quietly. "Don't worry."

He went right back to his work, moving from Laurie's head to the side of her iron lung. He put his hands through the portals and leaned over the machine.

"When will she wake up?" asked Dickie.

"In the morning," said the doctor. He moved back to her head and talked in whispers to Laurie.

The respirators whined and whooshed. Mr. Valentine snored in his chair. And the doctor kept working, talking in a quiet voice.

"You're safe now. Don't be frightened," he said, as though Laurie were already awake. "You're at Bishop's, Laurie."

Dickie asked, "Is she going to be all right?"

The doctor turned to him now, big as a polar bear in that white coat. "Yes, she'll be fine. Just sleep—hush now—and let me work."

Dickie couldn't see the man's face very clearly. But he saw his hand reaching out, as though floating toward him as gently as a falling feather. And he heard his voice saying, "I'm Dr. Wishman."

And just as Dickie felt the doctor's fingers touch his forehead, he was asleep again.

◆ ◆ ◆

It was a sound of tapping that woke Mr. Valentine just after dawn. In the dream that he was having, a big black bird was pecking at his bedroom window, trying to smash through the glass to get at him. He woke with a start, raising his arms to shield himself.

He saw right away that he wasn't in his bed at home, that no enormous bird was trying to kill him. But the great relief that came with that lasted less than a second. When he saw the iron lungs, his heart sank.

He realized only then that the sound that had woken him was still going on. It wasn't very loud at all, but it was hurried and frantic, and Mr. Valentine looked up to see Laurie's hand moving in the window of the iron lung.

Her fingernails were hitting the glass, tapping faintly on the little window.

Mr. Valentine was on his feet in an instant. "Laurie, I'm here," he said.

But she was still asleep; she couldn't hear him.

"Laurie!" Mr. Valentine gestured frantically with his hands, as though trying to hold on to her, but not seeing how to do it. He grabbed the legs of the iron lung and shook the whole machine.

He shook everyone awake.

◆ ◆ ◆

For Dickie, the room was suddenly full of light and noise. He had been awake in the night, in the quiet and the dark, and now—the next instant, it seemed—Mr. Valentine was shouting beside him, and on the other side Carolyn was crying out with each breath of her respirator, "What's going on?"

But Mr. Valentine just kept shaking the legs of the iron

lung, shouting his daughter's name. He made so much noise that Mrs. Glass came barging into the room, bringing a doctor behind her.

"She's moving!" said Mr. Valentine. "She's moving in there!"

In his mirror, Dickie watched the doctor rushing by. He turned his head and saw him push Mr. Valentine out of the way, then bend down to peer through the window of the iron lung.

"She's not moving," said the doctor.

"She was," said Mr. Valentine. "She was still asleep, but she was tapping at the glass."

"Well, that's a good sign. A very good sign," said the doctor.

He was young and tanned, more like a lifeguard than a doctor. He put his hand on Laurie's forehead. "She's been in a coma how long?"

Mr. Valentine had to count back through the days. "I can't remember," he said. "It's all a blur."

Dickie grunted, but nobody looked toward him.

The doctor took a small flashlight from his pocket. He pried Laurie's eyelids open and peered this way and that. When he finished he turned off the flashlight and spun it absently in his fingers, like a gun slinger with a six-shooter.

"Well?" Mr. Valentine was squeezing one hand with the other. "When will she wake up?"

"A coma's a strange animal, Mr. Valentine." The doctor slipped the flashlight back in his pocket. "There's no telling how long it will last."

Dickie grunted again. He piped up from his pillow. "She

was kind of awake in the night. When the other doctor was here."

Mr. Valentine glanced at Dickie. So did Mrs. Glass and the doctor. They all gave him the same sort of look—puzzled and disbelieving. And Dickie sensed that Carolyn and Chip were doing the same thing on his other side; he could feel them looking at him.

"What doctor's that?" asked Mrs. Glass, too casually. Dickie knew she didn't believe he had seen a doctor at all, that *none* of them believed it.

"He came in the middle of the night," said Dickie. "His name was—" Suddenly, he didn't want to say it.

"His name was *what?*" asked Mrs. Glass. She looked at him sharply. "Dickie, what was his name?"

"Dr. Wishman," he said.

Chip didn't laugh. Neither did Carolyn, though she did say, "Oh, Dickie." She said it in the very nicest way, just as kindly as Miss Freeman would have done. "Oh, Dickie," she said, "you got that name from the story."

"No I never," he said. "That's what the doctor told me himself. He was here."

"I think you were having a dream," said Mrs. Glass.

"It wasn't a dream," said Dickie.

The doctor was watching more intently than anyone. Now he raised his eyes to look beyond Dickie, over his head to Carolyn and Chip. "Did either of you see this?" he asked.

"No, they were asleep," said Dickie. "But *I* was awake, and I know it's true. I talked to Dr. Wishman."

They began to look away from him now. Mr. Valentine

turned back toward Laurie. Mrs. Glass straightened her little nursing hat and fussed with one of the envelopes of papers on Laurie's iron lung. Only the young doctor kept looking at Dickie. He said, "A dream can fool anyone, you know."

"But it wasn't a dream," said Dickie. "Dr. Wishman was here."

"Okay, Dickie," said Mrs. Glass. She came and fluffed his pillow with her big callused hands.

"It's true," said Dickie. "He told me that Laurie would wake up in the morning. He said she was going to be okay."

"And I'm sure he was right," said Mrs. Glass, smiling down at him. "Now let's let the doctor do his work."

It didn't take long for that; there wasn't much the doctor could do. Mr. Valentine hovered around him, asking questions that didn't really have answers.

"I'm sure it's no comfort," the doctor said, "but your daughter's not alone with this. There was a problem at one of the labs, Mr. Valentine. Maybe a live vaccine."

"Yes, I understand that," said Mr. Valentine. "I know about the Cutter lab. I work for the Foundation. The only thing I want to know is this: what will happen to my daughter?"

"It's my hunch that she'll be fine," said the doctor. "I'm sorry that it all comes down to a hunch, but it's the best I can do. Every day improves her chances."

"Yes," said Mr. Valentine. He knew the odds very well. Twenty percent of the deaths in the first day, eighty-five percent in the first three weeks. It was a long way to go until anyone could say she was safe.

Little Dickie was looking up. "Don't worry, Mr. Valentine," he said. "She's going to be okay. She really is."

And he was right.

Laurie came out of her coma not an hour later. She could move her arms and legs, her fingers and toes, and before noon she could manage just fine without a plastic tube in her throat.

The doctor took it out. But he left the girl in the iron lung. "Just for a night or two," he said. "I've never seen a patient recover so quickly."

◆ ◆ ◆

In her iron lung, Laurie listened as Dickie told her how the story had unfolded. He brought her up to Piper's Pond, with the Wishman there, and the Gypsy King. The others interrupted now and then when they thought he'd got it wrong, then Laurie asked one question: "So what did they wish for? The one wish for all three."

"Yeah, what *was* that wish?" asked Dickie, turning to look at Carolyn.

She blushed. She shook her head, and the long braid of hair swished from the pillow. "It's stupid," she said.

"Aw, come on. Tell us," said Dickie.

"Well, it sounds dumb," said Carolyn. "But they all wished to live happily ever after. And that's how the story ends."

No one spoke. There was just the huffing of the iron lungs as Dickie and Chip frowned at each other. Laurie stared into her mirror, out at the window behind her.

Finally, Dickie spoke up. "What do you mean, that's how it ends?" The coonskin cap dangled in front of him, beside the wooden tomahawk and the pictures of Davy Crockett. "Boy, there's got to be more than that. What happened to Khan and Finnegan Flanders? What about the Swamp Witch and the Woman and the Gypsy King?"

"Beats me," said Carolyn. "I think Laurie should finish it."

Dickie turned the other way now, and grinned at Laurie. "So what happened next?" he asked.

It seemed to Laurie that Carolyn knew very well how the story would end. Giving it back was a kindness, she thought, the first gesture of friendship she'd ever seen Carolyn make.

With her head on the pillow, the iron lung pulling her breaths in and out, Laurie felt herself floating from her world of hospitals and machines, into the land of her story. In the tilted mirror, there was a strip of sky with big round clouds made silver by the sunlight.

But in her mind she saw the fire blazing in the grove at Piper's Pond. She could hear the laughter and the music, and watch the Gypsies dancing.

◆ ◆ ◆

In firelight, the Gypsies reeled in a huge circle. Their clothes were swirling, their rings and bracelets flashing. Sparks flew up from the fire, and the fiddles screeched, and the Wishman played his pipes.

Jimmy the giant-slayer danced three times with every

girl, until he was exhausted. But the Woman danced only with the King.

Jimmy watched his mother twirl and laugh, and could not remember a time when she had been so happy. And when she was as tired as he, they sat together through the night and listened to the music.

At the edge of the pond—not seen by anyone—the Swamp Witch crouched in the shallows. Beside her was the little basket, empty now.

Her throat bulged and shrank. A happy croaking sound, something like the purr of a cat, came from deep in her throat.

At midnight a Gypsy girl went to the pond for water. She carried a pot and a dipping ladle, and she tossed back her long hair as she knelt at the edge of the water.

The Gypsies were dancing behind her, whirling through the firelight.

A splash, or a swirl of water, made the girl sit up and stare into the darkness over the pond.

"Marla!" said the witch in the darkness.

The girl gasped to hear her name come from the black pool in a croaking sort of voice. "Who's there?" she asked.

"Marla, don't be scared," said the witch.

The girl stood up, staring. She saw a black shape hunched nearby. Behind her, the fire flared as someone added wood, and she saw the witch's eyes staring from the pond.

She dropped the pot; it clattered on a stone. She dropped the ladle. She opened her mouth to scream.

"It's me," said the witch. "Your sister."

The girl stepped back from the water. She held up the

{267}

hem of her long dress, ready to run. "Jessamine?" she whispered.

"Yes. Please stay," said the witch. "It's really me."

The girl hesitated. She looked back at the fire, again at the pond. She took another step from the water. Then she leaned forward and whispered into the shadows the beginning of a rhyme she had invented long ago. "The Gypsy King has dash and flair."

And back from the darkness came the rest of it. "And yellow spots in his underwear."

The girl laughed. She ran into the water, splashing through the shallows blindly.

Suddenly, a face loomed in the faintness of the fire; cold arms reached out and hugged her. She could see the witch's frog-like face. She could touch the knobs of lizard skin. But she could *feel* the soul of her sister, and that was all that mattered.

"Jessamine!" she said, and drew her toward the fire.

The dancing stopped as the pair came closer. The music faded away. Then every Gypsy stared as the Swamp Witch and the girl walked slowly round among them. The witch was wearing her Gypsy rings now, her earrings and bracelets, the very same jewelry that Jessamine had worn on the day she'd disappeared.

When she came to the King of the Gypsies, the Swamp Witch stopped and looked up. Her throat filled and emptied. She held out her webbed hands, the fingers long and knobby. "Father, I've come home," she said.

◆ ◆ ◆

Carolyn sighed. She was looking up at her mirror, or at least *toward* her mirror. In its surface she saw the darkness of Piper's Pond and the face of a Gypsy girl. "Gee, that's nice," she said. "That's keen."

"Huh?" said Dickie, beside her. "What's nice?"

"Just the way she went home," said Carolyn. "She was so different, so ugly, but she went home anyway."

Chip didn't seem as pleased with that part of the story. "But the King wouldn't even recognize her."

"Yeah, that's true," said Dickie.

"It wouldn't take him long; he's not stupid," said Carolyn. "On the inside, Jessamine's the same girl who got stolen. Maybe she's even better now. Maybe she's nicer."

Laurie nodded. This time it pleased her that Carolyn had seen right through the story. "That's what *I* was thinking."

"But what about the changeling?" said Chip. "When the witch stole Jessamine she left a changeling behind. That's what the hunter said."

"Yeah, what about that?" asked Dickie. "Boy, what's a changeling anyway?"

"It was a creature," said Laurie, "a *thing* made of wood and sticks and stuff. It looked like Jessamine. It talked and moved and everything, but it was evil and horrid. When the witch left it there, the Gypsy King couldn't understand how his lovely Jessamine had suddenly become so horrible."

"But the changeling didn't live very long," said Carolyn. "Did it?"

"A few weeks. That's all," said Laurie. "Then it withered away like a plant without water. It got dried-out and hollow, until all that was left was a thin, hard shell. Then the

King understood; he saw that this thing was really a changeling, nothing more than enchanted wood. From that day on he was haunted by the thought that his daughter was still alive, so he kept moving from place to place, hoping to find Jessamine."

"Maybe that's why Gypsies roam today," said Carolyn. "They got used to it."

Dickie was happy now, content. But Chip still looked puzzled. "So why does the King hate the Swamp Witch so much?"

"Gee, I know *that*," said Dickie.

"Does he think she's the one who stole Jessamine?"

"No," said Dickie, scornfully. "There wasn't even a Swamp Witch living then. It was just a story that she was a hundred years old. There wasn't a witch in the swamp until Jessamine went to live there. Right, Laurie?"

"Right," she said.

"So why does the King hate her?" asked Chip again.

"Boy, it's easy. Every time she came around the camp, and the dogs knew she was there, the King was afraid she'd steal another baby. He thought all witches stole babies."

"Oh!" said Chip. "*Now* I get it."

Carolyn rolled her eyes. "I hope the King was happy that day his daughter came home," she said. "What happened after that?"

◆ ◆ ◆

The witch was never changed back to the way she had looked as a girl. Forever she was froglike, with enormous yellow eyes and a mouth that barely had lips. But in the story the Gypsies told of that night, a tale that would live a thousand years, she had never seemed more lovely than she did in the light of the fire, as she came home from the bottomless swamp.

From then on she lived at Piper's Pond. Her father, the King, saw no need to wander anymore, and his caravan never moved again. The grass grew up above the wheels, twining round the spokes.

The Wishman too discovered a fondness for his home. Months later, he made one more journey down the Great North Road. He returned in seven weeks, with many small doilies, with samplers to put on his walls, and pretty little covers for the toilet paper, and a wedding ring for Jessamine.

But for Jimmy the giant-slayer, there was nothing better than traveling. He soon had his own caravan with a high seat, and a team of six black horses. For nine months of the year he drove all through the land, from one edge of the world to another. Only in winter did he settle down. Beside Piper's Pond his wagon sat warm and black in all the whiteness of the valley, with a thread of gray smoke rising from the chimney. There he stayed until the unicorns came down from the hills, sweeping silver through the valley.

◆ ◆ ◆

"What happened to Finnegan Flanders?" asked Chip.

"He settled in the village where the farmers lived," said Laurie. "For the first year, he did nothing but pose for statues."

"Then what?"

"He learned how to build wagons. He got an old wagon builder to show him how. Soon every farmer in the valley wanted a Flanders wagon."

"Did he have any more adventures?"

"He certainly did. Finnegan Flanders explored the land to the west of the swamp. He battled giants in the north and dragons in the south. When he was very old he went on a lecture tour that took him all through the east. So Finnegan Flanders saw the whole world."

"What about Fingal and the Woman?" asked Dickie.

◆ ◆ ◆

Fingal kept the Dragon's Tooth for the rest of his days. And he did rather well in the end. From far and wide, people traveled to the foot of the Great North Road to see the birthplace of Jimmy the giant-slayer. Fingal sold souvenirs—little chips of wood from Jimmy's cradle. But of course they were fake. Every night he made another batch by whittling at his firewood.

He lived to be more than a hundred, famous through the world as Fingal, father of Jimmy.

Whenever a traveler mentioned the bottomless swamp, Fingal was reminded of the Woman. He would always ask then if there had been any news of her, any sightings on the Great North Road. The answers were always the same: heads were scratched; chins were scraped; eyes looked off in the distance. "No," said the travelers, "no, I can't say I've seen her."

But far to the north, at the end of the Great North Road, the Woman lived happily. In the company of the Gypsy King, the Wishman, and Jessamine, she was more happy, in fact, than she had ever been with Fingal.

For years she never spoke about her days in the giant's castle. But then one morning when the sun was shining on Piper's Pond, she sat down with Jessamine and, holding hands, told her all. There were things too horrible to dwell upon, but now and then a bright moment made the Woman smile as she recalled it.

As they talked, children played around them. The giant-slayer took a fishing pole to the pond and cast out a line that split the bright surface. The Gypsy King was laughing.

In the end, said the Woman, it was maybe something of a blessing that she'd been captured by the giant. "I'm glad I'm not the way I was before," she said. "Now I have so very much."

◆ ◆ ◆

On her first day out of the iron lung, Laurie stood for a while at the window. She looked down at Piper's Pond and the green grass, and the driveway that was wet again with rain.

She looked at the spot where they said she had fallen, but she couldn't remember it happening. She couldn't remember getting polio, or waking in the iron lung. To her it seemed unreal, like something that had never happened.

Behind her, the machines kept breathing. And down below, a small figure appeared, a little boy hobbling on crutches. There was a nurse beside him, her white dress starched and bright. Her legs, in their white stockings, looked like bowling pins.

The boy was moving quickly on his crutches. Leaning forward, swaying from side to side, he swung his legs in that way that made him lurch and tip. The nurse kept reaching out her hand, ready to hold him if she had to. But she never did, and as they walked along the path toward the pond she looked like a swan protecting a cygnet, shielding it with her wing.

When they reached the pond, they sat on a bench. As the boy turned to arrange his crutches, Laurie saw his face. She had thought he was James Miner, and she was right. He looked proud and happy.

The nurse produced a paper bag that she set by his hip. And the ducks came surging across the water. And James began to feed them, tossing bread crumbs from the bag.

As Laurie watched, he looked up. It gave her the strangest feeling to see him from the window, as though she had become the prince in the tower and was now looking down at her young self. Then James waved at her, and she waved back, and that chased away the feeling.

Too tired to stand for long, she went back to the chair between Dickie and Chip, where she had sat for an hour that morning. She was helping Chip sort through the pictures on the front of his iron lung.

"That one at the top," he said now. "With the girl on the merry-go-round."

Laurie reached up. "This one?"

"Yes."

She took it down and set it on the pile. Nearly half of them were gone now, leaving pictures of different people in different places, and here and there a wild-haired boy looking scared or embarrassed, but seldom looking happy. At least they were the same boy, and Laurie at last could track him through the years as he moved in and out of different homes.

Carolyn was watching from one side, Dickie from the other.

"Now the one underneath," said Chip. "The boy in the hot rod. I don't know who that is."

They were still working on the pictures when Miss Freeman came into the room. She was even more happy than usual. "What are you doing?" she asked.

Laurie explained. Then Miss Freeman said, "You'd better give a picture to Carolyn. One of the real ones, I mean."

"Why?" asked Chip, sounding a bit suspicious.

"So she'll have something to remember you by."

Now it was Carolyn who didn't understand. She looked back with such a puzzled look that Miss Freeman laughed.

"Carolyn," said the nurse, "you're going home, sweetheart."

The rubber collar pulsed at Carolyn's neck like the throat of the Swamp Witch. "Home?" she said.

"We just got a call from your parents," said Miss Freeman. "They've bought a respirator; they're setting up a room right now. The March of Dimes is helping them out, and . . . " She looked at Carolyn with absolute kindness, in the same way that Chip had always looked at *her*. "Don't you see? You get to go home."

Carolyn smiled, but in a strange way. Chip and Dickie

{275}

seemed more excited than Carolyn did. They said, "Yay!" together, and then Chip said, "Don't you want to go home?"

"Yeah, sure I do," said Carolyn.

"Gee, I thought you'd be happier than that," said Miss Freeman. "I thought you'd be on cloud nine, all up in the air like one of those people on *Feather Your Nest*."

Carolyn nearly laughed at the image of that; she liked watching game shows, though she always saw them backward in her mirror.

"Are you worried?" asked Miss Freeman. "'Cause you don't have to worry, you know. You won't have to frog-breathe all the way, if that's what you're thinking. They'll move the respirator, with you inside it, all the way from here to your new house. The hand pump will get you downstairs. The ambulance will be all set up. The airplane will have a generator, and they'll plug you right in. You lucky dog, you can travel all over, and you don't even have to get out of bed."

"That's not it," said Carolyn. Her voice was quiet and serious.

"Then what's the matter?"

"I'm the Swamp Witch," said Carolyn. "It's really true." Her machine trembled as it breathed. "You can't take the ugly old witch out of the swamp. You have to take the swamp with her."

Miss Freeman didn't understand at all. "*Well!*" she said, a bit miffed. "A lot of people are going to a lot of trouble for you, Carolyn. I thought you'd changed, but I guess I was wrong." She started away in a huff.

"No, wait," said Carolyn. "Don't get frosted."

But it was too late. In the breathing of the machines, Miss Freeman had left the room.

"Miss Freeman!" said Carolyn.

"Forget it," said Dickie. They were staring straight up again, into the backward world of their mirrors. "She wouldn't believe you anyway."

"I don't know," said Carolyn. "She's pretty hip."

"Not *that* hip," said Dickie. He had never used slang words before, and it made him a bit embarrassed now.

"He's right," said Chip. "It sounds crazy: a story taking over."

They didn't look at each other. "It's keen, though," said Carolyn after a moment. "I'm going home." Then she smiled. "But I can't call it home. I've never been there. They've moved all over. Like Gypsies."

There was another silence. The respirators hummed and creaked; the shadows of the bellows moved across the floor. Chip said, "I wish we hadn't started the story."

"Why?" asked Carolyn. Then she understood. "Hey, you won't be alone. Dickie's here."

"Yeah, but not for long. He's going away too," said Chip.

"I am?" said Dickie.

"Sure. Didn't Khan disappear into the forest?" said Chip. "Remember? He sort of vanished into the mountains."

Dickie was frowning again.

"He went where it's wild and empty," said Chip. "Sure, that was in the story."

"I guess so," said Dickie. "He would have gone where the

unicorns live. Where it's always bright and clear. Where a man can ride forever, up at the edge of the sky."

His voice faded away. It seemed he was talking about heaven, and nobody moved or said a word. Into Laurie's mind came an image of James Miner looking fearfully from his treatment board and saying: *I think one of us is going to die.*

"I wonder what it's like up there," said Dickie.

"It's Frontierland!" said Chip loudly. "That's what I mean. You're going to get better, and your folks will take you to Disneyland. That's how it's supposed to happen, remember?"

"Yeah, you stupe," said Carolyn. She tried to make it sound like a joke, but nobody laughed. Then Dickie turned his head aside at last, so that he faced away from the others, and he lay sliding gently on his cot as the respirator drew him in and out.

"Boy, Chip. I'm sorry you'll be alone," he said.

◆ ◆ ◆

Laurie looked down from the window, across the grass toward the pond. James was still sitting on the bench, though not feeding the ducks anymore. They stood around him instead, gazing up like fat little people come to hear him talk.

"What do you see?" asked Carolyn.

Laurie felt a funny sense of déjà vu. It swept her back to her first day in the room, and she almost believed that if she turned around it would all begin again, that none of it had happened. When the sensation faded away, it was like waking from a dream.

"James is sitting at the pond," she said, poking her glasses. "Under the trees, on a bench. The willows are all droopy 'cause it was raining, but now the sun's out and they look shiny and bright, like rhinestone trees."

The red car—the Starlight—came into view below her. It went slowly down the driveway, paused at the gate with a red blink of its brake lights, and raced off down the road, heading north.

The gurgling roar of the engine made Chip strain his neck to see in the tilted mirror. "Was that the Starlight?" he asked.

"Yes," said Laurie.

Dickie asked, "Was Dr. Wishman driving?"

"I don't know," said Laurie.

"I bet he was. He's traveling on," said Dickie. "He's going to help someone else now."

"Where's he going?" asked Laurie.

"He doesn't know. Not yet."

Laurie was smiling. "He'll just keep driving north."

"I guess so," said Dickie. "He'll know where he's going when he gets there. He'll find someone who needs him."

"That's keen," said Laurie. "What will happen then?"

Dickie looked at Laurie in his mirror. He saw her poke her glasses into place and wondered how many times he had seen her do that already. She looked happier now than she had when he first met her, before summer, before polio. And she was looking at him with none of the pity she had shown before, as though she understood that he didn't really mind the iron lung. It made him feel safe, protected. It was more a cocoon than a prison. At night, in his dreams, he came out

{279}

of it, riding as Khan through the mountains, living forever at the edge of the sky.

◆ ◆ ◆

Laurie recovered completely from her polio. When Carolyn left later that month, Laurie walked beside her iron lung, down on the elevator, out to the ambulance.

It was a huge production that made Carolyn blush with embarrassment. There were two people spelling each other on the hand bellows, and a generator in the van that came to get her. It had a little elevator to hoist her up inside.

Laurie wished she could hold hands with the girl, but had to settle for putting her palm on the window of the respirator, just as Mr. Valentine had done for her.

"Good luck at home," she said.

"Thanks," said Carolyn. "Thanks for everything, Laurie."

As the van pulled away, Laurie ran beside it, round the curve past Piper's Pond, out to the gate where it speeded up and left her behind.

She said goodbye to Dickie and Chip a few days later, when both were moved to a bigger hospital. Chip kept gazing at Laurie, but he seemed shy and awkward surrounded by nurses and orderlies. "I'm going to miss you like crazy," he told her in the elevator. Then his face blushed a very bright red. Laurie smiled back at him. "I'll send you postcards," she promised. "Cross my heart. I'll write every week."

Dickie's parents were there that day, and they wept as he was loaded into the ambulance, because even they could see how small and weak he'd grown, though his grin was as big as ever.

"So long," he said, just before the doors were closed. "Pretend that I'm waving, Laurie."

His parents had their car all packed. They would follow the ambulance and settle in with a sister of Mrs. Espinosa. "We're taking everything," said Dickie's father. "I hope we're there a good long time."

From that day on, the polio ward seemed a little lonely. There was no wheeze and whirr from the iron lungs, no need for Laurie to go farther down the hall than the big room with the television set. But she often did, on her weekly visits. She would walk beside James as he lurched on his crutches, or with Ruth and Peter in their wheelchairs. And she would stand at the door of an empty room, thinking of things both sad and wonderful.

There was a day in the future when James Miner wouldn't struggle along beside her. On that morning he would come running instead, his crutches forgotten, his braces discarded. He would race down the hall with his knees kicking high, his hair blowing back, a huge grin on his face.

"Laurie!" he'd shout. "Laurie, I beat it!" He would hold out his little arms, and Laurie would sweep him up and hoist him to her shoulder, the way the crowd had lifted the giant-slayer at the edge of the world. She would stagger back with his weight, and the two of them would fall to the floor, laughing.

James would be first on his feet. He would reach down to help her as she lay sprawled on the floor, still giggling. And for a moment he would tower above her, below the poster of the striding boy.

His picture would be in the newspaper—not the big daily, but the local weekly. He would be part of a story about the March of Dimes, and Mr. Valentine would be in it too. It would tell how James had been a Polio Pioneer, "a hero," it would say. "Here's a boy who risked everything in the fight against polio. And that fight nearly cost him his life. But polio could not have been beaten without James and the others."

◆ ◆ ◆

In August of that year of 1955, Laurie Valentine sat with her father in the grass of the Shenandoah valley. The creek was nearly dry then, in the middle of a long, hot summer. The mud was gray and cracked. But a tiny stream still trickled from the culvert, and there a boy was building little weirs from willow sticks, trapping the black water into pools.

He was blond and big, not at all like Dickie. But Laurie felt a pang to see him.

"I hope that boy had his shots," said Mr. Valentine. He bit his lip and stared around the little park. "I wonder if I should find his parents and have a word with them."

"No, Dad, he's okay," said Laurie. "Don't worry about everybody."

Mr. Valentine was still wearing his tie, the one that he had worn home from work. But at least he had loosened the knot, and now he gave it another tug before he settled back on his elbows. "People think that it's over, but it's not," he said. "It will be years yet before polio's gone altogether. The war's won, but it isn't ended. There's a lot of mopping up to do."

Laurie looked up at her father's tired face. He looked like a very old soldier now, wearied by his work. "Will you have to get another job?" she asked.

He smiled sadly and shook his head. "The Foundation will go on as long as *I'm* alive," he told her. "We'll have to keep the respirators running. We'll have to pay for the wheelchairs and the crutches and braces. Every year we'll need more money, and it's going to be harder than ever to drum up donations for a beaten disease." He sighed; he scratched his head. "Laurie, I lay awake last night thinking about this. I'm afraid my work is really only starting."

She felt sorry for him because he seemed so desperate. But she was disappointed too. He was away so much already, and she hated the thought that he could somehow be even busier.

"But look," he said, reaching out to touch her arm. "We don't have to think about that today. And we don't have to think about it tomorrow, because we're going to do something together."

"Like what?"

"Whatever you want." He sat up, looking suddenly younger. "And in the evening I'll take you out for dinner. There's a place that was your mother's favorite."

"But, Dad," said Laurie, "tomorrow's Friday. It's not even the weekend yet."

"I know that," said Mr. Valentine. "Can't a man spend a Friday with his daughter every now and then?"

They leaned back until their shoulders were on the grass. The shadows of the clouds moved across their faces.

"I wish we could do it all the time," said Laurie.

"Now, now," said Mr. Valentine. "Be careful what you wish for."

# AUTHOR'S NOTE

There is an image in my mind of a child in leg braces, lurching on crutches while an adult towers at either side. It is my only memory of polio, and so faint that I wonder at times if it's really there.

I was born the year polio was beaten in North America, the year the vaccine developed by Jonas Salk was made available to millions of people. Polio still thrived in other parts of the world, and even lurked at the edges of my own, like a bogeyman in the darkness, leaping out now and then to strike down a child. But I never knew the terror that gripped whole towns and cities when polio appeared every summer.

It was a terrible disease, as old as civilization. There are drawings from ancient Egypt of polio-stricken people. In North America, the worst epidemics began right after World War II, with about 20,000 cases reported each year for the rest of that decade, and nearly 60,000 in 1952.

Polio attacked children more often than adults, paralyzing muscles in the arms, legs, and chest. For most who got it, the disease came and went as simply as a common cold, yet others were crippled, often for life, able to walk only with metal braces strapped around their legs. Those with paralyzed lungs spent months, or years—or sometimes all their lives—lying on their backs in iron lungs that did their breathing for them with mechanical pumps and bellows.

An iron lung was huge and hulking. It looked like an enormous metal barrel on a frame of legs and wheels. It encased a child from toe to neck, leaving only the head outside. The bellows that pushed air through the machine were so powerful that smaller children were sucked in a bit, and blown out a bit, with every breath. When the epidemics of the 1940s and '50s brought more and more polio patients into hospitals, some bigger iron lungs were built, able to stack the children into layers, with one set of bellows breathing for four or five patients. It was a photograph of one of those machines that inspired this story, a five-person iron lung the size of a small room, with the heads of four children poking out from its front like dice spots.

The children's heads rested on pillows, on shelves extending from the round openings of the respirator. Taped to the metal above one of the children's heads was a painting of a boy and his dog. A nurse stood off to the side, smiling, her white uniform crisp and perfect. She was smiling, but the picture was sad. It made me wonder how those children had passed endless days and weeks and months. I imagined that the picture showed them in a rare moment of happiness, in lives full of sorrow and anger.

But I was wrong to think that. I had no idea of the strength of childhood spirit until I met a man who had lived in an iron lung.

His name is Richard Daggett. I've never seen him, or heard him speak, but I feel as though I know him well. By e-mail and Internet, he has told me the most private and intimate things imaginable.

Mr. Daggett contracted polio in 1953, just after his thirteenth birthday. He woke one day with a stiff neck, and ended the next in an iron lung, with his breaths whistling in and out through a hole that doctors had pierced in his throat. On a family Web site—www.downeydaggets.com— Mr. Daggett tells his amazing story of recovered strength. He got out of the iron lung; he learned to walk again. Now Mr. Daggett is president of the Polio Survivors Association, a writer and speaker, and an advocate to preserve the famous polio hospital, Rancho Los Amigos, where he struggled as a child.

Over the course of a year or so, Mr. Daggett taught me a lot, and not only about the polio. Among the things he most wanted me to know was the fact that a polio ward was not the terrible place I'd imagined, that there was laughter there, and hope and happiness. He felt that I'd made the children in my story too lonely, and not properly thrilled by each small success.

He recommended a few books that show how others lived with polio. My favorites included *In the Shadow of Polio,* a combination of history and memoir by Kathryn Black, and *Small Steps: The Year I Got Polio,* by Peg Kehret.

When Dr. Jonas Salk introduced his vaccine in 1955, he was hailed as a hero, the worker of miracles. He declined to patent the vaccine, not wanting any personal profit. Later, asked why, he said, "Could you patent the sun?"

A massive immunization began that year, and instances of polio plummeted. In 1953 there were 35,000 cases. In 1957 there were only 5,600.

But the vaccine brought a tragedy. Because of mistakes in a medical lab, a small number of people contracted polio from the vaccine that was meant to protect them. And because of that, thousands more shunned the immunizations while new epidemics burst out among them. Who can say what lives were changed as the result of a simple error?

In a way, that incident is at the heart of this story. It seems incredibly sad to me that the first people to hurry for the vaccine would fall victim to the disease. I don't like to think how it must have haunted Dr. Salk.

This story shifts back and forth between a grim reality and a fantasy that is perhaps a bit quirky. I found it hard sometimes to leave the world of Jimmy the Giant-Slayer and go back to iron lungs and paralyzed children. It was more fun to write about the imaginary place, where a woman without a name would put on lipstick before heading off to the swamp, where facts didn't matter so much.

But still, I wanted the fantasy world to have a truth of its own. I filled it with creatures from different mythologies, not thinking that it mattered where they came from, as I didn't think it would have mattered to Laurie Valentine. The hunter in her imagined world was as likely to bag a hydra as a manticore, though the hydra came from Greece, the manticore from Persia. It was as if he had the whole world to travel across, and held the beliefs of all men.

I wrote with a gnome perched in front of me. He sat on the top of my monitor, a bearded man about seven inches tall, dressed in red cap and striped shirt, holding a shovel with a copper blade. He was a gift from a Swiss-born friend, Maya Carson, the person I turned to to learn about gnomes, because I thought of the little men as belonging to middle Europe.

Maya grew up with tales about gnomes, believing the creatures lived in caves, that they worked underground to care for the earth. It surprised me that her gnomes were old men, every one, with never a woman nor child among them.

I took what she said to heart, and was pleased by the way my gnomes turned out. But Maya, I think, was disappointed. Very little of what I wrote matched her childhood stories. Her gnomes cared for the earth as selflessly as Jonas Salk, taking nothing for themselves. No one would be frightened of gnomes, she said; to see one was a blessing. Even the little coveralls I'd given the creatures didn't belong with the stories. Maya's gnomes worked in their floppy hats and slippers, dressed just like the one on my monitor. And gnomes could never, ever share a world with trolls.

I may regret that my gnomes and other creatures are not

more faithful to mythology. But they exist here as thoughts in the mind of an American girl from the 1950s. If you come away from the story thinking you've learned something about polio, I'll be happy. If the gnomes don't make sense, it's my own fault.

# ACKNOWLEDGMENTS

Many people helped with the research and writing of this story. These are just a few of them:

Kathleen Larkin of the Prince Rupert Library;

Richard Daggett of Downey, California;

Kathy O'Kane of Grande Prairie, Alberta;

Françoise Bui and everyone else at Delacorte Press, New York;

Bruce Wishart of Prince Rupert, British Columbia;

Darlene Mace of Gabriola Island, British Columbia;

Alysoun Wells of Grande Prairie, Alberta;

Kristin Miller of Gabriola Island;
and all the people, wherever they're from, who told me their own stories about polio, stories about fathers and brothers and sisters and friends.

Thank you, all of you.

# ABOUT THE AUTHOR

IAIN LAWRENCE studied journalism in Vancouver, British Columbia, and worked for small newspapers in the northern part of the province. He settled on the coast, living first in the port city of Prince Rupert and now on the Gulf Islands. His previous novels include the High Seas Trilogy: *The Wreckers, The Smugglers,* and *The Buccaneers;* and the Curse of the Jolly Stone Trilogy: *The Convicts, The Castaways,* and *The Cannibals;* as well as *The Séance, Gemini Summer, B for Buster, The Lightkeeper's Daughter, Lord of the Nutcracker Men,* and *Ghost Boy.*

You can find out more about Iain Lawrence at www .iainlawrence.com.